STAR TREK®
The Last Roundup

STAR TREK®
The Last Roundup

Christie Golden

Based upon Star Trek®
created by Gene Roddenberry

POCKET BOOKS
New York   London   Toronto   Sydney   Singapore

POCKET BOOKS, a division of Simon & Schuster, Inc.
1230 Avenue of the Americas, New York, NY 10020

ISBN: 0-7434-4909-6

First Pocket Books hardcover printing July 2002

10 9 8 7 6 5 4 3 2 1

POCKET and colophon are registered trademarks of Simon & Schuster, Inc.

For information regarding special discounts for bulk purchases, please contact Simon & Schuster Special Sales at 1-800-456-6798 or business@simonandschuster.com

Printed in the U.S.A.

This book is dedicated
to Three Wise Men:

Robert Amerman
Mark Anthony
and
Michael Georges

Thanks, guys.

PROLOGUE

Lights flickered on inside the last of the mighty skyships. Smoothly, the oval vessel rose into the air, caught the sunlight on its shiny, metallic surface, and then disappeared. The stoic façade of the abandoned people finally shattered. A cry of pain and agony swelled up, a cry that their proud natures would never have permitted them to utter while their so-called masters were present to scorn their torment.

Takarik heard the cry of his people, and his heart ached for them. He let them wail and scream, sounds that he had never before heard any of them make. They were left alone on this place now, with no way to ever return to their homeland.

No way that they had yet thought of, at least.

When at last the deep, mourning sobs had subsided into soft sighs and shuddering whispers, he spoke.

"What a glorious day is now dawning for our people!" Takarik cried, lifting his arms as if to embrace the world upon which they had been stranded. His people stared at him as if he had gone mad. He smiled, and his eyes twinkled. He meant every word.

"Those who believed themselves to be our betters think they have rid themselves of us. After so many years of doing their hard labor, they no longer found us necessary, so they placed us here. And in so doing, they did us a very great favor."

"Takarik!" called an angry voice. "We have been removed from all we know! We have been callously disposed of, as if we were nothing more than their waste matter!"

"What you say is true, Minkar," Takarik acknowledged. "But we are not they. We do not have to regard what has happened in the same light as they do. What they have done, I tell you truly, is freed us. The land is rich with fruit and game. We have a small amount of technology that will enable us to build shelters and communicate and find and prepare food. We have our hearts yet, and our keen minds. And we also have this!"

He gestured to a youth standing behind him, holding what seemed to be an innocuous box. It was scratched and dented, but within it . . . ah, within . . . Takarik had deliberately hidden it in this shabby box, tucked it away casually with clothes and supplies as if it had no more worth than those ordinary things. It had escaped discovery during a cursory search by a guard who obviously thought handling such tainted things was beneath him.

With a ceremonial flourish, Takarik lifted the lid and withdrew the precious contents. He held it aloft proudly, and heard some murmurs. The gem was as large as his head, and even though it had not been faceted as so many precious stones were, it caught and seemed to hold the very sun. It was almost completely transparent save for its amber tinting like liquid sunlight, and without flaw as far as Takarik could determine.

"That we were able to bring this safely from our homeworld to here, without our captors ever discovering it, tells me that we have a great destiny in this place," Takarik continued. "Many of you have glimpsed this as you labored for those who deemed themselves superior. But many more of you have never seen it. Oh, you have heard the tales; so have our captors, but as far as they know, they are children's stories.

"We do not yet know its true value, for we have never been permitted to reveal its existence to others, but its beauty alone inspires us. We took heart in our labors, knowing that it shone for us alone. Our captors never even knew it was there. This gem, this precious jewel, has made the bitter journey with us to symbolize hope."

Carefully, he replaced the stone in its deceptively nondescript box.

"This place will become our new home, but we will never forget our true heritage. We will thrive here, in a place where we will finally have the opportunity to govern ourselves. We will live in the shelters we build, and eat what we have harvested. We will devote our culture to knowledge and development. We will always remember the Great Stone and its beauty, and know that the gods gave it to us alone. And one day, we will take what is rightfully ours, earned by our labor, our blood, our sweat."

He looked at their eager, upturned faces. Such hope was another expression he had never seen on visages that were more accustomed to not revealing their emotions at all, lest they suffer for it.

"It will not be in my lifetime. Nor in hers," he said, pointing to an infant in her mother's arms. "Nor in her child's. But one day, I promise, it will happen.

"I swear to you by the beauty of the Great Stone—one day, we will go home."

STAR TREK®
The Last Roundup

Chapter One

It was a dead world.

It had never supported life of its own. The planet known in Federation records as Polluxara IV had no intelligent life that might interfere with the Prime Directive. It sported not so much as a microbe, but within its lifeless, rocky exterior had once flowed a rich vein of what was then one of the most precious substances in the universe—dilithium.

It was this deposit that had led Earth, almost a hundred and fifty years ago, to establish a colony in order to mine the mineral. But now, once again, Polluxara IV was lifeless, save for the twenty-seven souls that stood safely encased in environmental suits on its still-radioactive exterior.

Captain James Tiberius Kirk, once Admiral Kirk, and earlier and since captain of the *U.S.S. Enterprise,* was one of the twenty-seven. The others were much younger and, at this moment, were quieter than he had ever heard them.

Kirk wasn't surprised. Standing at the site of a great tragedy had that effect.

Towering above them were the ruins of what had once been a colony of vital importance to a pre-Federation Earth. There remained only sharp shards of metal and other materials, warped, melted, twisted, and pulverized. The bodies were long gone, of course. What the Earth forces could come and retrieve to honor with a hero's burial had been so gathered, decades past. But there hadn't been enough remains to bury of most of them; hadn't been enough to find.

Kirk didn't speak immediately after they materialized. He let the cadets look around and absorb what they saw for themselves. The wide-eyed solemnity he saw in their faces—a mixture of species that would have stunned those who had died here a century ago—-made him nod slightly in approval. Good kids, all of them. He'd been right to call in a few favors on this.

Time for the pop quiz.

"Cadet Singh," Kirk said sharply. Indira Singh's head whipped around.

"Sir!" she answered, snapping to attention despite the mute testimony to death that lay all around her.

"Tell me about Commander Lowe, if you please."

Light glimmered on her protective faceplate, but not so much that Kirk couldn't see her lick her lips nervously. "Commander Sabra Lowe led the mining colony here in the middle part of the twenty-second century. It was a state-of-the-art colony that turned out swift production of a very pure form of dilithium, almost ninety-two percent pure."

"How many other active dilithium mining colonies were there at that time?" Out of the corner of his eye, he saw Cadet Skalli Jksili raise her long, slender arm, but he ignored her.

"Only seven. Polluxara IV turned out—" Singh hesitated, and her dark eyes widened as she frantically sought the answer.

2

"Four point oh seven two times the amount of the others." She breathed easier.

"Very good. You've just made an excellent start on your final."

A chorus of protest rose as the students realized that Kirk was apparently springing at least part of the final exam of his course, "Command Decisions and Their Consequences," on them here, now, unannounced. The sounds were oddly comforting to Kirk, standing here among the ruins. It was a sound that reminded him that life had to go on, no matter how many colonies—

"I did tell you to do your research," Kirk reminded them mildly, raising a hand to still them. They quieted at once. "Now. Cadet Brown. Tell me what happened here a few years later." He could see Cadet Skalli shaking her head in disgust.

Cadet Christopher Brown stood at attention, trying not to smile. Kirk had given him an easier question.

"Commander Lowe received advance warning of an attack. The scout reported that the Romulans, then a relatively unknown species, were approaching."

"And their goal was to completely destroy the colony, in order to strike fear into the heart of Earth forces."

"Negative, sir!" Brown's smile widened as he caught Kirk's trick question. "Their goal was to take over the colony in order to harvest the dilithium."

"Which was to be used how?"

"To develop warp drive and create more ships to bring to bear against Earth forces in the war. Sir!"

"Very good. You too have a head start on the final, Mr. Brown. Cadet T'Pran, pick up the narrative from this point."

Cadet Skalli was now actually stomping in impatience. Kirk had once tried to curb these physical displays of her irritation,

3

but it was impossible. It was simply a part of what she was—a Huanni.

T'Pran, a coolly beautiful young Vulcan female whose calm demeanor was the antithesis of Skalli's, predictably showed no emotion as she obeyed Kirk's request.

"There was insufficient time for Earth to send defense vessels. The colony had no weapons other than approximately two hundred handheld phase guns, fourteen primitive torpedoes, sixteen assorted pieces of mining equipment, and four thousand, eight hundred and twenty-seven detonation devices."

Not for the first time, Kirk marveled at how Vulcans used the word *approximately.*

"Very good. Cadet Lasskas, continue."

The translator turned Lasskas's hissing dialect into intelligible Federation standard, though it played a bit with sentence structure.

"Commander Lowe choice had none. Selected she to colony destroy, detonation devices all deployed at time same. Not Romulan hands fall into, precious dilithium, at time of war when vulnerable Earth. Died eight and forty and one hundred males and females by order of Commander Lowe."

"Most of that is correct, but there's something very wrong with that answer. Do you know what it is?"

Lasskas's sharp-toothed muzzle opened and his thick, green, forked tongue fluttered. Since the rest of his face was unable to move, that long tongue was the only indicator of his emotions. He clearly had no idea what Kirk was getting at.

"Anybody know what was incorrect about Cadet Lasskas's answer?" He could all but see their sharp minds turning as they tried to find the factual flaw in Lasskas's statement. They were all being too literal. Not even Skalli's hand was up this time. Her pale purple face was screwed up in frustration.

Kirk didn't enlighten them at once. He began to walk around the area, carefully.

"We're in a place of death, cadets. Even safely in our environment suits, we can feel it, can sense it. This is sacred ground. A place where lives were sacrificed in order to preserve noble ideals. One day, any of you might be looking at a similar scenario. I want you to take a moment and put yourself in Commander Lowe's position. Imagine yourself as commander of a colony of over a hundred people—people who looked to you to keep them safe . . . their families safe. Most of them hadn't signed on for this out of a desire for adventure or even any particular sense of loyalty. There was good money to be had for hard work on this planet."

They were quiet now, attentive. For the first time since he started this class at the beginning of the semester, Kirk felt that he was finally managing to get through to them. Hitherto, he had thought them too starry-eyed to really listen. It had taken this—a risky visit to a devastated world that still leaked radiation from its death throes—to do it, but he thought he had succeeded. If they understood this one message, it wouldn't matter to him what they had scored the rest of the semester.

"And then you hear from one of your scouts, who is attacked and killed shortly after he sends the message, that Romulans are on the way," Kirk continued, his voice ringing in this silent place. "Romulans. You've never even seen them, only heard vague rumors about these faceless beings hitting outposts hard, then vanishing. And now, they're coming. For you."

A few of them shifted uneasily. Others gazed at him raptly. Chief among these was Skalli. Kirk quickly looked elsewhere. Skalli never needed much encouragement.

"They're coming for you," he repeated, "and your home planet can't do a damn thing to protect you. You're too far away.

You know what they want, and you know their tactics. They've never left anyone alive before." He paused in midstride and whirled back, catching their eyes with his own hazel ones.

"But they've never wanted anything from an outpost before. They might take you prisoner. They might agree to let you go. You just don't know. Now do you see why Cadet Lasskas's answer wasn't correct?"

They stared at him blankly. Skalli was obviously frustrated that she couldn't grasp what her instructor was getting at, and the rest seemed uneasy as well.

Kirk sighed. Maybe they were just too young. Maybe at their age, he wouldn't have been able to comprehend this either. After all, wasn't he the one who secretly reprogrammed the simulation computer in order to become the only Academy student able to wring victory from the *Kobayashi Maru* simulation?

"Cadet Lasskas's answer was factually correct. But you've got to take into consideration more than just facts if you're to be a good officer in Starfleet. You've got to consider things like hunches, intuitions, gut feelings . . . and knowing that you always have a choice." He glanced over at Lasskas, who was hanging his reptilian head. "You said Commander Lowe didn't have a choice. From our perspective, a hundred-odd years in the future, that statement seems obvious."

He spread his hands. *"Of course* she had to destroy the colony, and sacrifice every one of those one hundred and forty-eight men and women, didn't she? We *all* know that's what she had to do, don't we?" he said, exaggerating the words. "She couldn't risk having that much dilithium fall into Romulan hands at that crucial juncture. Just push a button. An easy decision. It's in all the textbooks, so it must have been obvious, an easy choice. It has as much relevance to us now as the fall of

Lamaria, or the losses at Normandy in 1944, back on Earth. Which is to say, not very much."

Again, he surveyed them, standing tall and imposing. He had come to realize, somewhat ruefully, that to many of these youngsters he was a living legend. If he could drum this lesson into their heads, he wouldn't mind the pedestal.

"But they *should* have meaning, damn it. Every single man who died on the beaches at Normandy had a life that was as dear, as precious to him as life is to any of you. Every single Lamarian who fell defending their home from a vicious onslaught once laughed, and cried, and loved."

He raised his arms and indicated their surroundings. "This particular site is unique. Because there's no atmosphere, it's going to be preserved this way forever. There's no grass here to soften this battlefield, no grave markers to bleach and fade in the sun. We'll always be able to stand here and look at what was willingly done for the good of others as if it happened yesterday. Just because these people died over a century past doesn't mean we should let their sacrifice count for nothing."

He softened his voice. "There is a quote from an ancient book on my world that says, 'Greater love hath no man than this, that a man lay down his life for his friends.' I disagree. It's noble to die for a friend, for someone you love and value. But how much nobler—and harder—is it to die for a stranger? Commander Sabra Lowe died for people she had never met. And she *made that choice freely.* Now that, cadets, is a command decision. And this is its consequence—both the ruins of Polluxara IV and the fact that you and I are able to stand here today, alive, free, and members of a Federation that values freedom and justice."

To his deep satisfaction, Kirk saw the flickering of understanding pass across some of the painfully youthful faces. He

7

heard a slight thump and turned in the direction of the sound. Not surprisingly, tears were flowing down Skalli's purple face. She had forgotten she was wearing the environmental suit and had bumped her hand on the faceplate in an effort to wipe the river away.

The Huanni had only recently joined the Federation. Kirk had never seen such an emotional race before. It in no way compromised their intelligence or skills, which were considerable, but they were as open in their emotions as the Vulcans were closed—which was saying a lot. Skalli, the very first of her species to be accepted at Starfleet Academy, had come a long way in the single semester Kirk had known her. By Huanni standards, she was coldly logical. He had tried to be understanding of the outbursts while at the same time helping her learn how to control herself. She had confided in him that she wanted to be an ambassador one day. Kirk thought this highly unlikely.

To help her focus, he addressed her. "Cadet Skalli," he said. "We will take a moment to think of those who have died here so that we might live. Please, recite their names, slowly and solemnly." He knew that she, like all her species, had an eidetic memory, and this would be no challenge for her. But she would see it as an honor.

She looked up at him, and in her enormous eyes shone pride and a very intense form of hero worship. Kirk managed not to cringe. She composed herself, and with tears still streaming down her face began to list the names of the colonists.

"Commander Sabra Lowe. First Officer Jason Riley. Second Officer Ramon Sanchez. Chief Engineer Jonathan Bedonie. . . ."

It took a long time, to recite a hundred and forty-eight names. When Kirk caught one of his students fidgeting, he glared at him until he stopped. They stood at attention, until finally, Skalli stated the last name.

Kirk waited a moment longer. At last he said, "We have twenty minutes before we return to the ship. I suggest you take the time to wander the colony and get to know it for yourself. Be mindful that though the residual radiation from the explosion is low it is still present, and that you are not under any circumstances to remove so much as a glove. Also be aware there are many opportunities for a careless cadet to slip and break a leg. I'd advise against it."

There were slight, wary chuckles at this. *It figures,* thought Kirk. *They finally start seeing me as a human being on the last day of class.* While it was obvious that the students were thrilled to be able to attend his class, he knew that they were more interested in seeing him than in what he was saying. But talking about major command decisions of the past few centuries—including a few historical ones he himself had made—had only served to remind him that all he was doing was talking. He was horribly bored, itching to get out and do something, which was one reason he had called in a few favors to authorize this field trip to a place that was still largely off-limits. Command decisions weren't textbook cases, they were real, and bloody, and bitter. And heaven knew he'd had more than his share.

"There will be an essay as part of the final exam. It is freeform, and all I want from you is your impressions of Polluxara IV and what happened here. It will be due in my hands when we return to Earth orbit. The students who correctly answered my questions will receive extra credit. Those of you who didn't have that opportunity will just have to make sure your essays are even better."

"Captain, that's not fair!" one of them piped up.

Kirk merely smiled. "It doesn't have to be. I'm the instructor, and you're the students. You'll find that a lot in this universe isn't fair, but it has to be dealt with nonetheless. That, too, is part of being a Starfleet officer. Dismissed."

There were always those who loved writing essays in any class, and these students were abuzz with excitement as they hastened off to explore. And, of course, there were always those who loathed essays, and Kirk overheard the predictable grumbling from this segment as they departed with much less enthusiasm.

Kirk wasn't overly concerned. Most of them were outstanding students, and would pass even if they failed the final. He welcomed the solitude, for he, too, wanted a chance to roam this place and soak up the atmosphere.

"Captain Kirk?" The voice was bubbly, feminine, and quivering.

Kirk closed his eyes, gathering strength. He forced a pleasant expression on his face.

"What is it, Cadet?"

It was of course Skalli. She was nearly as tall as he was, though far more slender of build than most humanoids. Her large ears were perforce flattened against her head by the suit's headpiece and gave her a particularly mournful look. Her mercurial features set in an expression of sorrow completed the impression, and her large eyes still brimmed with tears, although Kirk was pleased to see that at least she wasn't actually crying now.

"Permission to speak freely?"

"Go ahead."

"Captain . . . do you. . . ." Skalli swallowed hard. "Do you think they were afraid? Commander Lowe and the others?"

"You heard the message they sent back to Starfleet before Lowe destroyed the colony. What do you think?"

Skalli tilted her head. "She did not sound afraid."

Kirk raised an eyebrow, silently encouraging Skalli to continue voicing her thoughts. "So . . . I suppose she wasn't."

"You still have much to learn about humans, Skalli. I can't know personally, of course, but I'm certain she was indeed afraid." He looked around. "To take that responsibility—to end your own life and that of so many others . . . you can't do it without wondering, without second guessing yourself." He looked back at her kindly. "Without being afraid."

"But her voice was so calm. . . ."

"One thing you'll need to learn if you want to be an ambassador, Skalli, is that you don't have to surrender to your emotions all the time."

She looked at him with a mixture of awe and disbelief. "So I have heard . . . but, Captain, I must confess, that seems impossible to me!"

"It certainly doesn't seem to come easily to your people," Kirk agreed. "But it can be learned."

He nodded in Cadet T'Pran's direction. She was standing on a jagged outcropping of metal, her hands clasped in front of her, her head bowed in meditation. "Vulcans used to be highly emotional, until they decided to embrace logic instead. Now they still have emotions, but they know how to control them."

Skalli laughed brightly, shifting from compassionate sorrow to mirth in an instant. "That, too, seems impossible!"

Some of the students frowned, clearly thinking Skalli—and by association Kirk—must be being disrespectful of the solemnity he had just encouraged them to experience. After laughing, Skalli continued to talk.

Kirk didn't dislike Skalli, but she was certainly a trial. *So was Spock, at first,* he reminded himself. *And look what happened there.*

But he was too old to take so young a creature through something as important as disciplining her emotions. It was just as well that this semester was over and he wouldn't be seeing the youngster on a regular basis. He didn't have the patience to—

"What?" he asked, hoping he had misunderstood Skalli's chatter.

"My personal advisor," she said brightly. "There was such a long waiting list for you! But because I'm the first Huanni to attend the Academy, they made a special exception for me and moved me right to the top of the line. Wasn't that kind! So now I'll get to meet with you every day, no matter *what* classes I'm taking!"

To his keen embarrassment, she threw her arms around him and hugged him tightly, then hugged herself and whirled around a few times.

"Imagine what they'll think back on Huan . . . little Skalli, who has the great, famous Captain James T. Kirk as her advisor!" She stopped and gazed at him with shining eyes. "It's going to be wonderful!"

"Wonderful," Kirk echoed, and wondered how the hell he was going to get out of this one.

Chapter Two

The transport vessel was small. Too small for Kirk's comfort, anyway. It might have had a crew of eight, a mess hall and even a room for recreational activities and exercise, but it was not sufficiently large for him to feel truly away from his charges. Alone in his cramped quarters, still imagining he could hear laughter outside his door, Kirk tapped the computer.

The image of a beautiful Native American woman appeared on the screen. She was approximately Kirk's age. Silver threads wound through her long, braided hair, echoing the twist of real silver necklaces about her elegant throat. Her dark brown eyes sparkled as she recognized her old friend, and her broad face lit up with a smile.

"Hello, Jim. You know, somehow I figured I'd hear from you any day now," Admiral Laura Standing Crane said, chuckling.

"How long have you known?" Kirk said dryly.

"A few days." She raised a raven eyebrow. "I was the one who authorized it."

Kirk leaned back in his chair and rubbed his hazel eyes. "Laura, Laura," he sighed, "what did I ever do to you?"

"Oh, come now, Jim, Skalli's a good kid. And you know how important it is to make new Federation members feel welcome at all levels in Starfleet—from the Academy on up. Who better than the great Captain James T. Kirk to help her learn how to get along with humans?"

Kirk winced slightly. "I think if I hear 'the great Captain James T. Kirk' one more time, I'm going to get myself surgically altered again and go hide out on Vulcan."

That made Standing Crane laugh openly. "You may have passed for a Romulan, but the Vulcans would spot you in a moment. Skalli requested that she be the one to tell you. I'm only sorry I wasn't there to see the expression on your face." She grew more serious. "How did the field trip go? No difficulties, I hope? It's my neck on the line, you know."

"No problems at all. It was sobering," Kirk said, "which was exactly what I wanted. Not even freshman cadets can stand on Polluxara IV and not think a bit. Thanks for authorizing it."

She nodded. "Of course. You know you've got a waiting list a kilometer long for next semester's class. Now that they know they're going to a quote-unquote off-limits area there'll be no stopping the flood of applications. What are you going to do with your summer?"

Kirk frowned. "Hadn't thought about it. Don't suppose that there's anything going on at Starfleet Command that a living legend could help with?"

"Jim, take a little time and rest on your laurels. God knows you've earned a break after the Camp Khitomer negotiations. How about exploring those caves on Paggaru Two? I hear they're a real challenge."

"I don't want to rest on my laurels, I want to *do* something.

Something other than standing at a podium reciting history to dewy-eyed kids who are only there because of who I am, not what I know."

Standing Crane leaned forward and regarded him with sympathy. "Jim, we've been friends for over thirty years. I know you're chafing, but there's really nothing here for you now. Unless you really *want* to help Spock negotiate with the Klingons."

Kirk laughed a little and held up both hands in a "back off" gesture. "While I respect Chancellor Azetbur greatly, I think I have had enough of the Klingons to last me for the rest of my life. At least tell me what you can about what's going on. I can pretend I'm not rotting away in obscurity on a transport ship crammed with twenty-six cadets, racing along at a heart-stopping warp two."

Standing Crane laughed again. "I suppose I have a few moments to humor an old friend. Actually, you might be interested in this, since Skalli's now your pet project."

Kirk rolled his eyes.

"The inhabitants of Falor, a planet in a solar system right next door to Huan's system, are now petitioning to join the Federation. We've just played host to a very large delegation of Falorians and it has been a time, I'll tell you."

"Anything like the Huanni?"

"Hmm, yes and no. They were clearly once members of the same species. Similar in appearance, but much stockier, less ethereal." Kirk knew what she meant. Skalli evoked images of a dryad from ancient Earth mythology. Huanni were humanoid in appearance, with long ears like a horse's and pale purple skin and hair. Skalli was tall and thin, her bones almost as delicate and light as an avian's. It seemed as though one good gust of wind would blow her away.

"How about the emotions?"

"They're much more controlled than the Huanni, thank goodness," Standing Crane replied. "But they have an insatiable curiosity and don't quite understand certain etiquettes. They're into everything, like children. They pelted us with more questions than a normal five-year-old would."

Suddenly Skalli seemed to Kirk to be significantly less annoying.

"They've asked to see every single starbase, visit every single member planet, tour as many starships as are available—frankly, Jim, we're getting overwhelmed! The Federation likes to be accessible to potential members, but this is just getting ridiculous. We found one of them in the kitchens before last night's farewell banquet. He had almost gotten stuck inside a cabinet and was meticulously examining—and sampling!—every single spice we had. One doesn't like to laugh at a respected member of an honored entourage, but honestly it pushed our limits!"

"I hope he didn't get into the Sakerlian spice. A mouthful of that stuff would have caused a diplomatic incident."

"Too true," Standing Crane said. She sighed. "Oh, Jim, it is good to see you. It's been too long."

"So, maybe I purchase the lovely lady a drink at Gaston's when I return," Kirk said.

"Maybe the lovely lady will take you up on that when she can spare a moment," Standing Crane replied.

"Maybe that," Kirk said ruefully, "will be a while."

"More's the pity. Enjoy the rest of the trip . . . if you can," Standing Crane said. "Good-bye, Jim. And you be nice to Skalli!"

She was still smiling when her image disappeared, to be replaced with a blue screen sporting the official circular insignia of Starfleet Command.

Kirk leaned back in his chair and stretched. He eyed what he had brought for entertainment: old copies of fine books he'd read several times, a tattered deck of cards over which he, McCoy, and Scotty—the only other members of his old senior staff who enjoyed gambling—had spent many an hour.

But he was not about to ask these cadets, to him barely out of diapers, to join him in a game of poker, or even fizzbin. And he was heartily sick of solitaire.

There was a sound on the computer indicating that he had a message and Kirk smiled. Perhaps Laura had found that "moment." He thumbed the control and said, "Changed your mind about that drink?"

The words stuck in his throat. Onscreen was not the friendly, attractive face of Laura Standing Crane but the stern, haughty visage of Chancellor Azetbur of the Klingon High Council. She cocked her head, clearly puzzled at his comment.

"Captain?"

Recovering immediately, Kirk smiled his easy smile and waved a hand dismissively. "Forgive me, Chancellor, I was expecting someone else. How are the negotiations coming?"

"Very well indeed," she replied. "Your friend Spock has a gift for bringing together at a table many who might otherwise prefer a fight. The others involved are also welcome contributors toward the peace we all seek."

"I'm delighted to hear it, but after serving with them so long, I confess I expected no less. Now, Chancellor, what can I do for you?"

"It is not what you can do for me, Captain Kirk." Her voice was as icy as he remembered it, even though they both knew now that he was no enemy to the Klingons, indeed one of their best friends by virtue of his salvaging of the peace negotiations. "It is what I am planning on doing for you."

"I'm . . . not sure I understand, Chancellor."

"You saved many lives a few months ago," she continued. "You perhaps saved my entire race."

He laughed slightly. "Come now, Chancellor. You give me too much credit."

"Indeed, I do not think so." Her eyes flashed briefly and Kirk wondered, as he so often did when dealing with Klingons, if he had inadvertently given offense. "I wish to repay you for what you have done. I owe you an honor debt, and Klingons always repay honor debts. I am invoking the *DIS jaj je.*"

Although Klingon had been in the computer's translation banks for several decades now, every now and then a phrase would be uttered that had the computer scurrying to catch up with the translation. This was such a moment, and Kirk and Azetbur stared at one another for an uncomfortably long few seconds before the computer offered the words, "The Year and the Day" as the proper translation.

Kirk was still baffled. He had no doubt that the translation was technically accurate as far as it went, but he remained unenlightened as to what it really *meant.*

Azetbur was regarding him expectantly. Her eyes were bright and her color was high. Clearly what she had just said meant a great deal to her.

With a silent prayer to whatever god controlled effective and harmonious communication, Kirk said, "Chancellor, I thank you, but this is not necessary. What I did, I did freely. There is no honor debt between us."

The god who controlled effective and harmonious communication clearly had the day off, because Azetbur tensed. "We wrongfully put you in prison, you and your chief medical officer. We expected you to die, James Kirk, and would have been glad of it. Despite this ultimately unjust treatment at our hands, you risked your life to save mine and those of numberless Klingons, those alive and those generations yet to be born."

The last thing Kirk wanted—well, the last thing other than to not have Skalli as his pet project—was to be in any way, shape or form further entangled with Klingons.

"I have no wish to offend you, Chancellor, but as far as I am concerned, all debts are paid. There's no need for. . . ." For the briefest of moments Kirk debated trying to twist his tongue around the guttural, consonant-laden language, then opted for the Federation standard words instead. "For 'The Year and the Day.'"

For a long, very bad moment Kirk worried that Azetbur would try to leap for his throat through the screen. Then, oddly, she smiled, showing sharp teeth, and settled in her chair. She looked like a cat who'd just cornered a particularly tasty-looking mouse, and he worried about *that,* too.

"As you wish, Captain Kirk. As far as you are concerned, then, there shall be no The Year and the Day. You will at least permit me to thank you again?"

"Chancellor, I was honored to be of service in so high a cause," he said, and meant every word. He hoped his sincerity would come through.

Apparently it did. She nodded, and seemed satisfied. "Then I wish you good day, Captain."

"And you, Chancellor."

Their eyes locked, then her image blipped out. Kirk blew out a breath. The Chancellor of the Klingon High Council wanted him to accept an honor debt. Well, that was something you didn't see every day. He congratulated himself for getting off so easily.

His door chimed. "Come in," he called, rubbing his eyes.

There was a slight hiss and Skalli stood in the doorway.

"It's nineteen hundred hours and five minutes," she said. "We're all waiting for you, and we're hungry!"

Kirk regarded her for a moment, then rose. "Far be it from me to keep a roomful of hungry cadets waiting," he said. "After you."

Azetbur stared at the dark screen after the image of Kirk had disappeared, playing a little game with herself. She wanted to see how long it would take before her right hand, Brigadier Kerla, exploded in fury.

"Arrogant human *pahtk!*" Kerla spat. Azetbur permitted herself a slight smile.

"It took you three entire seconds," she said calmly. "I am pleased to see you are learning restraint. It will serve us well in our interaction with humans."

"He spurned the *DIS jaj je!*" raged Kerla, stamping about the small room, ignoring Azetbur's gibe. "That pompous, self-centered—-"

"Patience, my old friend," Azetbur soothed. "He is only a human, after all. He does not know our customs. He could not possibly understand the honor I offered him." She rose. "Besides, he did not spurn it."

"With all due respect, Chancellor," said Kerla, "I was by your side the entire time. I heard what he—"

"He may have meant to *decline* the offer of the honor debt," replied Azetbur, choosing her words very carefully. "But one cannot decline such a thing. It will happen, whether he wills it or no. I have sworn the oath of *DIS jaj je.* I will honor it. No one can forswear me!"

Her voice rang clearly, and with an effort she brought her own bubbling rage under control. She knew that Kirk was a good person. He had overcome his own prejudices to save people he had very good cause to regard as enemies. It was a misunderstanding, not an insult. She would not permit Kerla to view it as such, nor would she.

"But if you try to enact it, he will surely notice," said Kerla. "Notice, and protest."

Azetbur shook her head slowly. "He will not know of it. I will keep my word, and he will think he has . . . disentangled himself from us. Brigadier, I want you to contact the *K'Rator.* I have a mission for her captain."

Chapter Three

Commander Uhura contorted her beautiful dark face into a snarl and spat forth a string of harsh-sounding words. Fiercely, she brandished her *bat'leth*, then leaped forward. Blood-red robes trimmed in black fur swirled around her.

> *"Son of a black-hearted dog,*
> *My body is not thine,*
> *My heart is not thine,*
> *But my blade—yes, ah, yes,*
> *This I offer to thee,*
> *I offer to thy heart!"*

A mere meter away, Karglak offered his own guttural challenge, which climaxed with an earsplitting screech. He was clad in black and silver armor, and sprang forward to meet his adversary.

> *"In this conflict shall I scream my battle cry,*
> *Death is but another foe to defeat.*

It is you who shall board the Barge of the Dead
In dishonor so great
That none shall remember your name!"

Their *bat'leths* clashed, then clashed again. Uhura's muscles quivered under the strain and she knew a flash of fear. Good thing she kept in decent shape—

Grunting, they sprang apart. Thrice they circled, and then leapt at one another. This time Uhura felt the wind rush past her face as she narrowly avoided the curving blade. She uttered a single word with all the strength she possessed: *"Qapla'!"* and charged him.

Karglak fell beneath her, his own weapon knocked from his hands to skitter to a halt three meters away. Uhura straddled his waist. She was sweating profusely and breathing heavily. Under the hot lights, she could see the bare skin of her own arms gleaming with moisture.

Quick as a thought, she brought the *bat'leth* down and pressed it against his throat. For a long moment, they stared into one another's eyes.

Slowly, she eased back and removed the deadly blade. He was faster, and before she knew it she was caught up in his arms, his sharp-tooth mouth pressed down on hers, and they were locked in an embrace as violent as their battle had been.

A sudden silence and utter blackness descended.

"Hey, watch the teeth," Uhura grumbled, clambering off the most famous opera singer ever to have graced the planet Qo'noS. She dabbed at her lip gently, wincing. Her finger came away red.

Karglak leapt to his feet, gallantly extending a hand to help her up. She took it. "I regret any pain I may have caused you," he said. "But that was marvelous! Marvelous! I was so caught up in the drama I was . . . how do you put it . . . carried away."

She smiled at him. At least he'd agreed to start using a mouthwash during their up-close-and-personal duets. "It's all right, Karglak. I'll take it as a compliment."

"As you should," purred Lamork, the director of the specially written operetta. "Karglak is notorious for discourtesy to his leading ladies."

"An exaggeration," Karglak scoffed. "They are—what is your word—prima donnas. Anyone of an artistic temperament would have difficulty performing with such arrogant females. You, dear lady, are a professional." He put his hand on his heart, and executed a bow.

The operetta would be performed in conjunction with a medley of songs that represented the finest of Earth's musical traditions: ancient Peruvian and Aboriginal melodies, "Greensleeves," some Gershwin tunes, two arias from *Madame Butterfly*, "Ole Man River," "Bring Him Home," China's famous "Moon and Sun Song," among others, and of course the famous "First Contact, First Touch" from the opera *Songs from Space and Time*, widely regarded as Earth's finest musical piece since humans first made contact with other species.

Despite the bruises, scrapes, and occasional cuts Uhura was forced to endure as part of this historic extravaganza, she had to confess she was enjoying herself hugely. Music had always been a great love. When but a young woman she had been forced to choose between two promising careers: opera performer or Starfleet Officer. She had chosen the latter and never regretted it, but was delighted that her voice was now considered as valuable a tool in the peace negotiations as her diplomatic skills.

She had been surprised to learn how much Klingons loved

opera, and what a long, rich history it had on their homeworld. Uhura couldn't help but smile as she remembered stumbling through rudimentary Klingon a few months ago, when the *Enterprise* was attempting to rescue its imprisoned captain. She had thought the language unmusical and unpleasant. Certainly it had challenged a human throat and tongue. But the more she heard it, the more intriguing it sounded to her, and when, at Captain Spock's gentle suggestion, she had finally listened to Klingon opera, she had been captivated. What power it had! What grand, sweeping stories it told!

When she approached Spock with the concept of a "musical exchange," an evening of Klingon opera and human song, he had seemed surprised. It had taken her a week or two, but she finally realized that it had been Spock's idea all along. He had only let Uhura think it had been her idea.

She, however, had been the one doing all the work: compiling the pieces and going over them with Qo'noS's most famous opera singer, Karglak. She had anticipated a difficult time, but to her delight and surprise Karglak was as eager as she to learn about new musical styles. They had each agreed to learn each other's languages, if possible, to honor the other's culture. He had taken smoothly to English and Italian, and she had to admit that despite his fearsome exterior, part of her melted—just a little—when he gazed into her eyes and sang "Some Enchanted Evening."

The mesmerizing effect he had on her ended after the performance, thank goodness. Positive cultural exchange was one thing, but the interspecies romance made so famous by *Songs from Space and Time* notwithstanding, she had no desire to exchange anything more intimate.

She mopped her soaking brow and gulped water with lemon while Lamork gave them notes. "Commander, you are doing a fine job with the range of the piece, but I would ask you to reexamine your Klingon. The 'r' comes from the back of the throat, not from the tip of the tongue. And the glottal stops are—"

Uhura sighed. "Lamork, I've no desire to permanently ruin my voice for one evening's performance. If I can approximate the sound well enough to be understood, what's the problem?"

Lamork frowned terribly. "You show disrespect for the composer's vision, *that* is the problem."

She kept her gaze locked with his, refusing to rise to the bait. "And Karglak hardly sounds French when he's performing as Emile de Becque, but you haven't heard me complaining."

"Commander," came a calm, cool voice from the back of the room. "Director Lamork. Please. We have no wish to start a new war on the eve of peace."

The voice, of course, belonged to Captain Spock. He was out of uniform and gliding down the aisle to meet them in flowing blue, silver, and gold robes, the traditional garb of his people. "This was meant to bring two races together with a love of music, not divide them by the finer details."

Lamork turned his fearsome glower upon Spock, but did not respond to the Vulcan's chiding. Instead, he changed the subject. "I dare not hope," he said, sarcasm creeping into his voice, "that you are here just to be uplifted by the music."

"You assume incorrectly if you think that Vulcans have no appreciation for music and art, Lamork. Simply because we control our emotions does not mean we cannot appreciate beauty. Rest assured that on the night of the performance, it is unlikely that you will have a more attentive listener than myself. However, you are correct—I did come here to speak with Commander Uhura. Commander, if you please?"

Taking her lemon water with her and nodding to her fellow

performer, Uhura stepped off the stage and followed Spock up a ways toward the end of the hall.

"How are the rehearsals progressing?" Spock wanted to know.

"Very well, actually," Uhura said. "Karglak is surprisingly easy to work with, though Lamork's a hell of a taskmaster."

"Any sign of conflict? Resentment?"

"Not really. Except over things like accents and hitting the notes right." She smiled, wincing a little as she did so as a brief stab reminded her of her cut lip. "It looks like artists remain artists, no matter what the culture. I don't think there's anything going on here except old-fashioned theater politics."

Spock frowned, noticing her wince and the swelling on her lip. "You are injured," he said.

"Oh, that," Uhura said, laughing a little. "Seems our Karglak got a little carried away during our duet."

"I would be mindful, Commander. It is my understanding that biting, especially around the mouth and face, is part of a Klingon mating ritual."

She stared at him, her jaw dropping slightly. He raised an eyebrow. Slowly, Uhura turned to look back at the stage. Karglak was watching them and as she looked at him, he smiled and waved a little.

"Uh oh," she said.

"No, no, no," said McCoy, his voice rising despite the delicacy of the situation. "Remember the heart is *there*, not there. That's the—" He glanced up at his Klingon counterpart. "That's the liver, right?"

Doctor Q'ulagh frowned terribly, and McCoy got the feeling that he, too, was running out of patience with the dissection. McCoy couldn't blame him. It had taken a lot of discussion—all right, call a spade a spade, *begging*—in order to convince the Klingon government to donate a cadaver in the first place. And now McCoy was watching some of the Federation's finest give damn good impressions of medieval barbers as they hacked at the corpse.

"It is not the liver," Q'ulagh responded, his teeth clenched and his eyes flashing. "It is the first of the two . . ." And the translator shut down, not even trying to translate the long flow of seeming gibberish that ensued. McCoy recognized it and nodded. The two whatziz were extraneous organs not found in any other humanoid species. He recalled what he knew to make sure he had his ducks in a row.

"These . . . uh . . . highly specialized organs secrete anti-inflammatory fluids and natural painkillers when the skin is damaged," he said. "It keeps a warrior on his feet longer. It is part of what makes a Klingon such a fearsome enemy in battle."

He threw that last part in on a whim. It was sincere enough, but this whole honor code thing was starting to wear a bit thin. However, when Q'ulagh visibly calmed and even nodded his head in admiration at McCoy's statement, the elderly Southern doctor recalled a statement his mama had made many years past: *You catch more flies with honey than vinegar, son.*

To his relief, his team of Starfleet doctors, some of them heads of medical schools, followed his lead. The Klingon doctors accepted the compliment and the tension in the room eased.

Dr. Malcolm Simpson, one of the finest surgeons to ever grace Starfleet, continued the dissection. One by one, the mysterious Klingon organs were removed and themselves dissected. The Klingons didn't understand it, but they didn't have to. Their chancellor, Azetbur, had told them to participate whole-heartedly in this special meeting of minds, so that an incident like the death of her father, Gorkon, would never again happen.

To this day, McCoy had dreams about that dreadful, tragic night. In his nightmares he again straddled the dying chancellor, who looked up at him with imploring eyes. McCoy read in their depths Gorkon's fierce desire to live, not so much for himself as for his people. Gorkon knew if this assassination attempt was successful, the tentative alliance the Federation and the Klingon Empire had formed would shatter like glass dropped on a stone floor. As it damn near had.

He vividly recalled the strange purple-magenta color of Klingon blood on his hands, searching frantically for the heart, doing everything he would normally do to save a dying human, and knowing that he was failing utterly with this Klingon.

I tried to save him, McCoy remembered crying aloud at his trial, a Klingon kangaroo court if there ever was one. *I was desperate to save him.*

Well, now he'd know how. And so would all these surgeons, who would teach their own students Klingon anatomy. There need never be another death on account of ignorance, not anymore. And the Klingons were learning the same things. There had been those who muttered that giving Klingons lessons in human anatomy was akin to providing them more efficient ways to butcher, but McCoy had shut up that line of talk quickly. They were becoming allies now, Klingons and humans, as unlikely as that seemed, and understanding one another physically was part of learning to understand one another culturally.

The dead Klingon was now empty of his organs. His belly and chest gaped open. The face was gone, peeled back early on in the autopsy in order to better access the brain. McCoy never liked being overlong with the dead; his job was to save the living. Seeing this corpse, which Q'ulagh had assured him had once been a proud warrior, McCoy felt sorrow brush him.

"Rest in peace," he murmured under his breath. Straightening, he cleared his throat. "Let's take a short break before we begin dissecting the human corpse."

"If you have no further need of the body, we will transport it into space. It is but an empty shell now." Q'ulagh said.

"Of course," McCoy said, although he was a bit taken aback by the Klingon's lack of desire for anything resembling a proper burial. Q'ulagh pulled out his communicator, uttered a few rough-sounding words, and the corpse and its attendant organs dematerialized.

As they were heading out the door, McCoy caught a whisper: "There went a good Klingon." Stifled laughter greeted the comment.

Fortunately, the Klingons were already gone. It was also fortunate that had they even heard the muttered words they would have taken them at face value. McCoy, however, knew what they were intended to mean. He whirled and grabbed Dr. Phillip Kingston by his bloody scrubs, taking the much younger man by surprise.

"Isn't it funny," said McCoy softly, "how old phrases just don't want to die? 'The only good Indian is a dead Indian' could maybe be forgiven when uttered by a prejudiced, frightened white soldier a few hundred years ago. But I can't believe I'm hearing it from the lips of a Starfleet officer."

Blue eyes blazing, McCoy turned Kingston loose with a grunt of disgust. "You slip up one more time, and you're off this team."

The blond man's lip curled. "You can't do that," he said.

"The hell I can't. This was my project from the beginning.

You're here because you're a top-notch surgeon. But I'm beginning to think you're not such a great human being."

He turned and stalked off, following the rest to the break area.

Damn, damn. You think you've come so far, learned so much as a species, and then something like this happens.

As the late, greatly lamented Chancellor Gorkon said at that ill-fated dinner aboard the *Enterprise* not so long ago, "I can see we still have a long way to go."

Chapter Four

The San Francisco skyline was beautiful at night, and Kirk stood for a while simply gazing at it.

He was completely, utterly, and thoroughly bored.

He had returned to Earth two days ago and had bid an unfortunately temporary farewell to a clingy Skalli. Standing Crane, as she had warned, was far too busy even for a quick drink at Gaston's. Spock, Uhura and McCoy of course were so deeply entangled in the peace negotiations that they could barely spare a moment to chat, although Spock had told him that things were progressing surprisingly well. Sulu, lucky devil, had his own ship now and was off somewhere captaining it. Kirk had messages in to both Chekov and Scotty, but so far, they hadn't responded.

Everyone, it seemed, was terribly busy. Except for one James T. Kirk. He rattled the ice in his Scotch and took another sip.

His door buzzed. Kirk glanced at the chronometer. It was after midnight. Who could it be at this hour?

Whoever it is, he thought grimly, *is welcome . . . unless it's Skalli.*

"Come in," he called, not bothering to see who it was.

The door hissed open and two handsome blond men stood in its frame. One was in his mid-thirties, well built and solid looking. The other, who hung back a little, was younger and slighter. They looked familiar, but Kirk couldn't place them at once.

Then the older one of them smiled, and the memory clicked into place.

"Hi, Uncle Jim," Kirk's nephew, Alexander, said.

"Good Lord," Kirk said, feeling a smile stretch across his face. "Alex . . . Julius . . . come in, come in! Is it really you?"

They stepped inside. "Nice place," said Julius, the youngest of Kirk's three nephews. How old was he now—twenty-seven? Twenty-eight?

A long, uncomfortable moment ensued as the three men regarded one another. Had they been the youngsters Kirk remembered, he'd have known what to do—fold them into a big, avuncular hug. But they were men, not boys, and it had been so long since he'd seen them. . . .

It was Alex who broke the ice by suddenly laughing and embracing his uncle. Alex was now bigger than Kirk, taller and broader, and Kirk felt a distinctly odd sensation that was both familiar and completely strange. Slowly, he reached up and returned the hug. He had a sudden, painful flashback to when he had first embraced his son David. He forced that memory down. David was dead, killed by—

—(Klingons)—

—a madman. Alexander and Julius were here, alive, and it felt very, very good to see them.

Julius forestalled an embrace by extending his hand, smiling stiffly. Kirk grasped the hand.

"I suppose it has been a bit too long for you to want to hug your Uncle Jim, Julius," he said as gently as he could.

Julius's smile froze on his lips. "I wasn't trying to—" he began. Kirk held up a hand, forestalling his comment.

"You look good, both of you. I saw your brother just recently." Peter, the eldest son of Kirk's late, beloved brother Sam, was active in Starfleet Diplomatic Corps. While not part of the group that had been selected to travel to the Klingon homeworld, Peter was nonetheless heavily involved in the peace process. He and Kirk had managed to grab a few moments for a cup of coffee together before their respective duties had called them away. It was, unfortunately, a very typical encounter for both of them.

Julius didn't react, but Alex brightened visibly. "Peter! How is he? We don't hear from him much."

Kirk heard the unspoken word "either," but ignored it. "He's doing very well. Quite active in the peace negotiations. Have a seat, both of you. What can I get you?"

Julius nodded at the small glass of amber fluid Kirk was carrying. "That Scotch?"

"Indeed it is. A parting gift from my chief engineer. You can practically cut the peat."

A quick, genuine smile flitted across Julius's sharp features, softening them for an instant. "Sounds perfect. Neat, please."

Kirk turned to the bar and poured Julius two fingers' worth of the twenty-four-year-old Bunnahabhain. "How about you, Alex? Scotch, wine . . ." He turned with a smile. "Romulan ale?"

Alex looked puzzled. "I thought that was illegal," he said.

"It is, but you don't look official to me." A thought crossed his mind. "And if you are, that was just a joke."

Alex laughed. "No, we're not official, Uncle Jim. I'll just have some ice water with lemon, thanks."

Kirk finished preparing the drinks, then handed them to his nephews. "To family reunions," he toasted, lifting his glass. Both young men did likewise, and then each took a sip. Kirk sat in a chair opposite Alex and Julius.

"I must confess, I'm quite surprised to see you two, especially at this hour," he said. "To what do I owe the pleasure?"

The Kirk brothers looked at each other. Julius, who was sitting on the arm of the couch, sat back a little, swirling his scotch. Alex put his glass of water down on the coffee table and leaned forward.

"I didn't think you'd think it was just a social call," he said. Kirk smiled faintly and took another sip. Alex ran a hand through his thick fair hair and laughed uneasily. "For months I've rehearsed this, and now that I'm here, it's all gone right out of my head."

"We're all family here," Kirk said. "Speak from the heart, Alex. It'll come out all right. Trust me."

Alex licked his lips and looked down at his entwined hands. He took a deep breath. "We, uh, didn't see much of you after Mom and Dad died. And I know that it wasn't your fault. I mean, you were a captain of a starship, and they don't let you take families with you on those. We couldn't go with you, even if you'd wanted us, and we know that. Peter was at the starbase for so long and then went back to Earth with Grandma and Grampa. And we stayed with the Pearsons on Rigel VI."

Kirk regarded his nephew steadily. "I know all this, Alex. Why are you mentioning it now?"

"Because the Pearsons treated us like cattle," said Julius unexpectedly. "And we've been on our own for the last several years. Something you might have known if you'd bothered—"

"Julius!" snapped Alex, his mild face flushed and angry. At once, his younger brother subsided.

Kirk was immediately attentive. "Alex . . . were you and Julius abused in any way?"

"Oh, no, Uncle Jim, nothing like that. But it was clear that we weren't wanted. I don't think they realized how much of a handful we would turn out to be! So when I was twenty I . . . well, I just took Julius with me and left. They didn't seem to care too much. Anyway, that's not the point. The point is, we've been doing a lot of traveling, and over the years we realized what we really wanted: a home."

Guilt warred with indignation within Kirk. Alex had been right—even if he'd wanted to adopt his three nephews, which he was unhappily certain he hadn't, he wouldn't have been able to. There was no place for children aboard a starship. And then one thing led to another, and the next thing he knew he had contacted the Pearsons and they told him that Alex and Julius were all grown up and striking out on their own as young men.

He'd sent a message on each of their birthdays, every year, along with what he hoped were suitable gifts. Every time he'd been near Rigel VI, which wasn't often, he'd arranged to visit them. He had adored his big brother, George Samuel Kirk, but even they had fallen out of touch once they had reached adulthood. The Kirks just weren't a close-knit family, that was all there was to it, especially with their divergent interests that took them all over the galaxy.

But this revelation about the Pearsons disturbed him greatly. "I didn't know that you weren't happy," he said. "You were visiting the Pearsons when your parents died, and it seemed the right place for you. You have a home here, with me, if you want it."

"It's all right, Uncle Jim. We don't want to move in!" Alex forced a laugh. The turn of the conversation was clearly as uncomfortable to him as it was to Kirk. "We want our own home. Our own place. And we've met with many others who share our vision."

He leaned forward, his eyes sparkling. "Uncle Jim, we want to found a colony."

Now I understand, Kirk thought. *They want me to pull some strings and find them a suitable place.* The thought that they had sought him out not for his own sake, but what he could do for them, pained him a little, but he supposed he couldn't blame them. Clearly they, too, thought of him not as a person, not as Uncle Jim, but the Great Captain James T. Kirk.

"I'll see what I can do," he began. "Most of Starfleet's attention is on this conference, and they're not going to be able to spare a lot of people to help you find a place."

"Oh, no, you've got it all wrong," Alex said. "We've found a planet already."

"Really? Where?"

"It's in the Besar system, very remote, freely donated as a goodwill gesture by a race that is negotiating with the Federation for admittance. I call it . . . Sanctuary." His face softened and his eyes lost focus. "It's beautiful, Uncle Jim. We're going to make it our own little corner of paradise. Here's a list of those who have already agreed to go."

Alex handed Kirk a padd and Kirk quickly scanned the names. The list of scientists and engineers was lengthy, and most of them were renowned for their cutting-edge discoveries and developments. Whatever else this colony might be, it would certainly be very high-tech.

"Alex, I'm impressed. You seem to have the cream of the crop here."

"Yes, we do," Alex continued eagerly. "There aren't that many ideal places out there anymore, as I'm sure you know."

"How fortunate that these . . . who's donating the planet?"

"Falorians."

"That's the second time this week I've heard their name crop up," Kirk said. "A friend of mine greeted their diplomatic delegation. Very friendly, very curious, is that correct?" He tried and failed to get Standing Crane's story of the Falorian scooping out a fingerful of every spice in Starfleet Headquarters' banquet kitchen out of his mind.

"Oh, yes," Alex said. "So open-handed."

"There's no such thing as a free lunch," Kirk reminded him.

"I know that," Alex said, and bridled a little. "It's obvious that they're hoping to win favor for their admittance by letting us have the colony. And we've negotiated certain rights to anything we might learn. Not all, of course," he hastened to add. "They've never had any desire to colonize it themselves or else they'd have done so centuries ago. It works out to be a good thing for everyone involved."

"How did you manage to snag this gem of a world?" Kirk wanted to know.

"It's all thanks to Julius," Alex replied, turning to regard his brother with affection. "He's been amazing. I've been working hard to get people to sign on for it, but he's been the one out there talking to all kinds of alien races to find us our Sanctuary."

Julius flushed a little—that pale coloring didn't serve him well—and looked down at his empty glass as if he wished there were more Scotch in it.

"Really?" Kirk said, trying to not sound too surprised. "Starfleet has a whole section with dozens of people devoted to that kind of wrangling. How did you manage it on your own?"

Julius's jaw tensed almost imperceptibly and Kirk wished he could rephrase the question. "This is the culmination of many years of discussions with many different species, Uncle

Jim. Let me assure you Alex and I have had our share of false starts and deals falling through. We were able to contact the Falorians at the right time, when they were trying to look good to the Federation."

"So, luck, skill, and hard work, is that what you're saying?"

Julius shrugged. "Pretty much."

"A wise man once said, the harder you work, the luckier you get," Kirk said. "It sounds to me as if you are both very lucky, from that standpoint. Tell me a little more about . . . about your vision, Alex."

Those were apparently the magic words, for Alex lit up immediately. "You've seen the list I gave you. You know these people, what they're known for, their personalities."

"Iconoclastic geniuses might not be too strong a term," Kirk said.

"Individualists," Alex insisted. "Dreamers who can back up their dreams with concrete realities. But we don't want to just hand over the results of our hard work to someone else—we want it for our own. We'll share everything, for the betterment of all peace-loving species, but we won't just surrender what we know, what we've made, without long, careful thought. And we'll make sure it's all used for the right purposes. We'll make sure our knowledge doesn't ever fall into the wrong hands."

Kirk felt a quick stab of pity for Alex's naïveté. He'd been that idealistic once. He thought of Oppenheimer, of Lu Wang Hu, of the Vulcan teacher Sekur. All of them had used their genius to break barriers; all of them had eventually seen their creations turned into weapons of mass destruction. He hoped this wouldn't happen to Alex.

"We're taking as our inspiration the Amish and the Quakers," Alex was saying. "They've made it through centuries still holding onto their ideals of nonviolence. So can we."

"The Amish don't exactly approve of cutting-edge technology," Kirk reminded him.

Alex laughed. "No, that's true. But we don't have to be Amish to respect them and learn from their wisdom."

Kirk gestured with the padd. "And all these famous people have agreed to this?"

"Absolutely. We are committed to this, Uncle Jim."

Kirk looked at him for a long moment. "Your father would be so proud," he said quietly. "Of both of you," he added, including the more withdrawn Julius as well as the open, talkative Alex.

"I wish you both all the luck in the universe," Kirk continued.

Alex and Julius exchanged amused glances. "He hasn't figured it out yet," Julius said with a slight smirk.

"Figured what out?"

"Uncle Jim," Alex said, "We didn't come all this way and show up at your door at midnight just to *tell* you about our colony. We came to ask you to come with us."

Chapter Five

"Out of the question," Kirk said automatically. "I have responsibilities here. I can't just go galloping across the galaxy as if I were your age again."

"Why not?" The question was uttered in absolute innocence and Alex seemed genuinely puzzled by his uncle's abrupt refusal. "You could help us so much. You have so many years of experience!"

"Experience in captaining a starship, yes," Kirk said. "Experience in protecting and defending a colony from hostile forces. But I don't know how much use I'll be to you and your people. What could I possibly do?"

"You could give me excellent advice," Alex said promptly. "You could help Julius with the Falorians." He grinned sheepishly and added, "And if I may be frank, having someone with your reputation join the colony will be a real feather in our cap. It would give us a great deal of legitimacy in the Federation's eyes, some negotiating clout when it comes to that."

"Please come, Uncle Jim." Surprised, Kirk turned to look at

his youngest nephew. "We've worked so hard. It would mean so much to Alex . . . to me . . . if you would come with us."

"Worried about your old uncle, is that it?" Kirk asked. "I appreciate your concern, but I'm not ready to be farmed out to pasture just yet, thank you very much."

"Then what are you doing right now?" Julius challenged. He leaned forward. His blue eyes were intense in his lean face, his body taut with emotions Kirk couldn't quite decipher. "Don't you think we've been keeping tabs on you? We needed to know if you'd be in a position to even consider our offer, and you most certainly are."

"Juley—" began Alex, worried.

"Don't 'Juley' me, not now, Alex," Julius shot back. "We're too close to let him stop us."

Kirk began to speak. "Julius, I can understand—"

"Shut up!" cried Julius, startling both his brother and his uncle into a momentary silence. "You have no idea what we've been through the last few years, Uncle Jim. No idea. You don't know the, the begging and pleading Alex has had to do, the crawling through mud and getting sick and being literally scared for my *life* half the time that I've done to get this thing to fly. We've got names, we've got backing, we've got a beautiful, unspoiled world owned by friendly aliens, and the last piece of the puzzle is *you*."

He paused, swallowing hard, then continued. "It was part of the dream from the beginning, having us all together again. We know we can't get Peter. We know what he's dealing with and as peace-loving people ourselves we have respect for that. But you're done, Uncle Jim. You're hanging around Starfleet hoping they'll toss you a bone, and all they've done is given you classes at the Academy. I heard about your "Command Decisions and Their Consequences" class. The kids loved it, but I bet it rankled, having to stand up in front of a class and just talk about the glory days instead of living them."

Kirk had gone from startled to angry to amused. "Please, don't stop now, Julius. Keep telling me how I feel."

The youth was too wrapped up in his own emotions to take offense at the gibe. "You're a legend. And your career speaks for itself. You like to act, to be involved, to do things, just like we like to do things. Just like Alex tells me Dad and Mom liked to. I have to take his word for that; I don't have any memories of them. I think it's in our blood, this—this love of doing. And I can't believe that you're happy with these so-called responsibilities.

"Tell us, Uncle Jim. Look us in the eye and tell us that you are happy where you are, teaching eighteen-year-olds ancient history, when you could be part of an experiment working alongside your own blood to bring about things that can change the universe. You tell me this and we'll go away and not try any more to drag you out of this early grave you've dug for yourself. Can you do it, Uncle Jim? Huh? Can you?"

The amusement had faded and the anger had surged back. Coolly, but with an edge to his voice, Kirk replied, "It's been good seeing you both. I wish you luck with Sanctuary."

For a moment, Julius stared. He seemed more distressed than Alex at Kirk's blunt refusal.

It was Alex who finally broke the taut silence. "I told you he wouldn't come, Juley," he said heavily. "But you were right about one thing. We had to try."

Julius still seemed to be in shock. "I can't believe it," he whispered. "I can't believe you'd just . . . without even . . . ah, the hell with it. And the hell with you, *Captain.*" He slid off the back of the sofa and strode toward the door. It hissed open and he was gone, without a backward glance.

"I apologize for Julius, Uncle Jim," Alex said. He was still seated on the couch. "You'll have to forgive him. We really have been through a lot in getting this colony pulled together, and it would have been the jewel in the crown if you could have been part of it. He was so insistent that we come talk to you in person about it. I think he really thought we'd be able to convince you."

"You didn't seem so sure," Kirk said softly.

"No. I figured you were pretty well entrenched in whatever it was you were doing. We'd have to catch you at just the right moment, and that would be hard." He rose and smiled awkwardly. "Admiral Karen Berg is one of our sponsors. She'll be able to contact us if . . . if you change your mind."

"Alex, I'm sorry. I think Julius believes it has to do with you, but it doesn't. It has everything to do with my responsibilities."

"Oh, sure, Uncle Jim. He'll understand. Well, I better get going if I'm to catch up to Julius." He smiled sadly, and again reached out to his uncle. But there was a resignation in the hug that had not been there the first time.

They drew apart and looked into one another's eyes. "I'm sure Sanctuary will live up to its name with you as the leader, Alex," Kirk said.

Alex seemed about to say something, then apparently thought better of it. He smiled, squeezed Kirk's shoulder one last time, then turned and followed his brother into the night.

The silence was absolute. Slowly, Kirk picked up the discarded glasses, took them to the sink, washed them, and went to bed.

It was still dark out when his door chimed. Kirk bolted upright and glanced at the chronometer. Who would possibly be at his door at 5:30 A.M.? Maybe it was Julius and Alex, back to try to convince him again. For some reason, he was pleased at the prospect.

He fumbled for a robe, hastily sashed it closed, then stumbled into the living room. He glanced up to see who it was and groaned softly. It was not Julius and Alex. It was not anyone he had any desire to see.

Steeling himself, he opened the door. "Good morning, Skalli."

She bounced a little, standing in the doorway with a big grin on her lively face, then scampered inside. She carried a large basket, which she summarily plopped down on the kitchen table.

"Good morning, Captain Kirk! I brought us breakfast before our hike."

Kirk sighed. "Skalli," he began, "it's really not appropriate for you to be here at all, especially at this hour of the morning." *Let alone,* he thought, glancing down at his black terrycloth robe, *when your instructor is wearing just a bathrobe.*

Skalli had turned and followed his gaze. "Oh, you mean because of the possibilities of sexual relations between student and teacher. Don't worry. You are absolutely *not* of interest to me sexually."

Kirk didn't believe it, but he felt himself blushing at her frank conversation.

Skalli's hand flew to her mouth. "I didn't mean that to sound the way it did . . . oh, dear . . . Not that you're not attractive . . . I mean, in your own human way, but to Huanni aesthetics humans aren't . . . there's not a *chance* that—"

Kirk held up a hand, growing slightly desperate to change the subject. "That will do, Cadet. All questions of impropriety aside . . . what *are* you doing here at five-thirty in the morning?"

She tilted her head in the expression that he had come to

recognize as confusion. Her large ears flapped twice, then stood at full attention. "I thought I told you . . . I brought breakfast—"

"Before our hike, I got that. Didn't you think that perhaps I might have made my own plans about how I wanted to spend my day?"

"No," she said. "*Do* you have other plans?"

"No, but that's not the point. Why are you here?"

"For breakfast and—"

"I got that part," Kirk almost bellowed. "But why are we having breakfast and hiking? And you are not permitted to say because it will be healthy."

"But, you're my personal advisor. I thought we should get started immediately. Now that I have you all to myself, I have so many questions!"

Kirk ran a hand through his hair. "Skalli, that's during the semester."

Her ears sagged slightly and drooped like dying flowers down either side of her head. "You . . . you don't want to see me. Oh. I understand. I'm sorry. I'll go now."

He caught her by her long arm as she headed for the door, tears brimming in her enormous eyes. "It's not that, it's just . . . There are certain protocols and etiquette we have in place that you'll need to familiarize yourself with. One of them is, cadets don't interact with faculty members except during the school year. Another is, you schedule your meetings, which usually last about an hour. A third is, you never show up at a faculty member's home even if you're not sexually attracted to them."

He paused. That somehow hadn't come out quite right.

She listened with an earnestness and an intensity that was a bit unnerving. "I understand, Captain," she said firmly. "I apologize for my breach of protocol."

Kirk dropped his hand. "Apology accepted, Cadet." She still looked so distressed that he softened. "Tell you what. Since you went to all the trouble to make us breakfast, let's not let it go to waste. Let me get dressed. We'll eat, talk, then say good-bye, and I'll see you in September when the semester starts."

Her smile lit up her face. "That sounds great, Captain!"

It was a long breakfast, but it was delicious: blueberry muffins, fresh-squeezed orange juice, fresh fruits that Kirk didn't recognize but were delectable, and a thermos of a wonderfully aromatic beverage that was a kissing cousin to coffee but even tastier. Skalli talked incessantly, pummeling Kirk with questions, as the sun rose.

Finally, after every last crumb had been devoured, Skalli sadly slid off the chair and packed up the basket. "Let me apologize again, Captain."

"No need, Cadet. Thanks for breakfast. Have a good summer."

Her ears drooped. "You too, sir." The very personification of dejection, she slumped to the door, looked back at him sadly, and was gone.

The door had scarcely closed behind her when Kirk was at the computer. "Computer, contact and leave a message for Admiral Karen Berg. Please inform her that Jim Kirk needs to contact his nephews as soon as possible."

Shortly after Kirk had showered and shaved, a soft chime from his computer told him that someone was trying to contact him. It was Alex, managing to look both wary and hopeful at the same time.

"Got your message, Uncle Jim. What's going on?"

Kirk smiled. "You and Julius were right. There's nothing for me here that can't be resumed later. I'm not ready to make a long-term commitment right now, but . . . is the offer still open for me to come for a few months?"

He heard a faint whoop from somewhere in the room, and Alex's face split into an enormous grin. "You bet, Uncle Jim! Stay as short or long a time as you want. I'm sure though once you're there, you'll never want to leave!"

Kirk didn't share Alex's certainty, but he did know one thing: He was dying a slow death here, teaching classes and putting up with Skalli's boundless enthusiasm. He needed to be away, out there . . . *doing* something.

"You've got a great list of people, but you could probably stand to use a few old hands. Mind if I bring along some friends?"

"Absolutely not! Any friend of our Uncle Jim is a friend of Sanctuary," Alex said. "Who did you have in mind?"

Chapter Six

"I'm afraid not, Pavel," said Admiral Gray. "There's been no change since our last conversation."

"I see," said Commander Pavel Chekov, striving not to let the disappointment show.

"Captain Sheridan keeps asking about you," Gray continued, his dark face expressionless. "That first officer position is still open."

"Yes, sir. I know, sir."

"Pavel, I really suggest you take it. With all the hullabaloo going on with the Klingons, there aren't going to be many changes in the upper ranks. I don't think a captaincy is going to come along any time soon, and in the meantime, you're just sitting at that starbase wasting your time."

Part of Chekov thought that Gray was absolutely right. He was going mad here at Starbase 14, twiddling his thumbs. Ostensibly he was there as a "Starfleet presence," whatever the heck *that* meant. He was coming to the conclusion that it meant twiddling one's thumbs.

But he knew that he was ready for a captaincy. His last job as first officer of the *Reliant* had been a trying one. He'd distinguished himself very well since, but the thought of going back to the same position when his old helmsbuddy Sulu had been given the *Excelsior* felt to him like he was giving up. It was just a bad time, that was all. He'd ride it out and surely something would turn up.

"Please tell Captain Sheridan that I am flattered by his obvious respect," he told Gray. "But I can't accept."

Gray sighed. A handsome man of African descent, he'd been doing a lot of string-pulling on Chekov's behalf recently, and Chekov doubted he'd continue to do much more.

"I appreciate everything you've done for me, sir," he said. "But I know I'm on the right path."

Gray smiled wryly. "That makes one of us, Pavel. You're a good man, but you're like that former captain of yours. Stubborn as they come."

"Any comparison to Captain Kirk I will take as a compliment," Chekov responded, bridling a little on Kirk's behalf.

"As well you should," Gray said, still smiling. "Gray out."

Chekov leaned back in his chair, took a deep breath, puffed out his cheeks, and exhaled. He laced his fingers at the back of his neck and cradled his head, thinking hard. Was he really on the right path? Or was he on a wild goose chase? Gray might come back with one more offer, but that would certainly be it.

If only he had some kind of a sign—

His computer beeped, indicating a message. Chekov tapped it. "Commander Chek—*Captain!*"

On the viewscreen was an image of Captain Kirk. "Hello, Pavel," he said. "How are you doing? I thought you'd have a command of your own by this time."

"Thanks for the vote of confidence," Chekov answered, grimacing a little. "But, strangely enough, Starfleet doesn't seem to share our opinion. How is your class going?"

"Over and done with," Kirk said, "as is my tenure at the Academy. I've got a proposition to make, if you're in a position to think it over."

Chekov felt his mouth curve into a smile. Hell, it stretched into a grin. Anything Jim Kirk was going to get him into was going to be exciting, and he could use some excitement along about now. Sooner or later, there'd be a captaincy for him. In the meantime, he'd listen to what Kirk had to say.

"I'm all ears," he said, seeing in his mind's eye Spock's reaction to the colorful phrase. Ah, those were the good old days.

Commander Montgomery Scott was freezing his rear off.

It had been decades since he'd been home to bonnie Scotland, and while for the first few weeks it had been a true delight, he was forced to admit that he'd forgotten just how cold, wet and, if one were to be honest, miserable the place could get.

Now, mind, that wasn't when one was sitting back in a cozy pub with the fire burning, sipping on a dram of the finest alcoholic beverage in the galaxy (Romulan ale, bah!), playing a round of darts. Or on a summer's day, strolling happily through Edinburgh. Or dancing at a ceili with the fair-skinned, rosy-cheeked lasses . . . ah, now that was Scotland at her sweetest.

But fishing in the high country . . . now that was a wee bit different.

Even in summer, storms would arise and the temperature would plummet. As now. Scott's little boat, *Highland Lassie,* rocked furiously. Scott looked at the gray, choppy water, the gray, cloudy sky, the gray, frigid rain that was suddenly starting to pepper him with cold wet droplets. He had worn rain gear, of course—one never ventured outside for any length of time without wellies and macs—but the thermos of hot spiked coffee he brought for just such occasions wasn't going to get him through this one. Grumbling and muttering to himself, he tapped the controls and took *Highland Lassie* back to the rocky shoreline. The rain and wind picked up and he barely managed to get his little boat safely ashore and secured. Cursing roundly, Scott stumbled up the rickety steps that led from the shoreline to his cottage. He'd thought it quaint and charming that sunny day he'd decided he had to have it; now nearly every day he cursed its antiquated "quaintness." What he wouldn't give for an upscale apartment in Edinburgh right now. . . .

He stumbled inside, his gray hair plastered to his skull, and began shedding clothes as he made his way to the bathroom. A hot shower steamed up the bathroom and revived him, and by the time he had wrapped himself in an old, beloved robe and started water boiling for a pot of tea he was feeling almost human again.

The rain pounded on the roof and lashed at the windows. He gazed at it for a moment, sluicing down in gray sheets, and then gave it a rude gesture.

He turned back to check on the kettle. Out of the corner of his eye, he saw a green light flashing. It was the computer alerting him that he had received a message. He hit the controls and finished toweling his hair dry as the Starfleet insignia filled the screen.

Then a familiar visage took its place. "Captain Kirk!" Scott cried delightedly, even though it was a recorded message and Kirk couldn't hear him.

"Hello, Scotty." Aye, but it had been a long time since Scott had heard that particular affectionate nickname. "I hope you're out on that boat you bought, landing one that's this big." He spread his arms wide, and Scott chuckled. "I don't know how well retirement is treating you, but if you're anything like me, you're bored silly."

Scott sighed, shaking his head ruefully. "Too true, lad," he said.

"I've got a proposition for you. My nephews Alexander and Julius are getting ready to depart for a planet they call Sanctuary, to found a new colony."

"A game for the young," Scotty said, still speaking aloud as if he were addressing Kirk. "I've no time nor back strength for diggin' in the dirt."

"It's going to be a site where cutting-edge technology is going to be developed," Kirk said, as if anticipating Scott's response. "I've sent you a list of names of those who have already committed. Its mission is completely one of peace— we'll have no weapons being developed here of any sort." Scott punched a button and a list of names began scrolling across the screen to the left of Kirk's image. His eyes widened.

Kirk leaned forward. "Think of it, Scotty. All this new technology, and you'll get to be an intrinsic part of its development. You'll have a chance to work with some of the most famous people in the galaxy, not just the Federation. And they'll have the chance to work with you." He smiled. "We have to resign ourselves to being living legends, my friend. Let me know if you're interested. Kirk out."

The list continued to scroll across the screen even though the image of Kirk had gone. Scott couldn't believe it. His heart began to quicken at the thought of getting his hands on this stuff. . . .

But what about *Highland Lassie?* Bonnie Scotland, home of his birth?

He looked out the window again, at the storm that continued to rage.

"Hell with the boat," Scott said.

They met for a pre-departure dinner at a banquet hall in one of San Francisco's finest hotels, a scant three weeks later. Kirk had barely had enough time to get his affairs in order, and was mildly amused at how easy it had been to talk Scotty and Chekov into coming. They must be itching for action, just as he was.

The banquet hall was lavishly decorated and the drinks flowed freely. Some of the faces were familiar, and it was obvious that he was recognized. When eye contact was made, Kirk smiled pleasantly. Many of the future colonists introduced themselves. They seemed all of a type to Kirk, regardless of gender or species: young, eager, bright-eyed and oh so very sincere.

It was a petty thought, but he figured that a few weeks on an alien world they'd have to build from scratch would take some of the shine off them.

"Captain!"

Kirk, who had just taken a refill of scotch on the rocks from the cheery female Bolian bartender, cringed. Oh, no. It couldn't be. Not here, not now. . . . The Bolian winced sympathetically.

"Ooh, that bad, huh, sweetie?" she whispered.

"Yep," Kirk said quietly, forcing his features into a pleasant expression. He turned around. "I didn't expect—"

He should have seen the bone-crushing hug coming, but he didn't, and all the air rushed out of his lungs in a *whoosh*.

"Are you surprised to see me?" Skalli chirped.

He stretched his lips into a rictus of a smile. "'Surprised' doesn't even begin to describe it," he said.

She let him go and jumped up and down, her large ears flapping excitedly. The other soon-to-be colonists, including both nephews and his old *Enterprise* crewmen, stared.

Kirk ignored them. "It was . . . kind of you to come see me off," he said.

Skalli laughed. "I'm not here to see you off, Captain. I'm here to join the colony!"

"What?" Kirk realized he had raised his voice and quickly lowered it to a more conversational tone. "Skalli, you don't mean to tell me you dropped out of the Academy to follow me?"

"I sure did!"

He groped for words. "Skalli, you're putting your whole future at risk. You want to be an ambassador. You'll get so much out of Starfleet Academy that will—"

"I can always reenroll later," she said, dismissing his argument.

"How did you even find out about this?" Kirk had kept news of his departure close to his chest. Only a few people knew.

"Well, when I learned that you weren't going to be teaching next semester, I got worried. I went to our embassy and had someone find out what was going on. Then I got to thinking, well, Skalli, why don't *you* go along with the colony? There are so many reasons for me to go! For one thing, you're getting older, and who knows how much longer you'll be around for me to learn from."

"Thank you, Skalli, I feel so much better now."

She beamed, clearly not recognizing sarcasm when she heard it, and continued. "And second, what a unique chance to really learn from and bond with such a variety of people! Finally, it's almost in my own backyard. I'll get the chance to meet a Falorian!"

Her revelation distracted him from the innocent insult she'd delivered earlier. "You're in neighboring star systems and you've never met a Falorian?"

"Never. We're . . . a bit distant, the Huanni and the Falorians."

Kirk was now completely alert. "Were there hostilities between your people in the past?"

"Oh, no. Neither of us is an aggressive people." She wrinkled her nose at the thought of violence. "That's another reason I wanted to join the colony—their ideology is so profound. Technology can mean lasting peace, ways to help people, grow better crops, and provide shelter. It doesn't have to lead to war. Why do we always have to manufacture weapons? Why—"

Kirk steered her back to the subject of Huanni and Falorian relations. "It's hard for me to understand that two species in neighboring star systems didn't interact without there being some hostility between them."

Skalli sighed. "There was contact, many centuries ago. We developed on the same world—my world—but the Falorians wanted their own planet. So they left, went to another hospitable planet the next system over, and became Falorians. As I understand it everyone was pretty annoyed with everyone else, so there followed a custom of noncontact. Now that we have applied to the Federation and they are considering it too, though, we'll have something to talk about!"

Her expression had been unhappy when she began speaking, but by the end she had brightened back to her normal, almost unbearably cheerful self. Kirk didn't know whether to be pleased or regretful; the sad Skalli was much quieter.

The tinkling of a bell sounded, and the buzz of conversation in the hall quieted. Alexander and Julius were at the front of the room. Alexander stood behind a podium, while Julius hung back, off to the side and slightly behind his brother. Not for the first time, Kirk wondered at the difference between the three of his nephews. There was a definite physical resemblance between them all, but there the similarities stopped. Each had his own distinct personality.

Alexander almost glowed. Even when he tried to look more serious, it appeared as though it was impossible for him to wipe a delighted smile off his face.

"Good evening, ladies and gentlemen," he said. "I hope you've been enjoying the event thus far. We'll be heading in to dinner soon, but before we do, I would like to take this opportunity to thank you for your faith in Project Sanctuary. This has been a dream that my brother Julius Kirk and I have shared for many years. It's taken a lot of work, and the road has been far from easy. But we've done it.

"In approximately two weeks we will arrive on the prettiest planet I think I've ever laid eyes on. We will enjoy the natural beauty of Sanctuary. We will do our best not to despoil this lovely place. But we will also gracefully welcome her gifts. Those gifts, combined with our own skills and technology, will bring forth a society that exemplifies the best the civilized worlds have to offer. Nature and technology do not have to be opposed. Peace and progress can go hand in hand, if the minds and hearts of those who create them will it so.

"You'll have plenty of time to meet and get to know one another when we depart. The *Mayflower II* departs spacedock at oh-eight-hundred sharp. We'll all be eager to get underway and we won't be happy to wait for stragglers, so be on time!"

He grinned, and the crowd chuckled kindly, not so much at Alex's humor as at his obvious excitement and eagerness.

"Before we sit down for dinner, there is someone I'd particularly like to thank. Uncle Jim, where are you?"

Damn, Kirk thought. *More living legend nonsense.* Nonetheless, he forced a smile on his face and waved. Alex's lit up even more, if such a thing was possible.

"Folks, I'd like to introduce you to my uncle, James T. Kirk. Most of you have heard of him. I'm delighted to say that he will be joining us for at least a few months. Let's see what we can do to convince him to stay longer, shall we?"

And to Kirk's utter chagrin, Alex began to applaud. Julius joined in. For an uncomfortable moment, they were the only ones clapping, but slowly the others started to applaud as well, though with an obvious lack of enthusiasm. Kirk smiled graciously, waved a bit, and waited for the noise to subside.

He was beginning to regret this. He had a feeling he was in for a long several months.

Despite Alex's warning, the *Mayflower II* left spacedock late at 0934. It settled into a steady warp five and soon left the Sol system behind.

Shortly afterward, a cloaked Klingon bird-of-prey, careful to keep its presence undetected, began to follow.

Chapter Seven

Kirk hadn't been aboard for fifteen minutes when the trouble started. He, Scott, and Chekov were unpacking in the cramped quarters that would serve as home for the duration of the trip. None of the three had shared such close quarters with anyone else for a long time, and there was much joking and bumping of elbows. They left the door open and at one point Scott was looking down the corridor.

"Ah, looks like there's someone coming to see us," he remarked.

Kirk's head came up. "Female?"

"Aye."

Kirk swore underneath his breath. Would Skalli never leave him alone? He backed off to the side and said in a whisper, "Tell her I'm not here." Damn it, she ought to at least let him unpack before she came to harass him.

Scott and Chekov looked at him oddly, then Scott shrugged. He stepped into the doorway and leaned against the frame, effectively blocking Skalli's entrance. Kirk flattened himself against a wall.

"Hey," said a voice that was definitely not Skalli's. "Name's Kate Gallagher."

"The captain's not here," Scott said, and at the same time, Kirk stepped forward to greet the new visitor. There was an awkward silence. Kirk smiled faintly, embarrassed at having been caught trying to duck someone.

The human female who stood just outside the doorway had short brown hair, wore the loose khaki pants and white sleeveless shirt that served as an informal uniform here, and had no jewelry or cosmetics on. Her frame was lean and wiry, and judging by the collection of freckles on her face she'd spent a lot of time in the sun. She stuck out a callused hand.

Kirk hesitated for just a moment at the incredible informality, realized he'd better get used to it, and shook the proffered hand. "I'm Jim Kirk."

"Yeah, I know. Looks like you are here after all. Nice to meet—" Gallagher broke off in midsentence, staring past Kirk at the half-unpacked suitcase on the cot.

"Is there a problem?" Kirk asked.

"Yeah," she said, as if he were stupid. Gallagher pointed at the phaser. "That. We don't allow weapons. I'm surprised you were able to smuggle it aboard."

Kirk bridled at the implication that he had sneaked the weapon on. "Alex knows I have it. He gave us special permission." The ship, of course, had ample defense technology, but regarding additional weapons Alex had made it clear that as far as he was concerned there was no need for them, not even to protect themselves from the planet's native creatures, and to arrive in a place called Sanctuary bristling with tools of violence would only send the wrong message to the Falorians. Kirk's nephew had relented, very reluctantly, for the three Starfleet men only because Kirk had told him that he and his two friends would either have handheld phasers or they wouldn't come.

"This is a peaceful mission," Gallagher said, her eyes going hard and flinty. "We don't need weapons where we're going. Biggest predator there is a *miyanlak*. It's about the size of a coyote and very shy."

"Look, Kate," Kirk began in a placating tone, but Gallagher had obviously found something else about which to wax wroth.

"Oh, my God," she said, "is that *fur?*" She pointed at something furry and plaid in Scott's bag.

"Aye, that's rabbit fur. It's a sporran," Scott said defensively. "It's been passed down in my family for almost two hundred years. It's part of my formal dress uniform."

Kate laughed, but it wasn't a friendly sound. She crossed her hands over her chest in a defensive posture. "You know, I was going to give you guys the benefit of the doubt. I thought you'd at least try to respect our beliefs, work with us. You bring weapons, dead animals—I just don't know."

She turned and stalked out. Kirk stared after her, hardly believing the whirlwind of rudeness and aggression that had just swept through the tiny cabin.

"Well," Chekov said, "I feel so welcome now."

"Ah," Scott said, as if he'd just figured that out. "That's Kate then, is it?"

"What do you know about her? Other than that she's blunter than a Klingon," Kirk asked.

"Great lover of peace, that one. And beasties. I remember reading her bio—she's devoted to figuring out ways to protect endangered species. Can't suppose I blame the lassie. In this day and age, we don't need to make coats out o' their fur. But I tell you, Captain, this wee bunny would have been dead a long time ago o' natural causes."

"Don't let her get to you, Scotty. We knew we'd rub some

people the wrong way. I'm sure that once we get to know these people, it'll all work out.

He was sure of nothing of the sort.

During the trip, the old *Enterprise* crew members did indeed get to know some of the colonists. A few seemed approachable: Dr. Leah Cohen, an oceanographer; Alys Harper, a linguist and communications expert; the head geologist Mark Veta; and Dr. Theodore Simon, the medical doctor for the colony. Others, like Gallagher, the Talgart botanist Mattkah, and the taciturn engineer Kevin Talbot, seemed to take an instant and permanent dislike to the three Starfleet officers. The rest fell into a swirl of names and faces that never particularly stood out. They would come to the mess hall, eat quickly, and scurry back to their quarters.

The only exceptions were, of course, Skalli, who ambushed Kirk for chats repeatedly, and Alex. Alexander alone sought out his uncle and his friends. When he was with Kirk, the others all relaxed and risked friendly smiles and hellos. They followed his lead almost like dogs awaiting commands from their master. They might clash with one another—and Kirk was witness to a few arguments, particularly between Mattkah and Gallagher—but they all turned toward Alex like flowers to the sun. Kirk realized that Alex was, like George Washington on Earth in the eighteenth century, the "indispensable man." One thing he seemed to do with ease was bring disparate people together and focus them on a mutually beneficial goal.

Kirk, Scott, and Chekov found themselves seeking out one another's company almost constantly. At first, Kirk thought it was his imagination, but when both Scott and Chekov ruefully reported their own litany of polite refusals and occasional downright snubs, Kirk realized something he should have seen before: Among this group of peace-loving scientists and engineers, Starfleet's comparatively martial presence just wasn't welcome.

"How ironic," Kirk mused over lunch one day. As usual, he, Chekov, and Scotty were sitting by themselves. "I can't count the number of times that I've said the words 'we mean you no harm' or 'we are a peaceful people' in various alien encounters over the years, but that seems to count for nothing here."

"When I was first officer aboard the *Reliant,*" Chekov said, "I had to work closely with the scientific types. They are not easy to get to know, but they are good people."

"And an engineer is an engineer," Scott said between mouthfuls of reconstituted stew-like substance. "Scientist, Starfleet, peace lover, what have you. Scratch the surface of an engineer, and you'll find a heart of dilithium." His eyes crinkled at his joke, and even Kirk smiled a little.

"I'm certain we'll find that we have more in common than we think once we reach Sanctuary and get to work," Kirk said. "We'll be living together, working alongside one another. Our differences won't seem so great once we're working toward a common goal."

He knew his voice rang with assurance, but he had his doubts. And he was to be proved right.

The enormous transport that was the *Mayflower II* settled with surprising gentleness on the planet's surface. Kirk had had plenty of time alone to familiarize himself with what to expect.

Sanctuary was a Class-M planet, with all of the attendant climates that usually included. They had landed in the northern hemisphere in a temperate zone that would be pleasantly warm in the summers and occasionally snowy in the winters. Small teams utilizing the single shuttle called the *Drake* would explore in detail other climates, some of which, such as the desert area with its deadly sandstorms, were hostile indeed. That in-depth level of exploration and possible expansion was slated for what the colonists called Year Two. Today, the landing, was Day One of Year One. Kirk thought this new numbering of days and years was a bit silly, but the colonists liked it, so he said nothing.

There would be plenty of time to settle in before the winter approached; it was late spring, and when Kirk stepped out onto Sanctuary's soil for the first time, the smells that teased his nostrils made him smile. For the first time since they'd left Earth, he felt excited and hopeful about the project's success again. It was truly a beautiful place.

Standing ready to greet them were six beings that Kirk assumed were Falorians. Standing Crane had been right. They did resemble the Huanni, which of course made sense if indeed both species had originated on the same planet, as Skalli had said. But they were different, too; stockier, less animated in their movements. He smiled and automatically stepped forward, but a gentle hand on his arm stayed him.

"Julius has had the dealings with the Falorians, Uncle Jim," Alex said softly. "He should be the one to address them first."

Of course, Alex was right. "Sorry," Kirk said. "Old habits die hard."

He stood next to Alex, taking his cues from his nephew, as the colonists, all 108 of them, exited the *Mayflower II*. He expected them to form a line, but instead they all clustered together, talking animatedly. Kirk frowned to himself. This was hardly the way to greet one's host. A more formal appearance was called for. He bit his tongue.

Julius was the last one out. Kirk was certain this wasn't accidental. The young man ran lightly down the steps and stretched out a hand to one of the Falorians.

"Kal-Tor Lissan," Julius said. "It is good to see you again."

"And you, Julius Kirk," the Falorian leader said politely. Kirk assumed Kal-Tor was a title, but not a military one, much like "chieftain" or "leader" or "head." "We have long looked forward to this day."

Lissan was speaking with Julius, but his large, dark eyes were scanning the crowd. "Permit me to introduce my brother," Julius said. "Alexander, this is Kal-Tor Lissan, the person I've been in negotiations with."

"Julius speaks of you often and highly, Kal-Tor," Alex said, stepping forward to shake the alien's hand. "We are so grateful that you have entrusted us with Sanctuary. We will take good care of her."

"I'm certain you will," Lissan replied politely. His eyes fell upon Kirk. "Forgive me, but . . . do I detect a family resemblance with this person here as well?"

"You do," Alex said. "This is my uncle, Captain James T. Kirk."

"Ah," Lissan said, nodding. "Even out here on the edge of Federation space, we have heard of the famous Captain Kirk. We are honored to have you here, Captain."

"It's an honor to be here, Kal-Tor," Kirk replied. "I understand you are in negotiations to join the Federation. I wish you every success. You have shown good faith thus far."

Lissan seemed flattered and inclined his head. "We are eager to become a part of such a fine organization of worlds. Your people will see that we have much to offer." His eyes narrowed a little as he regarded Skalli, who was practically jumping up and down. "I see that you have brought a neighbor. What is your name, Huanni child?"

"I'm Skalli Jksili, Kal-Tor," she said, bowing deeply. "As a member of this colony, and especially as a Huanni, I look forward to getting to know you and your people better." For her, it was an extraordinarily restrained response. Kirk was surprised.

"We will be visiting from time to time, to discuss how things are progressing," Lissan said. "Perhaps there will be a chance for us to converse then. In the meantime, I see that you have much to do. Julius, you know how to contact us if you have problems."

He touched a bright button on his robe. "Please transport," he said, and he and the others vanished.

"Wow!" Skalli yelped, her composure evaporating like dew beneath a strong sun. "That was a Falorian! A real, live, Falorian! I can't believe it!"

"Believe it," Kirk said, putting a restraining hand on her slim shoulder. "Come on. Let's unpack and make this place home."

Despite the assurances of Kal-Tor Lissan, the colonists did not see a great deal of the Falorians, and most of them seemed to like it that way. The first few days were filled with the practical necessities of simply getting the colony up and running.

Most of the *Mayflower II*'s vast storage space had been devoted to materials that were now put to good use in constructing sound, stylish shelters. Part of the ship itself was broken down as well. They would need to keep her in flying order in case of an emergency evacuation, of course, but she could be largely stripped and much of her parts utilized. No rustic log cabins here; all was new, gleaming, and very high-tech.

In keeping with Alex's sentiment that he wanted this colony to feel like a family, there was only one large building. In the center was a room that could accommodate all the colonists with ease. Here was where reports on progress would be given and where weekly meetings would be held. Right off this room was a mess hall, with a large pantry to store food harvested from Sanctuary's bounty and top-of-the-line equipment for preparing it. The entire left section of the compound was composed of labs and testing areas; the right-hand side, of living quarters. Kirk was quite relieved when he learned that he would have a private room, although when he saw it, he thought it smaller than his ready room aboard the *Enterprise.*

A staggering quantity of delicate, complex equipment was hauled out and set up in the testing areas. Scott, who was finally actually able to get his hands on some of these technological beauties, was openly in awe of them. This endeared him to his fellow engineers, most of whom had had a hand in creating the obviously admired technology.

There was a wide-open field right in front of the building. When there was time, people dragged out chairs to watch the sunset before heading in to dinner. It had gotten the name of the Courtyard, although it wasn't one in the real sense of the word, and as names often do, this one stuck.

There was a new sense of camaraderie as the colonists worked together to build their new homes and workplaces. But once they had finished construction, the colonists dove for their laboratories like gophers for their holes, and Kirk again felt the discomfort he had experienced while they had traveled to get here.

He had expected that Skalli would be a complete nuisance, but she turned out to be only a moderate one. With her eidetic memory and the staggering rate at which she was able to absorb information, she quickly became rather popular among the Sanctuarians, as the colonists had taken to calling themselves. She flitted easily from engineering to chemistry to medicine to geothermal mapping, and was clearly enjoying herself immensely. Her eyes still lit up whenever Kirk entered a room, however, and whenever she had a free moment she would seek him out. But she was in great demand, and her time was rarely her own. Kirk imagined that eventually, once they had learned to control their emotions to some degree, the Huanni would be very valuable contributors to the Federation.

Even his old friends Scotty and Chekov were less frequent companions than he had expected. He wasn't surprised that Scotty had been so taken with the bright and shiny new engineering technology that was going to be experimented with and perfected here on Sanctuary; this was, after all, the man who had been delighted to be confined to quarters because it gave him a chance to catch up on his technical journals. It was Chekov's interest in, and proficiency with, scientific research that had surprised Kirk. He had clearly learned much as first officer aboard the *Reliant,* and despite his protests about wanting his own captaincy, was clearly enjoying himself.

For the first few nights, once they had erected such things as private quarters, Kirk and his nephews had dined together. It had been awkward and strained, more so than their midnight encounter a few weeks ago when they had turned up on Kirk's doorstep. This, however, did not surprise Kirk.

Up until this colonial venture, Kirk had been in command, wherever he was. Over many years he had come to accept, embrace, and excel in his role as a natural leader. Now, he wasn't sure *where* he fit in. Alexander was the founder and head of the colony, and clearly everyone adored him.

He had no particular interest in science or medicine, and any knowledge and training he had was hopelessly outdated when compared to the "it was just discovered last week" experience of this group. He had learned his way around the engine room of a starship, but he couldn't even begin to guess what those coils, pulsating colors, and humming sounds meant.

Alex had insisted that having the family together—what they could cobble together of it, anyway—was important to him, and Kirk had no doubt that Alex had meant it at the time. Alexander Kirk was like his father, nothing if not sincere and earnest. But the reality was that with Kirk present, Alex would be upstaged if he didn't assert his authority often and clearly. Kirk didn't blame the younger man; he'd have done the same in his position. An expedition like this needed a clear leader.

As for raising their profile with Starfleet and the Federation in general, Kirk had already done all he could. Now they were stuck out here on this rock, lovely though it was, and Kirk realized he wanted nothing more than to go back home. Even his apartment in San Francisco would be better than here; at least there, he was surrounded by familiar and loved things.

But Jim Kirk liked nothing better than a challenge, and so he determined that he would win over some of the people who seemed the least likely to befriend him. His first target was Kate Gallagher. He had downloaded her bio from the computer, and had to admit she was impressive. She was only thirty-four and had already won seven major awards, including the coveted Peace Star for Humanitarian Achievement. Gallagher was deeply passionate about her work, and Kirk figured that that much, at least, they had in common.

She kept the lab door open all the time, but Kirk knocked gently on the wall nonetheless. Kate turned from the computer, saw who it was, and a look of irritation crossed her sharp features.

"Thought even you would figure out that if a door was left open you could come in," she said.

"Just trying to be polite," Kirk said. "I've been reading your bio, Kate."

"It's a free colony," she said, keeping her eyes on the screen.

Her short-nailed fingers flew over the keyboard as she entered data.

"I'm very impressed. Why didn't you tell us you had won the Peace Star?"

"I know stuff like that matters to you Starfleet people, but I don't give a damn about it," she said.

"You give a damn about protecting innocent creatures," Kirk said, refusing to rise to the bait. "You were the only one who believed the Vree rats were sentient. You saved an entire species from being relocated—which would have led to their extinction."

Now she did turn and look at him. "Yeah," she said. "The rest of the team wanted to clear them out to study the other flora and fauna. Wanted to transport them across the planet to a comparable temperate zone."

"And you proved that doing so would remove them from their sole source of nourishment—insects that had fed on a certain type of honey. You believed, against every available shred of evidence, that those small rodents were intelligent."

"Thank God there was a Vulcan in the group willing to do a mind-meld," she said.

"Ever heard of the Horta?"

Kate looked down. Her cheeks were red. "Yeah."

"Kind of a similar situation, don't you think?"

"Jim, I've read your bio, too. About the Horta . . . and about all the space battles in which you participated."

"I'm not in battle now, and I don't want to be. Truce?"

She glowered, but she didn't say no. Encouraged, Kirk asked, "I hear you're working on something quite remarkable. Something that could protect endangered species all across the galaxy."

"I call it the Masker," Gallagher said. Was Kirk mistaken or was that the beginning of a smile playing at the edge of her lips? "Hundreds of years ago we tagged animals with primitive means, to keep track of their progress. We still do it now, though, of course, with a much less invasive method. There are so many animals that are being poached across the galaxy it just makes me sick. We can only do so much, but I got to thinking— today's poacher finds his prey by scanning for its signs on a tricorder. What if we tagged animals so that their signal was masked? It wouldn't be that hard—just insert a small chip under the skin that sends out a signal that confuses a tricorder. Suddenly, they're invisible."

"Of course, each species has a different type of tricorder," Kirk pointed out. "A signal that would confuse a Federation tricorder wouldn't protect an animal from a Klingon using his people's tricorder."

Her thin shoulders sagged. "Yeah, and that's the problem."

"Kate, I think it's a brilliant idea," Kirk said, and meant it. "Our Mr. Scott might be able to help you out a bit, if you'd let him know you were interested."

She hesitated. "I'll think about it." She turned back to the computer and Kirk knew he'd been dismissed. He turned to leave.

"Hey, Jim?"

He turned around. "Yes?"

She smiled, fully this time. "Good job with the Horta."

Chapter Eight

Encouraged by his progress with Gallagher, Kirk then tried to warm up to some of the others. He eventually was able to talk pleasantly with Cohen and Harper. The geologist, Mark Veta, also warmed up to him. Kirk tried, but couldn't share the man's enthusiasm for discussing the cave system that apparently riddled Sanctuary. Although at one point, when Veta asked if he was interested in spelunking, Kirk felt the first rush of pleasure he'd had since they had left Earth. Mattkah had apparently taken an extreme dislike to Kirk and Dr. Sherman's cool, formal demeanor did nothing but remind Kirk of how much he missed his old friend McCoy's folksy good humor.

Kirk's help was apparently not welcome in graphing the weather patterns, something of vital import in a world that had sudden flooding and sandstorms that could come out of nowhere and scour bones clean in five minutes. It was not welcome in charting this world's stars. It was not welcome in biology or botany or geology or engineering.

After the third week, when most of his attempts to assist had been politely but obviously rebuffed, Kirk learned that the Falorians were coming to visit and discuss the colony's progress. *I'm not much of a diplomat, but I've had more experience than these boys,* he thought. Perhaps this was a way he could contribute. Hell, Alex had even suggested as much.

The Falorians were to materialize in the same spot. Julius was already there to meet them, his hands clasping and unclasping as he paced back and forth. Kirk raised an eyebrow. Impatient boy, that one. He stepped forward. Julius froze in midstride and whirled to look at him.

"Uncle Jim," he said, clearly surprised. "What are you doing here?"

Kirk smiled. "I'm an old hand at negotiations," he said as mildly as he could. He didn't want to step on Julius's toes, and wasn't certain that his expertise would be welcomed. "I thought I might be able to assist."

Julius continued to glare, the surprised expression on his sharp features turning into annoyance. "I've been negotiating with the Falorians for some time now. I doubt I'll need any assistance." As an afterthought, he added, "Thanks, though."

Kirk decided to be as honest as possible. "Julius, I respect your familiarity with this matter. But," and he laughed a little self-deprecatingly, "I'm finding it hard to find a place here where I can contribute. You asked me to come here. You all but demanded it," he reminded his nephew. "So, I'm here. I came, as you wanted. Let me help."

Kirk couldn't read the myriad of emotions that flickered across Julius's face. Finally, the young man opened his mouth to answer. At that moment, Kirk heard the distinctive hum of a transporter and Lissan, along with two others, shimmered into existence.

Lissan blinked and drew his head back slightly. "Captain

Kirk," he said. "I did not expect to see you here. My meeting was with Julius."

Before Kirk could say anything, Julius interjected smoothly, "My uncle and I were exchanging pleasantries. He was just leaving." He turned and smiled. "I'll see you back at the colony for dinner this evening, Uncle."

The smile was pleasant, kind even, but Julius's blue eyes glittered like chips of ice. Kirk forced a smile onto his own face.

"Certainly, Julius. Until then."

It was obvious that Kirk's expertise would not be welcome in dealing with the Falorians.

After that conversation, Kirk decided he would benefit from a walk around the perimeter of the colony. The sun was just starting to set and it was quiet and peaceful. He shrugged into a light jacket against the chill of the evening and strode forth.

He moved briskly, not wanting to run for fear of spoiling the quietude but wanting more than a stroll. It smelled so fresh out here. He was reminded of his many camping trips and an idea occurred to him. Perhaps he could be useful as part of a scouting trip. All he'd need would be a tricorder, shelter, a knife and a pan to cook in. It would be a challenge to learn how to find and harvest the abundant foodstuffs Sanctuary offered, and sleep under the stars of this new world.

The more he thought about it the better the idea seemed. He breathed deeply of the cool twilight scents and felt himself calming down. These weren't Starfleet personnel; they were scientists, researchers, engineers. People who had spent most of their lives *avoiding* contact with people just like him. It was only natural that they'd take some time to warm up. In the meantime, he thought he'd finally come up with a way to contribute.

He was striding through a field now, and the heady scents of meadow flowers wafted up to his nostrils. He was disturbing some of them, and pale little spores flew up into the cool air, drifting to another spot upon which to settle and root, continuing the circle of life. Grinning a little, he created more breezes with his arms, sending them flying away to their new homes.

He felt better by the time darkness fell and he returned to the encampment. He'd missed dinner, so he went into the mess hall to see what he could rustle up. Mattkah, the irascible botanist, was there. Did the fellow ever stop eating? He knew that Talgarts had an unusually high metabolism, of course. Once he'd overheard another colonist refer to Mattkah as "the giant shrew." He was downing an enormous bowl of oatmeal and as Kirk entered was drizzling at least a cup of honey on it.

Kirk bit his tongue against a sarcastic remark and instead said simply, "Good evening, Mattkah," as he searched the cupboard for something quick, tasty, and nutritious.

Mattkah looked up with a surly expression on his flat face and then his eyes widened in horror. "Oh, no!" he yelped.

"What?" asked Kirk. "What's wrong?"

Mattkah had risen and was now pointing directly at Kirk. "The spores! You're completely covered with them!"

Kirk looked down and saw that indeed, his jacket and pants were dotted with tiny white spores from the little plants he'd walked through. He chuckled ruefully.

"It seems I am," he agreed. "Don't worry, there's nothing dangerous in any of the plant life that we—"

"It's ruined! You clumsy oaf, you've completely ruined the experiment! We started this on the second day we were here and now it's all for nothing." Mattkah had sunk back down in his chair, his head in all four of his hands. "We'll have to start all over again. Didn't you see the markers?"

Kirk closed his eyes briefly. Clearly, the flowery meadow through which he had so blithely trod was actually an outdoor laboratory. He had seen no markers in the darkling twilight, and even if he had, he wondered if he would have noticed them.

"Mattkah, I'm sorry, I didn't know. I would never have walked through the meadow had I known you were conducting research there."

The sour look Mattkah shot him told Kirk that the Talgart didn't believe him. Clearly, in his mind, Kirk was a lumbering elephant that had nothing better to do than to go gallivanting through delicate research areas, rendering weeks of work entirely useless. He gulped the rest of his oatmeal, helped himself to an armload of native fruits, and stormed out of the mess hall.

For a long moment, Kirk just stood there. Then he slowly returned the juicy, yellow-red fruit he'd been about to bite to the bowl on the center of one of the tables.

He'd lost his appetite.

He returned to his small, cramped but at least private quarters. Lying on the small bunk, he stared at the ceiling, counting the days until the next resupply ship would arrive and he could go home, where he belonged.

There was no place for him here.

Kirk's door chimed. He blinked awake, startled, and glanced at the chronometer to see that he'd slept through breakfast. He reached for his robe, sashed it, and called, "Come in."

The door hissed open. "Well, good morning, Mr. Chekov. I apologize for my present state. What can I do for you?"

"Sorry to intrude, sir, but there's something I think you should see." Kirk smiled wryly as he observed that although he was no longer in command, he was addressing Chekov, and Chekov was responding, just as they would have aboard the *Enterprise*.

"Sit down . . . if you can. It's tight quarters here on Sanctu-ary," Kirk said. Chekov took one of the two small chairs and Kirk took the other one. "What is it?"

Chekov frowned. "It may be nothing," he said.

"Or it may not," Kirk said.

"Well, I'm not particularly trained to contribute scientifi-cally, although I have been helping out. Most of the time I've been assisting Alys in downloading and sending messages," Chekov said. "You know, to loved ones back home."

Kirk nodded. He hadn't sent a single message. He had friends and acquaintances scattered throughout the galaxy, but unlike most of the colonists, there was no one on Earth—no one "back home"—he really felt like talking to.

"Subspace traffic has dramatically increased over the last four days," Chekov continued. "And I'm not certain of this, but I think . . . Captain, I believe our communications are being monitored."

"What makes you think that?"

Chekov shrugged, clearly troubled. "Nothing I can point to for certain. Little things. Echoes, blurry images, things like that."

"That's a pretty slender thread to hang charges of eaves-dropping on, Lieutenant."

"I know, sir. I probably shouldn't have troubled you with this, but I didn't know who else to take it to."

Kirk leaned back, thinking. "For now, take it to no one. I want you to spend as much time as you can on sending these messages, and I want you to document every glitch you encounter. If this keeps up, we'll tell Alex about it. It could be nothing more serious than the system needing to be fixed."

"Aye, sir." Chekov rose.

"And Chekov?"

"Aye, sir?"

Kirk grinned. "Thanks for thinking of me."

Chekov returned the smile. "You were the only one I did think of, Captain."

After he had gone, Kirk showered and dressed, thinking hard. One was trained to look for the most likely answer to any problem. Chances were, the equipment simply hadn't been set up properly and there was a glitch in the system. As for subspace traffic being heavy, well, maybe this was a hot time for space travel in this sector.

Still, he trusted Chekov, and he knew the younger man wouldn't have come to Kirk about this if he hadn't had some kind of feeling that there was something wrong.

Just like the feeling Kirk was starting to have.

Scott was thoroughly enjoying himself. He was having a "day off," as he put it, though others on the engineering team would have called it a day of hard labor. He, Alex, and Skalli were going to traverse the entire planet and tune up the monitoring posts they had set in each of the Sanctuary's ecosystems. This was done once a week, whether it was needed or not, as so much of the colony's research came from these posts. In Year Two, there would be much more extensive visitation of the areas, but for now, this sufficed.

There were eight of them: One in each icy heart of the arctic circles, two along the planet's equator, and one on each continent. Oceanographer Leah Cohen had bemoaned the fact that they didn't have the technology to put a few on the ocean floor, to which Scott had gallantly replied that in a few years he was certain the brilliant engineering team would figure out a way to do so. The bonnie lassie had rewarded him with a sweet smile.

The posts retrieved data from the surrounding area twenty-seven hours a day, data that was carefully analyzed. Each week (of course, the weeks here were a long nine days and three hours) someone would come and make sure everything was functioning correctly, and now it was Scott, Alex, and Skalli's turn. Today, they were having problems with what Scott called The Desert One. Technically, it was Monitoring Post AE-584-B2, stationed in the arid climate of one of the major continents, but Scott preferred to keep things simple.

Alex was piloting, humming happily to himself, while Skalli was talking animatedly with Chekov, back at Sanctuary Heart, as the base itself was called, as the little shuttle *Drake* flew over the brown-yellow sands. Not for the first time, Scott admired the sleek design of the craft, the ease with which Alex was able to maneuver her. Aye, she was a bonnie one, all right.

His stomach rumbled. When they'd finished with this one, it would be time to take a break for lunch.

"Where's a nice spot to have our picnic?" he asked Alex. Alex grinned over his shoulder.

"There are the most spectacular waterfalls near the top of the continent," he said. "We stop for lunch every time we check out the post there and have never been disappointed yet. But you've got to keep the secret—don't want everyone volunteering for post-check duty!"

"Ooh, a waterfall!" cooed Skalli, her eyes wide with anticipation. She was oblivious to the glares Alex and Scott were giving her. "Yes, Chekov, you heard right—we're going to a waterfall for lunch when we finish. Won't that be fun!"

Scott and Alex exchanged rueful glances. "Looks like somebody let the cat out of the bag," Scott muttered.

"Yes," Skalli was saying. "We only have—Chekov? Pavel, are you there? Hello? *Drake* to Sanctuary Heart, come in. Uh oh." She turned to look at Alex. "It sounds as though we lost him."

* * *

"Skalli, come in," Chekov said urgently. "Skalli—Sanctuary Heart to *Drake,* please come in." Silence. Damn it. Once again, they'd lost communications. In frustration, Chekov slammed his fist on the console.

"Hey, take it easy," said Alys Harper, the blond human female who was serving communication duty along with Chekov. "No need to break it more than it already is."

Chekov gnawed his lower lip, then made a decision. "Alys, go find Captain Kirk."

"Kirk?" He couldn't see her expression, but he didn't need to. She managed to cram a great deal of distaste into the single syllable word. "Why? Julius is in command whenever—"

"Just go find him, all right?"

"Okay, okay, calm down, sheesh." Muttering under her breath, she left to do as he had asked. Chekov found himself longing for the days when orders were given and followed without commentary, critique, or discussion.

He took a deep breath, calmed himself, and methodically began to check everything that could possibly be wrong on his end with the communications.

He had a gut feeling he wouldn't find anything.

"Hello? Hello? Hmmm," Skalli said. "Looks like we've lost communication for some reason." She frowned, turning the problem over in her mind, then seemed to dismiss it. "Oh, well. We're almost at the post anyway."

Scott was rather more disturbed at the abrupt termination of communication than Skalli was, but she was right about one thing. Alex was already beginning their descent. He could see the landing area now, the only flat rock in a sea of sand and jagged peaks.

Alex eased the craft down smoothly and they gathered their tools, putting on their protective glasses and gloves. The sun's glare was almost unbearable, and the post would be far too hot to touch with bare hands.

"One quick check before we go," Alex said. He nodded. "Good. No sandstorms in the vicinity. We've got a window."

When Scott opened the door, a blast of heat hit him with almost palpable force. For a brief moment, he recalled with longing the chilly rainstorm that had driven him to embrace this mission. Then he took a cautious breath of the hot air and jumped down into the sand.

They had a long walk ahead of them before they would see those waterfalls.

Kirk listened attentively as Chekov described the problem and everything he'd tried to fix it. On a whim, Kirk opened his communicator. "Kirk to Julius." Nothing.

"Our communicators aren't even working, then," Chekov said. Kirk shook his head. Chekov pointed to the screen. "This is closing in on their area and we can't even alert them to it."

Kirk looked at the monitor and his grim mood worsened. A sandstorm was starting to form. Here on Sanctuary, that was a dangerous thing indeed. "If they're still in the shuttle, they'll detect it," he said.

"But if they're not, they could be caught in the open," Chekov said. Kirk knew what the team would be wearing: the usual Sanctuary garb of comfortable pants and shirts that permitted easy movement, boots, gloves and glasses. Nothing more. Nothing that would remotely protect them from the whipping winds of a sandstorm. Not for the first time, he wished that they had a second shuttle. There would be no time to get the *Mayflower II* prepared to fly.

"Keep trying to raise them," he told Chekov. "I'm going to go find Julius."

Several long minutes were wasted in searching, since the communicators weren't working. Kirk finally found Julius in his quarters. The door chimed several times before Julius answered the door. He was tired-looking and unshaven, and seemed surprised to see Kirk.

"What is it, Uncle Jim?"

"Your brother and two other members of this colony are about to be bombarded with a violent sandstorm, and we can't reach them," Kirk said bluntly.

Julius snapped to attention. "What the—what do you mean?"

"Communications are completely off-line," Kirk said. He flipped open the dead communicator. "Even these. There's a chance that they're still in the shuttle but if they're outside in this—"

"Oh no," Julius breathed.

After a ten-minute walk—more of an ordeal than a stroll, considering the terrible heat—the team reached the post. Although they had erected a protective physical shielding around it, it was obvious that the grit of the desert's sand was taking its toll. Scott proceeded to quickly clean the internal workings and then put it through a test run. This would take about twenty minutes. It wasn't enough time for them to hike back to the shuttle, so they resigned themselves to being hot for a while. They leaned up against a rock formation and waited. Scott closed his eyes.

"Hey, what's that?" Skalli asked. She pointed to a flurry of motion in the distance.

"Uh oh," Alex said. "That looks like a dust devil." He removed his communicator and flipped it open. "Alex to Sanctuary Heart. Hey, how come you didn't warn us about this sandstorm we're . . . damn it. It's dead!"

Scott felt a chill despite the severe heat. It was conceivable that the communications had been damaged on the shuttle, but for the individual communicators to quit working meant that something had occurred on a much larger scale. He rose, staring at the dust devil that was rapidly becoming a sandstorm.

"Alex, is there anyplace we could take shelter?" he asked. *Because if there isn't,* he thought grimly, *then all a rescue party will find will be three scoured, bleached skeletons.*

Alex didn't reply. He was fiddling with the communicator, still trying to raise Sanctuary Heart. Scott's eyes flicked from the youth and his communicator to the encroaching storm.

He reached out and shook Alex by the shoulder. "Lad, we've got to take shelter!" he said, raising his voice to be heard above the rising wind.

Alex looked up at him wildly. *Poor lad,* Scott thought with a twinge of sympathy. *This is his first real crisis.* Alex had the charm and charisma to get people to follow him, but he didn't seem to know a damn thing about how to lead when the chips were down.

"Over here!" It was Skalli, jumping up and down and waving her long arms. Scott hadn't even noticed her get up, but she had clearly done so and found them protection against the storm. Scott shifted his grip to hold Alex's upper arm and hauled the young man to his feet.

The sandstorm was beginning. As they stumbled to where Skalli stood, Scott was intensely grateful for the goggles. Grit scoured his face and even though he covered his mouth and nose with his hands, he felt the fine, powdery sand slip past his lips and into his nostrils. Alex was hacking violently by the time they squeezed into the crevice. It was easy enough for Skalli, but Scott reluctantly admitted to himself he'd had one too many desserts as he nearly got wedged tight. By sheer stubbornness he forced his way inside.

There was no light save what filtered in from the crevice, and they needed to get as far away from that as possible as wind and sand continued to find their way into their shelter.

"This way!" cried Skalli. "Follow my voice!"

Alex was able to stand on his own now. Coughing and gasping for air, both men stumbled toward the back of the cave. It grew darker and darker until finally Scott could see nothing. He still walked forward as quickly as he could, arms extended to feel his way, until Skalli's slender, gloved fingers closed about his hands and guided him forward to sit on the floor.

They could still hear the wind crying and moaning like a wounded beast. Pressed together for warmth, for the cave was cold after the unforgiving heat outside, Scott felt Skalli shiver.

"It's scary," she said, voicing something that would probably have gotten her kicked off Kirk's bridge. "It sounds like a monster or something."

Scott was not inclined to reprimand her, as she was directly responsible for all of them surviving this in the first place. "Good job, lass," he said, squeezing her shoulder.

Alexander Kirk, who had coaxed over a hundred people to pack up and move in pursuit of a dream, and who had completely panicked at the first sign of a real problem, said nothing.

Chapter Nine

"I don't care if Lissan isn't scheduled to return for three days, I want him here *now*." Kirk was aware that he was close to bellowing but frankly didn't give a damn. They still hadn't been able to communicate with the away team and had watched in quiet apprehension as the fierce storm had settled directly over the monitoring post for almost two hours. Kirk and the others knew that if the party had been caught outside, they'd be dead by now.

"But you don't understand," said Julius, flushing a little. "I can't just order them to—"

"Fine. Then I will," Kirk shot back.

"Hey," snapped Julius, stepping in toward Kirk and looking him in the eye. "I'm the one who deals with the Falorians. You keep your Starfleet nose out of it."

Kirk smiled without humor. "I seem to recall that my Starfleet nose—or at least my Starfleet self—was one of the things you and your brother desperately wanted to get to Sanctuary."

He took a deep breath and calmed himself. He reached to put his hands on Julius's shoulders but the youth angrily shook them off.

"Julius, listen to me. Something is going on that is causing our communications to be disrupted. Because of it we weren't able to warn the team about the sandstorm. They could be dead as a result of that. It's your own brother. Aren't you worried?"

Julius's blue eyes continued to bore into Kirk's, but a muscle in his jaw tightened. "It could be equipment malfunction," he said, sounding to Kirk's ears like a stubborn child.

"We've checked everything out. Besides, that wouldn't take into account the communicators," Kirk replied. "Something external is jamming the frequencies. I'm not accusing the Falorians of anything. I'm sure they don't even realize what's going on, but I'm also sure that they are the ones responsible, even if it's indirectly. Now, will you contact them or shall I?"

Julius's shoulders drooped slightly. "I'll do it," he said. "Once we have communication again."

Uncle and nephew stood side by side in the communications room for the next twenty-three minutes, arms folded across their chests in almost identical poses, until with a burst of static a welcome, lively female voice was heard.

"—Heart. Come in, Sanctuary Heart. Repeat, we have minor injuries and are returning to home base, do you copy?"

With a relieved grin, Kirk leaned forward to reply. Julius's hand blocked the motion and the younger Kirk said, "We read you loud and clear, Skalli. What is the nature of your injuries? Is everyone accounted for?"

"We're fine, Juley," came Alex's voice, turning warm with affection. "We lost communications and were right at the monitoring post when the storm hit. I've no doubt you saw it on your sensors."

"We did indeed," Julius said. "Pretty big one."

"We have some minor dermal abrasions but were able to find shelter in time," Alex continued.

"Thank God for that," Julius said, sounding more sincere than Kirk had ever heard him. He glanced at his nephew and saw that Julius was pale and shaking a little. And were those tears he was blinking back? For the first time, Kirk realized just how deeply these two brothers were bonded.

"Did you figure out what was causing the malfunction?"

Julius, who was leaning over the console, looked up at Kirk. The cautious, hard mask was back in place. "Not exactly," he said. "We think perhaps the Falorians may have accidentally jammed the signal. We're going to try to talk to them."

"Good thinking, Julius," Alex said approvingly.

Julius scowled.

When the shuttle finally arrived, Julius hurried to embrace his brother. Six engineers scuttled out to attend to the *Drake,* looking for all the world like busy ants. Kirk felt a strong hand on his arm and glanced up to see Scott propelling him to a quiet corner.

"What happened out there, Scotty?" Kirk asked.

"Your nephew cracked," Scott said. "He's a good lad, mind, and I'm not passing judgment, but he panicked."

"You were the one who found the shelter, then?"

"Och, no, can't take that credit. Young Skalli kept her wits about her and found it for us."

Surprised and impressed, Kirk looked up to see Skalli talking with Chekov, waving her arms, flapping her ears, and pointing back at the shuttle.

"Good for her. How bad was Alex?" he asked quietly.

Scott shrugged. "Och, he'll be fine for the most part. But let me say I'm glad we're here if there's any real trouble."

Julius was able to reach Lissan, who showed up by evening the next day. Kirk, who had agreed to let Julius do most of the talking but had insisted on being present, was champing at the bit but managed to restrain himself. Communications continued to be erratic, and Kirk knew it was by sheer luck that he hadn't lost three crewmen, including his nephew, the first Huanni to attend Starfleet Academy, and one of his oldest, dearest friends.

Lissan materialized in the Courtyard. "Good evening," he said. "Julius, it is good to see you again. Alexander, let me express my pleasure that you are all right. Ah, and Captain. It is good to see you again as well. Julius has informed me of your communication difficulties. It's rather embarrassing, but . . . well, I'm afraid they're not going to end any time soon."

"Why not?" Kirk said, before he could stop himself. Julius glared at him.

"We are planning to reopen an old facility on the other side of the planet," Lissan continued. "You have inspired us with your colony, you see. We realized that we, too, could make use of Sanctuary."

"It was my understanding that you had given Sanctuary to us, freely, as a goodwill gesture," Alex said.

"And so we have! We will do nothing to hinder you, Alexander. You won't even know we're here."

"Well, it's difficult not to know you're here when your facility is interfering with our ability to communicate with anyone off world," Kirk said. He was just going to ignore Julius. "What kind of facility are we talking about?"

"Merely a resupply base for trading with various cargo ships."

"That accounts for the increase in subspace communication," Julius said, as if it explained everything.

"What about the problems in our communications?" Kirk pressed.

"We have erected a shield over the trading facility, and it appears to be that which is interfering with your communications," Lissan said.

"A shield? To protect you from what?" Kirk continued.

Lissan looked embarrassed. "Well, you see, Captain . . . some people with whom we trade are . . . one hates to say it . . . not entirely trustworthy, and might attempt to take cargo on without paying for it. The shield prevents them from absconding with anything of value. They have to be let in and out, one at a time. There is no chance of anyone attempting a quick transport that way."

It made sense, but there was still something wrong about the explanation to Kirk. Julius had given up trying to interrupt and now simply leaned back in his chair, arms folded across his chest, and an obvious, open scowl on his face. Alex leaned forward, clearly interested in following the discussion.

"I see your predicament," Kirk said, hoping to put the alien at ease.

"Not everyone is as honest as the Federation and the Sanctuary colonists," Lissan said generously.

"Clearly you need this shield. Equally clearly, we need to communicate with our friends and families. Is there any way you can change the shield's frequency so it doesn't interfere with our signals?"

Again, Lissan looked uncomfortable and apologetic. "Our technology is not nearly as advanced as yours. I regret to inform you that for now at least, we can only operate the shield on this specific frequency."

Keeping an open, honest expression on his face, Kirk spread his arms in an all-encompassing gesture. "It is my understanding that the reason you were willing to host this colony is to promote open exchange. Isn't that right, Alex?"

"Oh, yes!" Alex said eagerly. "We'd be happy to help you! It would be an honor to be able to assist our benefactors."

"We have a dozen or more highly skilled engineers, including one I can personally vouch for," Kirk continued. "We'd be happy to send them over to your . . . facility . . . and make whatever adjustments are necessary."

"Captain, you and Alex are most generous," Lissan said warmly. "But you have set us a challenge, you see."

"You mean, this is something you want to do on your own?" Julius said before either Alex or Kirk could speak.

"Precisely," Lissan said. "You are an inspiration to our own scientists. We would like to tackle this problem ourselves."

"But it would be so much quicker if—" began Alex, but his brother interrupted him.

"Come on, Alex! The Falorians have been so helpful to us in getting us Sanctuary and as Lissan says, we've been an inspiration to them. You don't want to take the thrill of discovery away from them, do you?"

"Please don't," Lissan said. "Trust us—when we are, how do you put it, at the end of our rope, we won't hesitate to contact you! In the meantime, we will enjoy figuring this out on our own."

"How long will it be until you reach the end of your rope?" Kirk demanded.

For the first time since Kirk had seen him, Lissan appeared to be caught offguard. "I really have no idea. I—"

"Give me your best guess."

"A—a few weeks," Lissan said.

Kirk had more to say—a lot more. But Julius stepped forward quickly. "Then it's settled," Julius said firmly. "The Falorians will work it out on their own and they'll ask for help if things don't look promising. Thanks, Uncle Jim, Alex. Lissan, I do have some questions on the specifics of something. A word?"

The two walked away together, chatting quietly. Alex smiled. "Well, that problem is solved."

"I hope so," Kirk said, but as he watched the alien and his nephew bow their heads together in close conversation, he had his doubts.

"So," Alexander said to his brother as they dined together late that night on leftover salad and pasta, "Everything *is* okay, isn't it?"

Julius sopped up some tomato sauce with his bread and popped it into his mouth. Chewing, he replied, "Oh, yeah. Everything's fine. The Falorians aren't as technologically advanced as we are, you know, so there are bound to be some glitches when they try something new." He twirled spaghetti around his fork. "Plenty of time to help them out when they get stuck and ask for our help."

"I never would have thought about it that way," Alex said. "But I suppose that's part of diplomacy, isn't it? Helping the other species save face."

"They're a good people, but are a little embarrassed about their personal lack of technology," Julius said facilely, pouring his third glass of robust red wine. "It's best to let them try everything they can first."

"You're right, as usual," smiled Alex. "You really do know these people well, don't you?"

"Yes," said Julius. "I do."

That night, as he lay in bed, Julius couldn't sleep. He tossed and turned, alternately sweating and chilled.

It had been close, today. Far too close for comfort. Alex could have died out there, and the Falorians hadn't said anything to Julius about jamming their communications.

He knew their messages were being monitored, of course. They had been since the beginning, but earlier, at least, Lissan and his cohorts had been very careful to disguise it. If Kirk hadn't brought that Russian along on the trip, Julius doubted if it would ever have been detected.

Damn Kirk! Always getting in the way, always acting so smug and superior with his "Starfleet does it *this* way" attitude. *Well, I've got news for you, Uncle Jim. You're not in Starfleet anymore. You're out here, in the wilderness, all alone.*

Julius groped for the cup of water on the bedside table and downed a large gulp. He badly wanted something alcoholic, but was smart enough to know that he'd drunk enough at dinner and would be feeling it if he didn't switch to water.

Lying back down on the pillow, he thought about his childhood and Kirk's part—or lack of a part—in it. Alex hadn't lied to Kirk about their boyhood with the Pearsons, but he hadn't told him everything, either. There had been no abuse, as far as it went. Neither foster parent had laid a hand on them. But they hadn't needed to in order to break them sufficiently.

They left the boys alone almost all the time. They ignored Alex and Julius when they could, said sharp, cruel things to them when they couldn't. Alex tried everything to get the Pearsons' attention and love: taking good care of Julius, earning excellent grades, taking on odd jobs. Nothing worked. Julius's tactics, which consisted of cutting classes, getting into trouble, and offering what Mrs. Pearson called "sassy backtalk" did get attention, but the wrong kind.

Alex had made the meals and told Julius bedtime stories. Alex had protected him from the bullies, and helped him with his homework. Alex had listened with a loving smile when Julius went through agonies about which little girl liked him and which didn't. Alex was the sun around which Julius revolved.

And every now and then, their Uncle Jim would show up. He was a kindly, but distant presence. He often brought gifts that served only to show how little he knew what his nephews were interested in. Julius hated him, because he knew—he *knew*—that life with Uncle Jim raising them would be sweeter and happier than life with the Pearsons, and Uncle Jim never offered to take them away and care for them.

Alexander had a forgiving nature, and he never blamed Uncle Jim for not saving them. *He's a starship captain, Juley. They can't have kids on starships.*

But Julius never forgot, nor forgave. And now Uncle Jim was here. Damn the Falorians! Why had they made that the deal-breaker?

He'd done everything they wanted. Even served some time in a pretty bad alien prison getting the things they had asked for. A few times, he'd try to talk to other species about colonies, but those were all dead ends.

He reached for the water again. He was getting the shakes just thinking about some of the places he'd been. Places he had willingly gone into for Alex's sake, places that Alex would have died rather than have Julius enter.

Gunrunner. Though the weapons to which the name referred were obsolete, the name had stuck through the centuries. It had sounded exciting, romantic, and as far away from anything the Pearsons represented as it was possible to get. And at first, it had been fun.

Why the hell had he gotten involved with the Orion Syndicate? The answer came back, *because they were the only ones*

who could get me what I wanted—a colony for Alexander.
Looking back on it, he could see each step down that dark path
had led him to the next, and the next. He couldn't believe he was
now trading in illegal weapons and information when the goal
had been to found a colony of peace and technology.

God, if Alex ever found out. . . .

Julius reached again for the water and this time knocked it
over. He swore, grabbed a towel, and began mopping it up. He
realized he was shaking.

He kept replaying the conversation he'd had with Lissan
today. *What the hell is going on?* he had demanded, forcing a
smile so false his mouth hurt. *My brother almost got killed
today! And what kind of facility is really going up? You said
nothing about that!*

Lissan had looked at him with those large, cold eyes, devoid
of any emotion save perhaps a flicker of amusement. *The danger to which your brother was exposed was not intended.*

*It damn well better not have been. I won't budge on that. No
harm comes to Alex, and he never knows about us.* He was not
the best of liars and he knew it, and it was a real struggle to
appear to be having a pleasant chat with this alien when he
really wanted to rip his throat out. But the appearance must be
maintained. . . .

What is going on with this facility?

Lissan had smiled. *The less you know, the better.*

Julius swore an old, ugly Anglo-Saxon word. *I got you
everything you wanted. Weapons. Information. Technology.
Even Kirk, damn it. I gave my own uncle to you. I have to know
what's going on.*

Lissan's unpleasant smile had widened. *No you don't,
Julius. No you don't.*

And Lissan had stepped away, ending the conversation.

Julius had stared. To follow him and pursue it would have tipped Kirk off. Alex, bless him, wouldn't have noticed, but Kirk would. Kirk would.

Julius didn't know what this mysterious facility was really for, but from what he knew of the Falorians and their goals, he knew its purpose wouldn't be that of innocently catering to trading vessels.

He had finally thought himself safe for the first time in his life. Safe and sound at last, on Sanctuary, with his brother. He'd sold his soul to pursue Alex's dream for him, and damn it, that ought to have been enough.

But it wasn't.

Julius Kirk didn't fall asleep until the small hours of the morning, and when he did, he dreamed of Alexander looking at him with sorrowful disillusionment in his eyes just before a cackling Lissan, firing the very weapons Julius had obtained for him, killed them both.

Chapter Ten

The representative of the Orion Syndicate known to Lissan only as 858 looked around speculatively at the spartan quarters that served as a conference room. There was only a single desk covered with padds and a computer, two chairs, and a dented old box shoved into a corner. His green lips curved in a smile that was more condescending than appreciative.

"Nice place," he said, and Lissan could hear the sarcasm in the words.

"It suffices," he said, his voice clipped.

"Aren't you going to offer me anything to drink? A little local delicacy to snack on, perhaps?"

"No," Lissan said.

"All right then. Let's get to business." He leaned forward and the humor had vanished. "You're behind schedule."

"It's been unavoidable," Lissan replied.

858 sighed. "You've been telling us that for too long already."

"It was the Syndicate's idea to have Captain Kirk come

along," Lissan reminded him. "He's been nothing but trouble."

The dark, steady gaze of the Orion male was unsettling. "Let us hope," 858 said softly, "that he does not suspect. Otherwise, *you* are going to be in a great *deal* of trouble."

As if we weren't already, Lissan thought sourly.

"Kirk doesn't suspect because we have been as cautious as we have," Lissan said. Even as he uttered the words, he knew they were a lie. Kirk suspected something, all right. Julius had promised he'd be able to keep his uncle under control, but clearly this James T. Kirk was more than anyone had bargained for. Pushing as hard as he had for getting the "communications problem" solved. . . .

"We are too close to success for us to risk being discovered before we are ready."

"But, Lissan, old friend," 858 said in a falsely comradely voice, "when *are* you going to be ready? We've been very patient. We've waited years, now, without seeing a single payment. But patience does run out."

The words sent shivers across Lissan's body, but he kept his face neutral. He was grateful for so many centuries of stoicism. A Huanni would be a blubbering heap right now.

He decided to play the Orion's own game. "We are very grateful for all your help and your remarkable patience," he said, forcing his voice to sound as sincere as possible. "But you must admit, when you will be paid, it will be quite the treasure for something that required relatively little effort from the Syndicate."

"It is the value of that treasure," 858 agreed silkily, "that made us agree to be paid later rather than sooner."

Lissan's mind raced. There was still so much to be done before they were ready, and yet 858 was quite right about one thing: Time was running out. The window of opportunity, which had yawned so wide for such a long time, was closing rapidly. All depended on them leaping through that window while they still could.

He decided to go on the offensive. "Part of the reason that time is so short is because the Syndicate failed to keep Huan out of the Federation. That's made everything incredibly difficult."

"The Syndicate agreed to do what it could," 858 said icily. "It did. The problem is yours, not ours. Our problem is, we need a timetable from you. And it needs to be a timetable we agree with. When can we begin?"

"We still have so much—"

"You know," 858 interrupted, a green hand reaching down to his waist, "I really wasn't the best contact for this job. I don't have a lot of patience, personally. And I have to be frank with you, Lissan. I need a specific and firm date. And if I don't come out of this meeting with one, you don't come out of this meeting at all."

In his long green fingers was a small disk, with an opening aimed directly at Lissan. He didn't recognize the weapon at all, but that was hardly surprising. Of course, agents of the Syndicate would be equipped with the latest technology that could be bought or stolen.

"You're bluffing," he stammered, then looked up from the weapon to 858's cold eyes.

The Orion wasn't bluffing.

"A date," 858 repeated, softly.

"Two months," blurted Lissan.

Almost sorrowfully, 858 shook his black head. "Not good enough, I'm afraid." His thumb moved.

"One month!"

The thumb paused a millimeter from a red button. "Two weeks."

"Yes, all right, two weeks, curse you!"

858 smiled pleasantly. The little weapon vanished into the folds of his clothes. "I do so enjoy the give and take of negotiation."

Kirk hadn't served in Starfleet for as long as he had without learning when to trust and when to be suspicious. And right now, he was suspicious.

He voiced his concerns only to his old, trusted friends. Alex was a good man, clearly, but the colony was his baby. And Julius . . . there was something about Julius that Kirk didn't like, something that went deeper than the obvious resentment of perceived past neglect. Skalli was Starfleet, but Skalli was also . . . well . . . Skalli.

The old comrades met each day for lunch. With their history, that wouldn't be noticed, but any more frequent encounters might. Spring was giving way to summer, and Kirk knew of a few places where they could dine al fresco and not be observed.

Kirk lay on his back, watching clouds move slowly across a blue sky. He bit into a carrot, looked over at Chekov, and said, "Status report?" He was not unaware of the incongruity of the conversation and the setting.

Sitting cross-legged on the blanket, Chekov replied, "Communications have cleared up slightly. We are able to communicate with one another here on Sanctuary, but I don't think we can successfully send or receive messages outside. And I still think someone is listening in."

Kirk finished the carrot and moved on to a roasted native bird of some sort. He bit into a drumstick and thought wryly, *tastes like chicken.* "Are you certain the messages aren't getting out?"

"No, Chekov replied. "In fact, they do appear to be getting

out, but the fact that we have never received any response makes me think that they really aren't being transmitted."

"Spock would praise your logical deduction," Kirk said approvingly. "As do I."

"One thing Chekov and I did notice," Scott added, "was that it looks like the Falorians are able to get messages through. We detected a narrow band subspace carrier wave in that facility of theirs. It's able to punch through their shield just fine, thank you very much."

"Curiouser and curiouser," Kirk said. "What's the engineering buzz?"

"They're so busy with their noses in the engines that they don't stop to look up," Scott said. Kirk thought the same could be said of Scotty from time to time, but he said nothing. "We're getting flyovers almost daily. Sometimes more than once a day. There's a lot of traffic up there, Captain."

"If the Falorians are telling the truth, then that would make sense," Kirk countered. "It's a resupply base. Of course there'd be a lot of ships coming to Sanctuary now."

Scott raised an eyebrow. "If the base is over on the other side of the planet, they wouldn't be needing to fly quite so directly over our little colony, though, now would they?"

"So we're being watched," Kirk said. His friends exchanged glances, then nodded their agreement.

Kirk permitted himself to finish the drumstick, then announced his decision.

"Gentlemen, I think this base needs to be investigated. Either of you like to accompany me?"

It was 0134 the following morning that Kirk, Chekov, and Scott rendezvoused at the *Drake*. The air was heavy with dew and they were all shivering in the early morning chill.

"Let's go," Kirk said. Quietly and quickly, they entered. With a deft touch born of years of coaxing obedience from delicate machinery, Scott started the atmosphere shuttle. Seconds later, they were aloft.

Chekov shook his head, smiling in amazement. "I can't believe it," he said. "I thought for certain we would have been noticed and challenged."

"I knew we wouldn't," Kirk said with just a touch of superiority.

"How?" For the briefest of moments, Pavel Chekov looked like the brash young ensign Kirk remembered from thirty years ago as he stared at Kirk in wonder.

"He asked for the shuttle," Scott said. Kirk grinned like a wolf, and Chekov threw back his head and laughed.

"Alex thinks we are on a research mission to document the cycle of a rare, night-blooming flower. Said mission is headed by you, Mr. Chekov, so you'll need to be able to answer any questions."

Chekov made a face.

"Coincidentally," Kirk continued, "it happens to grow in profusion very close to where Lissan's mysterious base is located. We'll just have to remember to get a few samples before we head back home."

While the little atmosphere shuttle was not designed to explore space, it excelled at what it was designed to do and sped along quite nicely. As they approached the continent, all three of them instinctively quieted and focused on the tasks at hand.

"There it is," Scotty said.

"It doesn't look big enough to be a resupply base," Chekov said.

"That's probably because it isn't," Kirk said. Resupply bases were enormous. They had to be, in order to house sufficient supplies and provide ample docking for those ships that could land planetside. They were sometimes the size of small cities. The facility he was looking at was hardly a full kilometer. Whatever it housed was protected by a shield that not only prohibited examination via a ship's computer, but any visual appraisal as well. It was a ghostly blue color and arched over the whole like an eggshell.

"Any sign we've been detected?" Kirk said, leaning over Scott's shoulder to look out through the *Drake's* large windows.

"Negative," said Scott. "There's very little in the way of scanning equipment."

"They apparently assume that no one will come looking for them," said Chekov. He didn't comment about how this directly contradicted Lissan's comments about erecting the shield as a precaution against the untrustworthy. He didn't have to. It was obvious that the entire story was one enormous lie, and with each new bit of information they gleaned that lie unraveled further.

Scott's fingers flew over the controls. He shook his gray head. "Their technology is a lot more sophisticated than they'd like us to believe," he said. "I've tried all the tricks in the book and I can't penetrate that shield."

Kirk made a decision. "Land us."

Scott and Chekov didn't bat an eyelash. They'd served with him long enough to know that any protest would go unheard by Kirk. It was one thing to just fly over and claim they were researching flowers. It was another thing to actually land the shuttle near the facility and do what Kirk was planning on doing. Scott maneuvered the small shuttle close to the earth, skimming along until he found a large copse of trees with a meadow in its center. With a surgeon's grace, he dropped lower still and eased the shuttle into the clearing. The

Drake hovered, then settled gently down onto the grass.

"They'll find us if they do any scans," Scott warned, "but with any luck, the trees'll at least provide visual camouflage."

"Well done, Scotty. You need to stay with the shuttle."

Scott's mustache drooped. "But Captain, I—"

"No buts. I need your expertise to get that shield down long enough for us to get inside. Once Chekov and I are in, bring the shield back up immediately and get out of here fast. I think we'll be able to figure out a way to get the shield open from the inside when we're done." He smiled wryly and added teasingly, "That's of course assuming that you've been doing your research."

"Ah, now, Captain," Scott scolded gently, his eyes sparkling.

"You *think* we'll be able to get the shield open?" Chekov exclaimed. "But if we can't—"

"Then Scotty will have to lead a rescue team," Kirk said wryly. "I'm not sure how much time we'll need, so keep monitoring for our life signs outside the shield. We'll head back for this copse. We won't be able to communicate with you once we're inside, so it's up to you to keep a sharp lookout and get us out of here. Go to our original destination—the flower field. It's within transport distance and a few seconds away at top speed. You may have to pick us up very quickly."

Obviously, Scott was disappointed. But he saw Kirk's logic and reluctantly nodded. "Aye, it's a good plan. But I'm not going to be likin' just leaving you here."

"There's less of a chance you'll be discovered than if you just stay in this copse," Kirk pointed out. He placed a hand on Scott's shoulder. "We need you with the shuttle, Scotty."

"Aye," Scotty said, straightening. He turned back to the computer and for a while the three old friends sat in silence, waiting. Finally, Scott grunted approvingly. "So that's how we do it, eh?"

With a flourish, he touched a few more controls, and then the screen began to display a series of complicated graphics and code.

Scott turned around to explain what he was doing to Kirk and Chekov. "All right. Here's the situation. I've been able to piggyback on that subspace carrier wave and I can disable their entire security system from here. Any monitors, screens, scanners—they'll all go out. The only thing you two will have to worry about is being physically seen. And the beauty of it is it'll look like a common, garden-variety glitch. They'll never know it was us."

"Scotty," Kirk breathed, "you're a genius!"

Scott inclined his head modestly. "You and Chekov go on, Captain. I'll have that thing open and shut for you in the blink of an eye. And unless anyone is actually looking at the controls at the time I do it, they won't notice *that,* either."

Kirk grinned, clapped the miracle-performing engineer on the back, and opened the shuttle door. He and Chekov dropped quietly down to the earth and sped for the Falorian "resupply base."

It loomed ahead of them, its pulsating blue glow eerie in the dark night. Kirk's eyes flicked from the approaching shield dome to his tricorder. No sign of humanoid life. So far as he could tell, they were still undetected.

He didn't slow as they drew closer, and Chekov matched his pace easily. Kirk trusted Scott completely, and just as it appeared that they were both about to slam into the shield and probably be killed, the shield disappeared.

They kept running.

* * *

Already aloft, Scott watched without blinking as the two dots that signified Kirk and Chekov entered the facility. The instant they had cleared the shield radius he jabbed a button and the shield was reerected.

They were in.

Smoothly, Scott maneuvered the little vessel toward the field of white flowers. "Godspeed," he wished his two friends, and began the wait.

Chapter Eleven

Commander T'SroH had never been more bored in his entire life.

Intellectually, he knew that he had been given a great honor: to assist his noble Chancellor in carrying out her vow of *DIS jaj je*. When Kerla had first contacted him and informed him of this important task, T'SroH had puffed his chest out with pride.

And then Kerla filled him in on the details.

The destruction of Praxis had been a disaster on a scale that most Klingons were only now truly beginning to appreciate. T'SroH, like Kerla, had not at first approved of Gorkon's peace initiatives, but with each day that passed, the unpleasant reality revealed itself more clearly: The Klingons needed peace if they were to survive as the passionate, proud people they had always been. The events at Khitomer regarding one James T. Kirk had startled T'SroH and many others, and when he learned that Kirk was the subject of Azetbur's *DIS jaj je,* he was not surprised.

If only Kirk had willingly accepted the great honor that Azetbur had bestowed! Then T'SroH would not be bored, as he was now. It was not the fact that he now owed a year and a day out of his life to fulfilling his chancellor's honor debt, but the manner in which he had to spend that year and day.

He had followed the large, ungainly ship called the *Mayflower II* to this planet, nauseatingly named Sanctuary. His ship, the proud and noble *K'Rator,* had maintained its cloak the entire time, running undetectable while any other ships were in the vicinity and scanning quickly, cautiously, when they were not.

Why had Captain Kirk, by all accounts an adventuresome human, come to this wretchedly peaceful place? The Klingon had been brought up to speed, of course, and knew that there was a blood bond between the starship captain and the younger colony founders. But what purpose would it serve? From what he knew of Kirk, T'SroH suspected the human was as bored as he.

Weeks had gone by in this manner. T'SroH was beginning to think he might go mad. His crew was beginning to grumble as well. At this rate, the entire Year and a Day would pass before Kirk would do so much as stub a toe.

At least there was *some* activity to break up the monotony. T'SroH had watched with mild interest as the Falorians worked without ceasing to build a spacedock close to Sanctuary. He had made note of the vessels that came and went. Many were large cargo vessels; some were sleek, dangerous-looking fighters. Still others were strange hybrids, clearly cobbled together of many different vessels from many different peoples. One or two T'SroH thought he recognized as belonging to members of the Orion Syndicate, but, of course, he could not be certain unless they chose to display their symbol of a circle and a lightning bolt. Which, naturally, they would be reluctant to do. He made a mental note and let it go. If the Falorians chose to deal with the scum, let them. His sole focus, his reason for being locked in orbit around this miserable place, was James Kirk. All else was extraneous.

To that end, of much greater interest were the daily flyovers the Falorian ships made of the colony. T'SroH kept hoping for some kind of attack to break the monotony, but none came.

T'SroH had also hoped this mysterious facility the Falorians had built on the far side of the planet would prove of interest, but thus far, the shields had only been lowered for the briefest of moments. There had been no time to execute an order to scan so they might discover what that shield protected.

The Klingons had long since adapted to the cycles of this planet's days and nights, and it was the small hours of the morning on Sanctuary. T'SroH lay in his bed, unable to sleep, although sleep would be an excellent way to pass the time that appeared to be on his hands.

There was a sharp whistle of the communications system. "Commander," came his second-in-command's voice.

"Speak," T'SroH grunted.

"Captain Kirk and two others have left the colony. I thought you would wish to be informed," continued Garthak.

At this hour? That was indeed unusual. T'SroH sat up in his bed. "What is their destination?"

"Uncertain." A pause. Then, his voice laced with excitement, "They are heading to the facility."

T'SroH growled his pleasure and leaped out of bed. *This should be interesting.* Perhaps the time had finally come to pay the *DIS jaj je.*

He hastened to the bridge just in time for Garthak to say, "They are right outside the perimeter."

T'SroH found himself breathing shallowly, his blood racing. Had it really been so long since anything had happened that the sight of two humans outside an alien facility would make him catch his breath so? He made a mental note to challenge Garthak to a good *bat'leth* practice later today.

But T'SroH was not the only one watching with excitement; he could feel the tension on the bridge. There he was, the famous James T. Kirk. He knew, as Kirk could not, how secure the Falorians were in the impenetrability of their base. Clearly, they thought the colonists would behave like good little Earth sheep and stay where they were supposed to; stay where the Falorians could keep watch over them.

He found himself doing something he thought he would never do—rooting for a human.

"I have heard of his Engineer Scott as well," T'SroH said. "If he is the one in the vessel, then it is likely that—"

He fell silent as in front of his eyes, the shield went down and the two humans raced inside. T'SroH caught only the briefest glimpses of the shapes of buildings before the blue, pulsating shield went back up.

The shield had only been down for half a second. With any luck, if it was even noticed by whatever security the Falorians had, the brief shutdown would be assumed to be a technical error.

He leaned forward in his command chair. After weeks of waiting, T'SroH wasn't about to miss a moment of this.

There was a low hum and a crackle as the shield went down. Phasers at the ready, Kirk and Chekov charged in. A fraction of a second later, the shield was back up. They remained tense, alert for any sign that they had been discovered, but all was quiet.

Kirk looked around while Chekov studied the tricorder. In the distance was a large tower. Scattered about were six or eight outbuildings, all small, utilitarian looking and single-story. There were a few lights on, but not many. The perimeter was only sparsely lit as well.

"Clearly, they put a lot of trust in that shield," Kirk said. "Scott said their security systems were a bit lax."

"I see no cargo areas, no ships, nothing that even remotely resembles a vessel," Chekov said. Sarcastically he added, "I wonder why that is?"

"But I do see the source of that subspace carrier wave," Kirk said, stepping forward and craning his neck to look up at the tower. "It dominates the entire area."

"It's a subspace relay, all right, but . . ." Chekov frowned. "This is a Starfleet issue relay, I'm certain of it."

"What?" Kirk looked with renewed interest at the relay. "No cargo areas, pirated technology . . . it's not looking very good for the Falorians' trustworthiness. Come on."

Carefully they moved toward the mostly darkened buildings. Scotty might have disabled the security system for the next few hours, but there was always the chance that they'd run into the old-fashioned security system—a guard. But the Falorians were diurnal, as were humans, and it looked as though most of them had gone to bed for the night.

Kirk heard a slight noise and, grabbing Chekov's arm, pulled him up close against the nearest building. Several meters away, a single bored-looking Falorian guard, carrying a Starfleet-issue phaser, strolled past.

"If that's their security system, I think we're a match for it," Chekov whispered.

"Did you see the phaser?"

"I'm holding one just like it."

Quietly, they moved on. A window was open across a wide patch of grass, and Kirk squinted, trying to see inside. He saw what appeared to be a bed and a desk, and then the room went dark. These were living quarters, then.

But who lived here?

"Captain," Chekov said quietly, "There's a large entrance into the soil at the center of the area. It seems to be a tunnel of some sort. I'm detecting more evidence of high-level technology there than in any of these outer buildings."

"Then that's where we should be," Kirk said. This area was better lit than the perimeter, but Chekov was able to pinpoint the presence of any Falorians. When all was clear, they sprinted for the tunnel.

The mouth was several hundred meters wide and narrowed as it went further into the ground. Kirk could catch glimpses of the technology that Chekov's tricorder had revealed. His eyes widened slightly. Lissan's claim that they didn't have the level of technology that the colonists possessed was clearly a lie of the most elaborate sort. At the end of the tunnel, there was no dirt or stone to be seen. All was metal and alloys, lights and gantries and lifts. Kirk caught a glimpse of similarly clad Falorians scurrying along corridors here and there, carrying padds and looking focused.

Quickly they stepped down onto a gantry and pressed back against cold metal. Chekov was still reading the tricorder.

"I'm detecting very little indication of weapons," he said as Kirk continued to take their bearings. "This may be a research facility."

"Let's find out what it is they're researching." It was clearly an enormous complex, and they were only two humans. With the security system disabled, luck ought to be with them. They hopped onto a lift and rode it down. Despite himself, Kirk felt his imagination stir at the sight of all the unfamiliar technology, much of it obviously new. It was probably just as well Scott wasn't with them. The engineer might have fallen in love.

The lift clanged to a stop. The corridor was empty and they jumped off, ducking into a darkened room. Chekov glanced at the tricorder and nodded that all was clear. Phasers drawn, they proceeded down the corridor.

"What are we looking for?" Chekov whispered.

"We'll know it when we see it," Kirk hissed back. Even as he spoke the words, he wondered if they were true. What they were looking for was some reason why the Falorians had woven such an extensive web of lies. Why had they given up an entire planet to an alien race, with the only stipulation being a share in the technology the colony developed, when it was clear they had advanced technology themselves? Why had they erected a shield over nothing more dangerous than a research facility, and called it a "resupply base"? Why were they lying about jamming the colony's frequencies, and why did they not want the colonists communicating with the outside world? What was a pirated Starfleet subspace relay system doing here, and how had they gotten a hold of it in the first place?

Answers were what he and Chekov were looking for. He only hoped they would indeed know them when they saw them.

Many of these rooms were storage facilities for equipment. And much of this equipment was Starfleet issue. It solved at least one problem. Kirk leaned over and whispered in Chekov's ear, "The Orion Syndicate."

Chekov nodded. "Cossacks," he muttered. Then, wordlessly, he hauled Kirk down behind a cabinet full of beakers of various shapes and sizes.

"Lights," came a voice. Footsteps passed them, hesitated. They heard the clink of glass, then the footsteps moved away. "Lights off," called the Falorian, and all was quiet again.

The next room into which they ventured was obviously a

laboratory. Kirk looked around, then spotted what he was searching for—access to a computer.

"Start downloading anything you can," he said. "I'll look around."

Chekov nodded, and immediately began configuring the tricorder to link up with the computer.

Kirk could have made a fair guess at navigating an alien bridge, but here in an alien laboratory, Kirk felt out of his element. Too bad Spock wasn't here. He'd know what to make of this confusing jumble of equipment and—

Notes.

A padd lay tossed on the table next to a cup of something that had been poured and forgotten and was now growing some kind of mold. That in itself would be an interesting project, but Kirk was certain that was only an accidental side effect of too many hours spent in painstaking research. It was funny how similar scientists were, whatever their species. He picked up the padd, careful not to accidentally erase any information. Of course, it was all written in Falorian, but translation would be easy once they got back to the colony.

"Captain, look at this," Chekov said. He was glancing back and forth from his tricorder to the screen. Kirk looked up to see a graphic of various shapes parading across the screen.

"What am I looking at?" Kirk asked, deferring to Chekov's greater familiarity with all things scientific.

"I'm not certain, of course, but I've got a general idea of the focus of their research. At least one focus. Nanotechnology."

Kirk watched, fascinated, as what he now realized were infinitesimally tiny machines marched about their business. "That covers a lot of ground," he said. "What are the nanotechs doing? Is the focus on medicine, repair, what?"

"They're not repairing anything," said Chekov. "I don't

have enough information yet, but my guess is they're going to be used as some kind of weapon."

Kirk's stomach clenched. "I want you to go to the deepest level of information they have in the computer," he said.

"That could take time."

"If they're formulating a weapon, then the clock's ticking already, Mr. Chekov."

"Aye, sir." He hesitated. "So far, I've only downloaded basic information. If I try to break into their encrypted files, I could alert someone to our presence."

"That's a risk we have to take. We must know what they're planning."

Chekov bit his lower lip. This wasn't his area of expertise, but he was still more familiar with something like this than Kirk would be. With clear reluctance, he sat down and began to try to bypass the security system around the computer.

Kirk's mind was racing. Everything was starting to make at least some kind of sense now. He looked down at his tricorder. This complex was enormous and extended for several hundred meters into the earth. It wasn't anything new, nor was it anything that had been abandoned long ago and recently reoccupied. The Falorians had to have been working on getting it up and running for some time now. How could Alex not have known about this?

The answer came to him almost immediately, but it was an answer that he almost would rather not have had.

Julius.

Julius had always been the liaison to the Falorians. It wasn't inconceivable that he had known what was going on from the very beginning, and had conspired with them to conceal evidence of this mammoth facility from any scans and reports.

Kirk's mind went back to that middle of the night conversation when Alexander and Julius had first shown up on his doorstep. How long ago it all seemed now. *It's all thanks to Julius,* Alex had said. *He's been amazing . . . he's been the one out there talking to all kinds of alien races to find us our Sanctuary.* And Julius's own words: *You have no idea what we've been through the last few years, Uncle Jim . . . the crawling through mud and getting sick and being literally scared for my life half the time that I've done to get this thing to fly.*

He thought of the Starfleet technology generously peppered through the complex. *Oh, Julius. I think I do know what you've been through . . . and what you've done.*

"I've done as much as I dare do," said Chekov, breaking into Kirk's thoughts.

"Good job. We've got one more stop on this pleasant little tour of the resupply station."

According to the tricorder readings there was an enormous cavern at the very bottom of the facility. They had seen dozens of labs, conference rooms and storage rooms, but nothing like this.

Kirk had to shake his head at how easy this all was. The shield and the system Scott had so easily cracked had lulled the Falorians into a false sense of security. Doors hissed open as readily for them as for the aliens, and after taking a long ride down on a lift, they stepped into what was clearly the heart of the complex.

Like everything they had seen thus far, this cavern was entirely Falorian-made. There was no glimpse of stone walls or dirt anywhere. Every wall was lined with panels, monitors (most of which, Kirk noticed appreciatively, were blank), switches, buttons, and blinking lights of every variety.

"We're in a control center," Chekov breathed, awe in his voice. "A very, very *big* control center."

Kirk had moved forward and was now looking at some of the images on the screens. Most of them were of places he didn't recognize.

But there was one he did, and his heart began to pound fiercely in his chest.

He was looking straight into the formal reception hall of Starfleet's headquarters in San Francisco.

Chapter Twelve

"That's . . ." Chekov's voice trailed off as he stepped beside Kirk and looked at the banquet hall.

"Yes," Kirk said grimly. "My friend Admiral Standing Crane told me that the Falorians were very curious people. They wanted to visit every starbase and member planet, tour every ship. And they were so pleasant, so charming about it that no one suspected anything. Not even Standing Crane, who's as sharp as they come. Whatever the Falorians are planning, there's a good chance it's going to affect the entire Federation." He nodded to one of the enormous consoles, and Chekov hastened up to it.

He touched the tricorder, and then frowned. "They have a heavy encryption on the data here, much more than they had in the labs."

Kirk knew what he was saying. Chekov had been able to break into the computer system fairly easily. It would be harder now, and every minute they lingered here meant a greater chance of discovery. Also, the deeper encryption clearly guarded information of greater import. Chekov wasn't an expert at this, and an attempt to access the information could trip some kind of security system.

"Continue, Mr. Chekov."

Chekov's eyes searched his for a moment, and then he nodded. He turned, took a breath, and touched the computer. His fingers flew over a few soft pads, and then the tricorder began to hum.

"It's work—"

A shrill alarm cut him off. And at the same time, he snatched his hands back with a cry of pain. His fingers were blackened and smoking. White bone peeked through. Kirk swore. He rushed forward and grabbed Chekov's tricorder and phaser.

"Let's go," he cried. They rushed back up the way they had come. Kirk heard Chekov trying and failing to stifle the occasional whimper of pain and he cursed himself. He knew that breaking into secure systems could be dangerous. Why hadn't he been the one to take the risks? Why had he put Pavel in jeopardy?

As they raced for the nearest lift Kirk heard a clatter of booted feet echo down the hallway. He looked around and saw metal rungs extending up as far as the eye could see. Despite Scott's efforts, Kirk had managed to trip the security system, and he knew that all the lifts would be shut down now. There was only one way out.

He glanced over at Chekov. The younger man's handsome face was twisted in a grimace of agony. His fingers were now black and swollen. Blood and pus crested and broke through the burned flesh.

"Can you climb?" Kirk asked.

Chekov forced a smile. "Do I have a choice?"

Despite the direness of the situation, Kirk smiled. "I don't think so. Go on. You first."

"But I'll slow us down—"

"That's an order, Mister," snapped Kirk. Chekov nodded, and set his teeth against the pain as he began to climb, slowly and in obvious agony.

Kirk followed, glancing down. Below him he saw a handful of guards come running into the corridor and into the chamber Kirk and Chekov had just vacated. It was huge and there were a number of places people could hide. With luck, that would keep them busy for a while.

They kept climbing. Chekov was deathly silent, but as he followed him, Kirk could feel the smear of fluid on each metal rung. Chekov began to breathe heavily. He alternated hands and tried to use his lower arms instead of grasping the rungs directly. Kirk looked up. They still had such a long way to go.

"You can do it, Pavel," he said, softly and urgently. "One rung at a time."

"Captain," gasped Chekov raggedly, "You should leave me behind. There's no point in both of us getting captured."

"I won't leave you. Keep going."

It seemed to take an eternity to get to the next level. Kirk ducked his head into the corridor and pulled back quickly. Guards. He touched Chekov on the leg to silently signal that he needed to keep going. After the briefest pause, Chekov gamely continued. Kirk wished that he could help Pavel, but he could do nothing except let him set the pace and be below him on the ladder to catch him in case he slipped.

Kirk didn't know how long it took, but they made their slow, agonizing way up ladder after ladder. When they could, they ducked into corridors and labs to catch their breath and give Chekov a respite, albeit a brief one, from the pain. If only the lifts hadn't been shut down! At the very least, they seemed able to avoid capture.

Finally, Kirk saw that they were close to the top. There were only two or three more ladders to climb. He checked the tricorder. All seemed clear in the nearest corridor, and he silently signaled Chekov that they should take a break. Before they could scramble over the lip and head to freedom, they had to get the shield down.

He leaned back, thinking. Next to him, he heard Pavel hissing softly through his teeth as he stretched his damaged hands out in front, keeping them as still as possible. Where would be the best place for security posts? In the center area, of course, since it appeared that the control room was the most sensitive area. And right near the top, to prevent exactly what he and Chekov had managed to do.

He checked the tricorder and nodded as it confirmed his logic. The top floor, which ran the circumference of the tunnel, was filled with weapons, technology, and Falorians.

"Here's the plan," he told Chekov.

Once Chekov was in position, Kirk stepped close to the edge of the corridor, aimed at a piece of equipment several meters below, and got off a single, rapid shot. At once he heard a commotion. Had anyone been watching, they would have seen the direction from which the phaser had been fired and could easily have traced him, but as it was, they didn't realize what had happened until it was too late and now congregated around the smoking, blasted piece of equipment.

While their attention was diverted, Kirk sprang onto the nearest ladder, scaled it swiftly, and ducked into the first security room he came to. He surprised a guard, who lifted a weapon in one hand even as he reached for an intercom button with another, but Kirk was faster. He fired and the guard crumpled. Kirk whirled and fired again, taking out two more guards. He leapt over the bodies and scanned the equipment.

Damn it, he had no idea what he was looking for. He'd relied on Chekov to do that. His pulse racing, Kirk examined alien lettering and various colored buttons. Pulsing lights in red, yellow, orange, indigo, and—

Blue. The same pale blue as the shield. Would it be that simple, that obvious? Kirk thought about the overconfidence the Falorians had, how easily their systems had been disabled, and decided that the gamble was worth it. He flipped open his communicator.

"I'm in. I'm going to press a button, Chekov. Let me know what happens."

"Aye, sir."

Without a moment's hesitation, Kirk pressed the blue button.

"It's down!" came Chekov's excited voice.

"I'm right behind you," Kirk said. He snapped the communicator closed and headed for the ladder.

But now he was spotted, and he heard shouts. A directed energy weapon blast struck inches from his head. A few centimeters above him was the lip of the tunnel and—

Kirk almost lost his grip as a booted foot kicked him in the face. Gray and white swirled in front of his eyes, but he refused to lose consciousness. He reached up in the gray swirl, grasped the leg attached to the boot that had kicked him, and pulled. Screaming, the Falorian hurtled down into the depths.

Bleeding from a broken nose, Kirk pulled himself over the lip of the tunnel. The shield was still down, and the stars arched above the complex. Their calm, cold twinkling was strangely incongruous to Kirk. He got to his feet and took off running.

He dematerialized in mid-stride.

Kirk treated his own and Chekov's more serious injuries with the medikit on board the *Drake,* filling Scotty in on what had transpired.

"I can't believe getting the shield down would be that easy," Kirk said. "You were right, Scotty—the Falorian security system is amazingly lax. Push a blue button, a blue shield comes down."

"Um," said Scott, looking uncomfortable.

Kirk looked up sharply from Chekov's hands. "What?"

"Well, um . . . the shield . . . I was fiddling with the signals and—"

"You got the shield down?"

"Um . . . aye, sir. Though I'm sure you would have been able to figure it out yourself had you had the time."

Kirk grinned weakly and turned back to Chekov. "It's good that you got that information, laddie," Scott said to Chekov, clearly trying to change the subject, "and we'll be able to translate it for sure. But if it's encrypted, I doubt there's anyone sufficiently trained back at the colony to break the code."

Kirk's heart sank at the words, but he didn't let his disappointment show. "We have at least three Starfleet officers here," he said. "Between us, we'll come up with something."

"I was never trained in such things," Scott said. "And unless you two have taken some courses I don't know about, neither were you."

"Damn it, we have to try!" Kirk cried. "The entire Federation could be at risk!"

At that moment, there was a crackle and then Alex's voice filled the little shuttle. "Uncle Jim! We're under attack! Repeat, we're under attack!"

* * *

Even at top speed it was several minutes before the *Drake* could reach the colony. They saw the brutal orange and crimson glow of the fire while still several kilometers away. There had been a few injuries, none of them serious, and no fatalities. The only true casualty had been the *Mayflower II* herself.

"They came out of nowhere," Alex had told them, his voice high-pitched with panic. "They came out of nowhere and just started firing on the ship!"

"But not on the colony itself?" Kirk had wanted to know.

"No, not on us. But the ship's gone, Uncle Jim. There's no way to repair this kind of damage."

Kirk had hoped his nephew had been wrong, but as they skimmed over the burning wreckage, he had to agree with Alex's assessment. As they settled in for a landing, Kirk saw the flames dying as chemicals were sprayed on them. As soon as they stepped out of the shuttle, Alex rushed up to them.

He looked dreadful. He was wild-eyed and sweating, and reached to clasp Kirk's arms. "I'm so glad you're back, Uncle Jim, we—what happened to your face?"

Kirk waved it off. "A little accident. Chekov is more in need of treatment than I am. A . . . wiring accident, which we've already taken care of."

He didn't particularly enjoy lying to his nephew, but it was obvious to him that the Falorians had fired on the colony in retaliation for the break-in. The less Alex knew, the better, at least until Kirk could better assess the situation. Alex ran his finger through his soot-darkened hair, his eyes drawn inexorably to the inferno.

"Did you see who did it?" Kirk asked.

"Huh? Oh. We've got their signal, but no one actually saw anything. We were all asleep. We don't recognize the ships at all."

Skalli came rushing up, her long legs carrying her swiftly across the dewy grass. "Oh, Captain Kirk!" she exclaimed. Tears of sympathy welled in her huge eyes. "Your face! What happened? Oh! And Mr. Chekov, your hands, your poor hands!"

"Pavel, go with Skalli to see Dr. Sherman. Skalli, stay with him." It would keep her out of his hair. "Alex, let's you and Scotty and I go look at the records."

Before they left, Kirk took a quick look back at the crowd that was busily damping the flames. Among them was Julius, bare chested and clad only in pajama bottoms. His torso glistened with sweat and looked orange in the light of the dying fire. As if feeling Kirk's gaze upon him, he turned. Their eyes locked, and Kirk saw a brief expression of anguish cross Julius's face before the younger man turned away quickly.

Kirk thought about the pirated equipment he'd seen in the complex, and then turned to follow Alex.

"See? It's nothing we know," Alex said as they looked at the images on the screen.

Kirk could make a pretty good guess, and so could Scott. They exchanged glances. Kirk wondered how much he ought to reveal at this juncture. He decided to start with the truth.

"That's a vessel built by a species that is known to have dealings with the Orion Syndicate," he said. "See that shadow on the hull?" He pointed to a thin, dark line. "That indicates a false panel. They can remove it to display the mark of the Syndicate when it serves them, and hide it when it doesn't."

Alex's eyes widened. "Really? Do you think they're dealing with the Falorians?"

Surprised, Kirk said, "Yes, we do."

"No wonder they wanted that shield," Alex said. "I'm sure they don't trust the Syndicate at all. Maybe they stopped dealing with them and the Syndicate retaliated by attacking our ship."

Kirk sighed quietly. Alex still bought Lissan's story about the facility being a resupply base. And now was not yet the time to disillusion him. Alex was not a liar, and if Lissan returned to the colony and Alex understood fully what was going on, Alex would give them all away.

"Maybe you're right," was all he said.

The cool night winds blew away the smoke, and the colony awoke to a crisp, bright dawn. Its cheerful roseate glow made the ruins of the mighty colony ship look even more stark and desolate. It was black and twisted, a dark skeleton silhouetted against the morning sky.

Kirk was up early, helping everyone scavenge what they could. According to Alex, all the damage had been caused by a single strafing run of the unknown vessel. It had not made a second pass, which would have utterly destroyed everything. Clearly the attack had been to simply make sure they had no means of escape. Utter destruction had not been deemed necessary.

Scarcely had he begun pitching in when he heard the hum of a transporter. Kirk glanced over to see Lissan materialize in the Courtyard. He choked back a wave of anger. If he had any hope of discovering and thwarting the Falorian plans, he had to maintain a façade of trust. He would let Lissan set the tone for this meeting.

"What happened here?" exclaimed Lissan, staring at the remains of the *Mayflower II.*

He was good. If Kirk hadn't known better, he'd have bought it hook, line, and sinker, just like Alex did. Alex and Julius stepped forward to greet the Falorian.

"It happened last night," Alex said. "This ship came out of

nowhere and just started firing. It was awful. Do you have any idea who it might be?"

Lissan shook his head, looking pained. "Regrettably, I do. It appears we are both victims. You see, last night our facility was broken into. Whoever it was did a great deal of damage and even stole some things. I would imagine it is those same people who destroyed your vessel."

He turned to look Kirk directly in the eye as he said this, and Kirk felt a chill. Lissan knew, all right. He knew who had broken into the facility and what they had taken. The stakes in this dangerous game had just gotten higher.

"Why?" Alex asked, all earnestness. "We've done nothing to anyone."

"I told you that we were dealing with some very unsavory people. We did our best to keep the riffraff out, but sometimes one fails." This was most definitely aimed at Kirk. Out of the corner of his eye Kirk saw Julius glancing from Lissan to Kirk.

"I don't suppose you'd be able to help us with repairs?" Kirk said, looking innocent.

"As I have told you, our technology is nowhere near your level," Lissan lied smoothly. "We have our hands full simply repairing our own damage."

"I see," Kirk said, and smiled gently.

"Please let us know if we can help," Alex said.

Lissan inclined his head. "You are most kind. I am certain that at some point you will be very helpful indeed to us. Farewell."

He touched a button on his chest and dematerialized. Kirk gave his nephews an avuncular smile and put a hand on each of their shoulders. He felt Julius stiffen beneath his touch.

"Let's go inside," he said. "There's something I need to talk to you about."

"I have to—" Julius began, but Kirk squeezed his shoulder. Once they were safely inside Alex's quarters, away from prying eyes, Kirk whirled. He seized his youngest living relative by the front of his shirt and shoved him into a chair, hard.

"I want to know what the hell is going on, Julius," he demanded. "You're going to tell us everything."

Chapter Thirteen

Julius's pale face flushed bright red. "I don't know what you're talking about!"

"Uncle Jim—" Alex interrupted, but Kirk pressed on.

"Come on, Julius. Alex may only want to see the good in you, but I'm a little more detached. I know you're involved in something, but I want to know just how deep it goes."

Julius laughed shakily, turning to Alex for support. "I don't know what's got into him."

"Yes you do. You know where we were last night, just like Lissan knows where we were. Did you tip him off, Julius? Were you happy to sell your old uncle down the river? You're damn lucky that Lissan decided to attack just the *Mayflower* and not the colony."

Julius said nothing, only glared at Kirk with an intense hatred.

"Uncle Jim . . . where were you last night?" Alex, his voice soft, pained.

"Tell him, Julius. Tell him where I was and what I saw."

"How the hell should I know?"

"Because you're in this so deep that you're about to drown," Kirk shot back. "I can't believe that my own nephew—"

"Oh, yes," Julius sneered, "your own nephew. The nephew of the great Captain James T. Kirk. God forbid that any of us should do anything to sully your spotless reputation. Well, you taught me better than you know, Uncle Jim. I'm not the first person in this family to break a few rules in order to get things done!"

The accusation stung, because Kirk knew Julius was right. "Yes, I've bent the rules. Sometimes I've even broken them. But I never would have sacrificed my own family—"

"I didn't know why they wanted you so badly!" Julius shouted. "They just—it was part of the deal, and we had to have Sanctuary, so—"

Alexander had gone pale. "Juley," he said, his voice alarmingly steady and calm, "Juley, what have you done?"

And like a twig snapping beneath a fierce wind, Julius Kirk broke. His body sagged, and all the tension drained out of him. Moisture filled his eyes and he wiped at them with the back of his hand. When he spoke, his voice was low and ragged with pain.

"I did what I had to do to get you Sanctuary," he said. "They wanted technology. I gave them technology. Then they wanted information. I got it for them. Then they wanted weapons. I got those too. Finally, they wanted you, Uncle Jim. That was the deal-breaker. I had to get you here, and now they're preventing us from communicating with the outside and have destroyed the only way we have to get off this damned planet. Oh, God, I'm such a fool."

Alex stared, open-mouthed. "Julius," Kirk said gently, laying a hand on his shoulder.

Violently, Julius wrenched away from the hand that was

meant to comfort. "Don't touch me, you bastard!" He was sobbing now. He turned his wet face to Alex and reached out a hand to his brother. "Alex, I'm sorry, I'm so sorry, but I had to do it. We spent years looking for a place. You know that. I didn't mean for it to . . . first it was just a little technology, nothing classified, and then some weapons . . . a couple of phasers or so . . . then they were going to leave us alone. We got the colony, just like you always wanted. I got it for you, Alex. I did everything for you, just like you used to do everything for me. I never forgot that."

Kirk's heart ached in sympathy for Alex as he stared at his brother. "Juley, my God, did you really think I wanted you to become a—a *gunrunner* for me? Do you think I wanted to buy Sanctuary at the price of the lives of innocent people? Am I that much of an obsessed, single-minded monster to you that—"

"Alex!" The anguish in Julius's cry would have melted the hardest of hearts, but Alex, dealing with his own pain of betrayal, turned away from his brother.

Slowly, Julius looked to his uncle. "This is all your fault," he said between clenched teeth. "You let us rot. You came just long enough to make yourself feel that you'd done your duty and then left again, whereas we had to—God, Uncle Jim! Why didn't you even *try* to find out what was really going on?"

"I'm sorry," Kirk said. Julius blinked, startled at the ready apology. "I didn't know, and you're right, I didn't try to find out. I had my career, and I thought I was doing something important, something useful for the betterment of humanity. I tried to be a good uncle to you, but I see now I didn't try hard enough. Maybe one day you'll forgive me. But right now, if you want to help, you have to tell me everything you've done and everything you know."

Julius took a deep, shuddering breath and wiped a final time at his wet eyes. He stole a quick glance at his brother, who still stood facing the wall.

"Okay," he said. "Okay." He paused, gathering his thoughts. "It started a few years ago. I'd tried to talk various alien species into giving us a planet, but without the backing of the Federation they weren't interested. I began to realize that I had to have something more to offer them than what Alex had authorized, so I started keeping my ears open for any edge I could find."

Kirk thought that Julius's obvious need and desperation must have made him an easy target. He could see Julius in his mind's eye now, frantic to help his brother fulfill his dream, and burning with a bitterness that made him seize the first opportunity that came along.

"It never seemed exactly innocent, but at first, they didn't seem to want a lot."

"They who?" Kirk suspected, but he had to know.

"The Orion Syndicate," Julius said. Alex made a small sound in his throat and shook his head. He still hadn't turned around to face his brother. "They said they could help, and they did. They helped me get what the Falorians wanted."

"Last night," Kirk said, deciding the time for his own confession had arrived, "Scott, Chekov, and I went to check out this so-called facility. Have you been there, Julius?"

The young man shook his head. "I didn't even know about it until they told us." His voice was filled with self-disgust.

"It's some kind of laboratory and research facility. In the very heart, deep in the earth, is an enormous control center. They're monitoring hundreds of places scattered throughout the Federation, including Starfleet Headquarters itself."

Alex had turned around now and stared at Kirk with wide eyes and parted lips. Julius's flushed face had paled again, and he looked slightly ill.

"Their technology level is much higher than they're letting on," Kirk continued. "And part of the reason is that this research facility is crammed with Starfleet technology. They even fired a standard-issue phaser at us."

Julius rested his elbows on his knees and cradled his head. Mercilessly, Kirk plowed on.

"Chekov was injured when we downloaded some information from their computer systems. I took this." He held up the padd, which he had safely ensconced in a jacket pocket. "We were able to determine that the research is centered around nanotechnology. They're planning something big, gentlemen. Something that could potentially harm the Federation. But we don't have enough information yet."

Kirk caught and held Alexander's gaze. "Alex, you've got some of the best minds in the quadrant assembled here. We've got to put them to work. The Falorians obviously don't have any intentions of letting us leave."

He glanced at Julius. "Was that it, Julius? Were we supposed to be hostages?"

Julius finally looked up, and he seemed to have aged a decade. Kirk had always thought the saying that one's eyes were "haunted" was a cliché of the worst sort, but now he vividly understood what the phrase meant. Julius did look haunted, by ghosts of his obviously rough childhood and the fear of what he might inadvertently have done to his own people.

"It never occurred to me, Uncle Jim. When they wanted you so badly, I assumed it was just to wave it in the faces of the Huanni. They hate them so much. I would never have put Alex in harm's way. Never. I'd die before I do that."

Kirk latched on to what Julius had said. "The Huanni—they hate them? Even now? Why?"

"I don't know. Some ancient racial thing, I think. I—I

thought that's what they wanted the weapons for, but they never asked for anything big enough to start a war with." A muscle twitched near his right eye. "At least, not from me. Guess I wasn't a big enough fish. Uncle Jim, it's obvious to me that I was just some kind of stepping-stone. They've cut me out of the loop, and from here on in, I swear to you, I don't know what they're planning."

"I believe you, Julius. Come on. We've got a job to do."

T'SroH stared at the images of flickering fire. "The colonists remain unharmed? Particularly Kirk?"

"It appears so," Garthak replied. "But their ship is completely destroyed."

"The colonists' ship is destroyed," T'SroH mused aloud. He drummed his sharp-nailed fingers on the arm of his chair. "Their communications are being monitored and all outside messages are not being transmitted. When the shield of this facility was lowered, we detected signs of advanced technology and not a few weapons. These Falorians have built an enormous spacedock about which the colonists know nothing. They are in contact with the Orion Syndicate. Kirk obviously knows something. He yet lives, which means that the Falorians deem his life has value to them."

He made his decision. "Contact the chancellor." He had enough to warrant alerting her to the situation. She might have a chance to complete her *DIS jaj je* sooner than anyone had expected.

Spock sat alone in his quarters, absently plucking the sweet-sounding strings of his Vulcan lyre. The act soothed him, though he was well aware that what he was doing was much more akin to what humans called "jamming" than performing the demanding, rigid, thousand-year-old Vulcan songs traditionally played on the instrument.

He permitted himself to continue. He found that this action busied his fingers while simultaneously freeing his mind. His thoughts turned now to the last, nearly disastrous meeting between himself and the High Council.

Gorkon's dream, even now, was far from universally shared among the Klingons. Spock had found Gorkon to be a reasoned, far-sighted individual, particularly so for a Klingon. While his daughter shared her father's dream, she did not have his temperament. Loud shouting matches often erupted when she spoke, in which her council eagerly joined. The cacophony was offensive to both Spock's ears and sensibilities, both of which were delicate. Yet he knew that peace was possible, and he recognized, as far too few of his contemporaries did, how much the Klingons could contribute to the Federation if they ever decided to officially seek membership.

Spock was pleased, however, with how well things were working on the less political front. McCoy's medical staff interchange was weeding out those who were far too biased to be effective ambassadorial doctors and bringing to the forefront those who might have fewer commendations but more open minds. And he had to confess, he personally was enjoying the rehearsals of Earth music and Klingon opera. Uhura had obviously greatly impressed the explosive Karglak. Wars had been won by less.

His door chimed. Spock raised an eyebrow. This was his private time, and he had left orders not to be disturbed. Curious as to who would violate his order for privacy and why, he called, "Enter."

The door hissed open. Chancellor Azetbur quickly stepped inside. The door closed behind her.

"Chancellor," Spock said pleasantly. "What may I do for you?"

"I have a favor to ask," Azetbur said, "and perhaps an even greater one to offer."

"Indeed? Please continue." With a wave of his hand, he indicated a chair. She moved toward it, then apparently decided not to sit and began to pace. Spock sat patiently, letting her take her time. She knew he was supposedly out of contact at this hour; there must be a pressing need for her to have sought him out.

Finally she stopped, planted her feet squarely, and regarded him with an intense gaze. "I have reason to believe your friend James Kirk is in danger," she said.

"I am curious as to what makes you come to that conclusion."

"A few weeks ago, I took the oath of the *DIS jaj je.*"

"The Year and the Day," Spock translated. "Klingons have many rituals to appease the honor code. This one stipulates that the one who swears the oath will protect the other for an entire Klingon year and a day."

"You have indeed familiarized yourself with our customs," she said, and there was note of approval in her voice.

Spock inclined his head. "It seemed the logical thing to do. What does not seem logical to me, knowing the captain as I do, is that he would accept such a commitment."

"He did not," said Azetbur. "Not knowingly, at least. But I took the oath and I would not be forsworn, so I have sent one of my most trusted men to guard Kirk without his knowing."

"This way, honor would be satisfied, and Kirk's pride would not be affronted," Spock said. "Brilliant, Chancellor. You are a better diplomat than you think. I take it then that this trusted man of yours deems that the hour has come for you to assist Captain Kirk?"

"He does. Kirk and a few others are on a planet called Sanctuary. My ship has been monitoring the situation." Briefly, Azetbur told Spock of the blocked communications, the increased presence of the Orion Syndicate, and the destroyed vessel.

Spock digested this in silence, doing everything he could to brush aside the distracting, illogical thought: *Jim never told me he was leaving.* He endeavored not to show his surprise, and apparently was successful.

"I have no wish to cause an incident by sending my own ships to Sanctuary," Azetbur said. "The colonists are members of the Federation, if not Starfleet. It is my thought that perhaps it would best be handled by the Federation."

"Thank you for your information, Chancellor. I will contact Starfleet immediately."

"You will let me know what transpires?" She struggled not to appear too anxious, too eager to fulfill her honor debt.

"Of course."

"I thank you." She nodded once, then left. Spock sat for a moment, his fingers steepled, thinking hard. Then, before he did what he had promised Azetbur he would do, he tapped the computer. "Dr. McCoy, Commander Uhura . . . please report to my quarters immediately. I may require your assistance."

Chapter Fourteen

"I understand how you must be feeling, Captain, but there's really nothing I can do." Admiral Standing Crane looked terribly apologetic, and Spock knew that much of her concern stemmed from genuine caring. She had known Jim Kirk almost as long as Spock had. "All you've given me thus far are unverified rumors and suppositions. I can't possibly get authorization to get a starship out there on just that."

"I understand your predicament, Admiral."

Standing Crane didn't seem content to just let it lie there, and continued, "You of all people know about the dozens of little fires we're putting out right now. Every single ship is spoken for. If we're to pull them off their already established duties, we'll have to have a lot more proof than what you've given me."

"As I said, I do understand."

Standing Crane sighed. "Listen, Spock. You know I trust your judgment and I believe everything you're telling me is true. But that's not enough. What I can do is give you my personal authorization to go and check it out for yourself, if you can find

137

a way to get there. You give me proof that Jim and those colonists are in real danger, and I'll get you starships so fast it will make your head spin."

"Your hyperbole is exaggerated, but I appreciate the confidence you are displaying in my discernment, Admiral. I will do what I can. Spock out."

"So what do we do now?" asked McCoy. He and Uhura stood behind the console. They had agreed it would be wisest if Standing Crane hadn't known they were all involved. "We can't leave Jim and the others there!"

"Indeed we cannot," said Spock. "The Klingons prize honor above all things. I trust Azetbur to tell me the truth as she knows it. The *DIS jaj je* is an ancient and revered tradition; she would not feign it if she had not actually sworn it. But Admiral Standing Crane is correct. It would be unwise to authorize a Starfleet vessel to depart without further proof."

"Like the doctor said, what do we do now? We don't have a ship of our own anymore," Uhura said.

Spock raised an eyebrow and looked at each of them in turn.

"Of course," said Azetbur. "My only regret is that I cannot accompany you myself."

"To the best of my admittedly limited knowledge," said Spock, "there is nothing that says that the *DIS jaj je* must personally be carried out by the invoker, as long as she is at least indirectly responsible for its completion."

Azetbur smiled faintly. "Your knowledge is not as limited as you think, Captain. I have a duty to see it carried out, yes, but I have an equally important duty to my people to be here, on our homeworld, to see that peace is achieved."

"Agreed."

"The *Kol'Targh,* a *K't'inga*-class battle cruiser, is under your command, Captain," Azetbur said. "Her crew is to obey you as they would obey my own word. You should encounter no resistance. Do not hesitate to contact me if you require anything further. Azetbur out." Her image disappeared from the viewscreen.

"I'm getting mighty tired of spending time on Klingon ships," McCoy muttered.

"We do seem to be doing an awful lot of it," Uhura said. "I hope we're not gone too long. I can't stomach food that looks back at me while I eat it."

"Then you should be about setting in what you can eat, Commander," Spock said. "I fear that this trip might be longer and more dangerous than we might desire."

"What did they get away with?" The green face of the Orion on the screen revealed no emotion, but Lissan shrank inwardly from 858's image nonetheless. "And do not think to lie," 858 added. "We know more than you think."

Which was, mused Lissan, either a very good bluff or the truth. "You know they broke in and you know what they must have seen," Lissan said. "Whether they understand what they witnessed or not, I do not know."

"Then what do you *think* they learned?" 858 said in a voice of exaggerated patience, as if talking to a child.

"They downloaded some information, but they have no cryptographer. It is highly unlikely they will be able to break the code at all, let alone do so before we are ready to begin the operation."

"You are right about that," 858 said, "because the operation will begin in three days."

"Three—" Lissan almost choked. "That is simply impossible."

"What a shame. Because if we're not ready to go within three days, you know what will happen."

Lissan did. Bitterly, he recalled the dozens of times 858 had made that threat: *We will descend upon your facility and take everything, then blast it, and you, out of existence.*

They had the ability to do it. Not for the first time, Lissan wished he had never set eyes upon the human known as Julius Kirk. Young Kirk had brought in the Syndicate, and they had wooed Lissan like he was a shy little girl. He closed his eyes briefly.

"We will be ready," he said, and in a fit of spite terminated the conversation.

He leaned back in his chair, feeling a wave of nausea crash over him. Things were getting very bad very quickly.

There was no way they were going to be ready in three days. His mind went over the various options. There was, of course, the obvious: move in and take the colonists, especially the very high profile and highly vexing James Kirk, hostage. It would buy them time, granted, but it could also alert the Federation that something was amiss.

He could show 858 how very close they were to being ready at the end of the three-day timetable. The Syndicate had been patient for years; surely they would not risk all so close to achieving their goal.

Or at least, thinking they were going to achieve their goal.

The third option was the one that Lissan personally liked best. It involved destroying a Syndicate ship and having a dead Orion pilot at the helm.

He smiled contentedly at the little fantasy, and then the smile faded. This was not what his heritage had bred him for. He was descended from a long line of proud people, who disliked violence and used it only as a last resort. Murder was the

Orion's passion, not his. Lissan's was only to help his people get what they should have been given a long, long time ago.

He rose and went to an ancient wooden box, shoved with seeming carelessness into a corner of the room. It was scratched and dented, completely unassuming. To look at it, one would have no idea of the value of its contents. It had come here hidden, and to all but a few, it remained so.

Gently, reverently, Lissan lifted the lid. He reached a respectful hand to touch the gleaming stone's rough surface, caressing it, connecting with the past that it represented now and the future it would embody.

Somehow, his ancestors had known the true value of the yellow-hued Great Stone. As time went by and the Falorians began to interact with other worlds, they learned exactly how precious this stone was. It was valued beyond measure in other worlds, and could have bought the Falorians freedom long ago. But now, it was going to bring Lissan and his people more than that. It was going to bring them justice.

With great affection, Lissan stroked the largest, most perfectly formed dilithium crystal in the known universe.

After Scott had thoroughly swept the conference room for any bugs, Kirk ordered that everyone assemble there within an hour of his confrontation of Julius. They came, annoyed at having their research interrupted, and sat down none too graciously.

Alex addressed them first. "My friends," he began, "what my uncle and I have to tell you is devastating. There is no other word for it. I ask for your patience in hearing Captain Kirk out. What he has to say will sound unbelievable, but it's true. I also ask that everyone remain calm, as what he has to say is . . . unsettling, to say the least."

He stepped back and indicated that Kirk proceed. Kirk

quickly glanced at Julius, who was seated in the back of the room. Kirk had recommended that, for now, Julius's role in their present situation not be mentioned. It was not out of a desire to shield his nephew, but rather an overriding need to maintain calm. If these people knew what Julius had done, there could be a riot. Right now, he needed their cool heads, concentration, and unquestioned genius.

. He spoke briefly, telling of his, Scott's and Chekov's trip to the facility. There were murmurs of indignation at first from the crowd, then a stunned silence as he proceeded to inform them of what he had seen. Kirk played on their sympathy, asking Chekov to rise and show his still-unhealed hands.

"I am now asking . . . begging . . . for your help," he finished. "We obtained this information at a great personal cost. It's up to you to help us determine what the Falorian plot really is." He looked at the assembled crowd and smiled at them. "We've got something going for us that the Falorians don't have—some of the best minds in the quadrant are seated in this room today. I don't think I can overstate this: not only do our lives depend on you right now, but possibly the lives of untold millions, perhaps even billions, of innocent people. The Falorians could descend at any moment. We have to use what precious time we have to the best of our ability."

He paused to take a breath in order to continue speaking, but the crowd of scientists and doctors began to pummel him with so many questions he couldn't even distinguish between them.

"When will the Falorians come for us?" Leah Cohen cried, her dark eyes large and frightened.

"What kind of plan should we put into action?" Of course Kate Gallagher would ask that. She was always ready to act.

"Should I prepare the hospital wing for casualties?" Dr.

Sherman's voice was high and frightened, though he tried to look calm.

"Please!" Kirk cried. "We've got to do this in an orderly manner! You're disciplined scholars and researchers, start behaving like it!"

Alex shot him a look but Kirk ignored it. There was no time to coddle these people. He was painfully aware of every second that ticked past.

"We've already instructed the computer to translate the data we obtained," he continued. "But it's encrypted so deep that we haven't been able to break the code. Is anyone here trained in encryption?"

Not a single hand went up. Kirk felt his heart sinking. "Anyone have any experience at all?" Still no hands.

The silence was palpable. Then, shyly, Skalli raised her hand.

"Captain Kirk? Would you let me try?"

Kirk opened his mouth to form a polite refusal but the words seemed to stick in his throat. The Huanni were shockingly quick and intelligent, and retained everything they learned. And unlike a computer, Skalli had hunches and guesses. Who knew but that her ancient link to the Falorians might serve them well now?

"All right," Kirk said, and he could see by the way her ears stood up that he had surprised her. "Give it the old Academy try, Skalli. Impress me."

She did.

At her own request, she sequestered herself in a room with a computer, a stack of sandwiches, and a pot of Vulcan spice tea ("I love this stuff!" she had gushed when Kirk himself brought her a full pot). The rest of the colony puttered about, waiting, looking at the chronometers, ready to spring into intellectual action the minute Kirk gave them the signal. Kirk himself paced in front of the door. No one was foolish enough to try to gain admittance.

After fourteen hours and twenty-two minutes, the door hissed open and Skalli emerged. She was trembling and looked exhausted, but there was a smile on her weary face. She extended a padd to him.

"I did it," she said, her voice tired. "It was pretty hard too. They had triple-encryption sequences that relied on a familiarity with their regional dialects and slang terms, which is why it took me so long. I had to go back through the database and cross-reference with everything we knew about the Falorian language and customs. I got a break in that their Taskirakti region has fourteen different terms in common with Huan's Urhark province, or I'd *never* have been able to do it."

"That's . . . very fortunate indeed," Kirk said.

"You're telling me! Glad I don't have to do that every day!" She grinned, and her normal cheery self emerged for a moment despite her obvious exhaustion.

"Skalli. . . ." Kirk began. He gestured with the padd. "This is amazing. I'm in awe of you, and I'm very, very proud. Well done, Cadet."

Skalli blushed and bounced up and down.

They made multiple copies of the decrypted information and handed them out to several different groups. The way the scholars greedily snatched at the information and hastened off to study it made Kirk think of handing off the baton in a relay race. Gallagher, Veta, and Talbot were the first in line. For the moment, until these little clusters of scientists reported back with their findings, there was little he could do. His part of the race was over, for the moment.

He poured himself a cup of coffee and went outside, suddenly craving the feel of real sun and air on his face. It was a beautiful day. The sun shone brightly in an azure sky, and soft white clouds drifted slowly by. The warm breeze was filled with the scent of flowers, and stirred his hair gently. The only thing that marred the vista was the blackened hulk of what had once been a proud ship. Kirk's hazel eyes lingered on the wreckage and he sipped his coffee slowly, thoughtfully.

The colony was on what would be called red alert if it were a Starfleet venture. Those who were not involved in analyzing the Falorian data were constantly monitoring the skies as best they could. Kirk knew, though, that even that would be little enough defense if—no, when—Lissan and his buddies decided to swoop down and make their hostage situation a formality. Alex's insistence that this be a peaceful colony with no weapons, not even for defense, would prove to be their downfall. He, Chekov, and Scott had discussed this briefly earlier today. The only weapons in the entire colony were their three handheld phasers, which Kirk had ordered that they wear at all times from here on in.

"Uncle Jim?" The voice was soft, hesitant—uncharacteristic for its owner.

"What is it, Julius?" Kirk took another sip of coffee and kept his eyes on the horizon. He heard Julius move toward him and stand next to him.

"I, uh . . . I can't get Alex to talk to me."

"I'm not surprised."

Julius took a shaky breath. "I guess I'm not, either. Which is why I never wanted him to find out. Why'd you have to tell him, Uncle Jim? Why couldn't you just have confronted me in private?"

Now Kirk did turn, slowly, and regarded his nephew with a mixture of pity and contempt. "With all that's going on right now, with the Federation itself possibly at stake, that's all you can say?"

"Frankly, I don't give a damn about the Federation," Julius said, sounding more like his old, sullen, hostile self. "Let the Federation rot. What I care about is the only person I've cared about since the day I was born." His voice caught. "I know what I did was wrong, but I did it all for him. I can't—if he hates me for this, I don't know what—"

"This isn't cheating on an exam, Julius. You deliberately and knowingly gave technology and weapons to a race of people who are clearly planning to use these things against someone else."

"The Falorians aren't aggressive, they've never—"

"They've never had the kind of an edge that you gave them," Kirk continued. "You don't know what they'll do now that they've got it. You've admitted that they've already double-crossed you, and God knows what they've got in mind for the Federation. Alex has every right to feel angry, betrayed, and disillusioned." His voice softened. "But I doubt very much that he hates you."

Julius didn't look at him. His jaw tightened and his throat worked. "I wish there was some way I could undo this. I wish I'd never laid eyes on this place, or the Orions, or Lissan."

"We can't do anything but wait until the scientists come back with their report," Kirk told him.

Julius groaned. "I hate waiting. I want to be doing something."

"Now that," Kirk said, "is one thing we have in common."

Scott stifled the urge to wrap his hands around Kevin Talbot's throat and throttle him. It was this desire, he mused, that had kept him from going into research and development and placed him in the engineering room of a starship instead. He was used to accomplishing his miracles quickly and under the sort of pressure that made today's situation feel like a day at the beach.

Despite Scott's efforts to keep up to date on the latest technological breakthroughs, he knew that Talbot was about three steps ahead of him in that respect. But och, it was agonizing watching him put the pieces together, slow as a bear in midwinter.

Finally, he could take it no longer. He leaned over and touched a few panels.

"Hey, what are you—" Talbot stopped in mid-sentence. "Oh. Oh, my." He, Scott, and the rest of the engineering team leaned over the screen, barely breathing, as they watched the nanoprobes dance across the screen.

They were witnessing a test, and as Scott began to understand exactly what was transpiring, he felt the skin at the back of his neck prickle.

"Lord ha' mercy on us all," he said, quietly.

Chapter Fifteen

"**D**ilithium crystals," was the first thing Scott said to Kirk, Chekov, Alex, Julius and Skalli as they entered the secured "debriefing room."

"What about them?"

"Think for just a moment about how important they are," Scott said, obviously savoring his knowledge even though his face was pale.

"Oooh!" Skalli waved her hand as if she were still in class at the Academy. Kirk winced. For all her staggering intelligence, she was still such a youngster. Such a *Huanni* youngster. "I know!" She cleared her throat and began to recite, word for word, information that had been printed in the Academy textbook on the subject. "Dilithium is a crystalline substance used in every warp propulsion system on every known type of starship. Its unique composition regulates the matter/antimatter reactions that provide the necessary energy to warp space and therefore travel faster than light. Dilithium in its natural state is extremely rare and is found on only a few planets. In 2286, Captain Spock traveled back in time and discovered a means of recrystalizing dilithium by exposing it to gamma radiation, but this technology is still in its infancy. The purer the form of naturally occurring dilithium, the more valuable it is because it will require less processing in order to render it usable. It will also last much longer than lower-grade dilithium because—"

"Thank you, Skalli, that will suffice," Kirk said. Skalli settled back in her chair, her ears flapping gently with satisfaction.

"The short version is," Scott said, "without dilithium to power our ships, the entire quadrant would slow to a grinding halt. Under those circumstances, he who has dilithium would be lord of all he surveys."

"So you're saying that the Falorians have found a way to destroy the present deposits of dilithium?"

"Not destroy, exactly. We've had a look-see at the nanotechnology they've developed, and judging by our computer simulations, the Falorians have concocted a nasty virus that will render dilithium crystals inert by altering their molecular structure. They'll be just as pretty to look at, but they'll no longer be suitable for regulating matter/antimatter reactions."

"And from the sound of it," Chekov said tiredly, "those Falorians have planted this virus everywhere."

"How stable is the virus?"

"Unfortunately for us, very stable," Scott growled. "It's smaller than a dust mote and can adhere to skin, clothing, damn near anything. So you'll be taking it with you when you go to check on your dilithium crystals."

"Or when the miners go into the dilithium mines," Kirk said, the memory of his own recent visit to Rura Penthe still quite vivid.

"Like I said," Chekov said, "it's everywhere."

"At least it's not weapons," Alex said. Everyone stared at

him. "I mean, we were thinking that the Falorians were going to start a war or something. We thought millions of people might die."

"They may not die initially," Kirk said, "but when it's learned that every starship, every major mining colony, every hunk of dilithium is now not worth a damn, then there'll be violence, all right. A hell of a lot of it." He looked up at his old friend. "Scotty. Tell me there's something you can do about this."

"Right now," Scott said grimly, "there's not a bloody thing. But I'll keep running the computer simulations. There could be a flaw somewhere, something we haven't thought about yet."

"Julius, do the Falorians have a lot of dilithium stockpiled?" Kirk asked.

"Not that I know of, but as we've learned, I certainly don't know everything about them."

"But that doesn't make sense," Kirk said, thinking aloud now. "The Falorians have been a spacefaring race for some few centuries now. If they had access to dilithium, they would have used it before now. We'd have known that Falor or a Falorian-owned planet would yield dilithium, it's easy enough to scan for. The Falorians could have been wealthy for hundreds of years. Why wait?"

"Maybe because they're just greedy," Julius said. "I mean, that I know. They are greedy little—well, they might have been willing to postpone immediate gratification for longer-range riches."

"Do they have that kind of patience, Julius?" asked Kirk.

Julius thought. "They do have patience, but we're talking the kind of patience that is going to take generations to see fulfillment. I don't know that many species have that."

"And it's a devil of a gamble," Kirk said, continuing to follow this train of thought. "Too many things would have to occur in exactly the right fashion for this to work out to their advantage. Call it a gut feeling, but I think they've only recently come into this dilithium. Or they may not even have it yet. Maybe that's why the Orion Syndicate is involved—to help them get this one last cache of dilithium."

"One thing that I did notice," Scott said, "was that the grade of dilithium the Falorians utilized in their testing was amazingly pure. About ninety-nine-point-nine-eight percent pure. I've never seen that level of purity before in my life. It must be a pretty bauble indeed to look at. And the value of such a thing on the black market would be staggering. I'll bet that's it, Captain. They've teamed up with the Orions to get a hold of and control this cache of pure dilithium."

"So, they have weapons, they have the Syndicate, and they have a target that's rich in dilithium," said Chekov. "The question now is, where would they strike?"

"Oh, no," Skalli breathed. Kirk looked over at her. Her ears drooped and she was trembling. "This . . . this can't be. . . ."

"Skalli, what is it?"

She turned a frightened gaze on him. "I can't tell you. I'm not allowed to tell."

"On whose orders?"

Tears welled in her eyes. "We are never supposed to speak of it, never, never. I'm sorry, I can't. . . ."

Kirk reached over and grabbed her arms, shaking her gently. "Skalli, listen to me. You've remembered something that clearly might have an impact on what we've just learned. Don't you think you need to tell us what it is?"

"You don't understand!" she cried, gulping hard. "My people . . . I can't, I just can't!"

Kirk released her. "Maybe you didn't understand the full

impact of what Mr. Scott has just said. Your people have recently joined the Federation, presumably because they share its ideals. Those ideals will be shattered like broken glass once dilithium becomes useless. Anyone who has any amount of dilithium will have the sort of power that could make him a god in some peoples' eyes. Everything the Federation has worked for will disappear overnight. The galaxy will be a place where those with dilithium rule with an iron fist over everyone else. It'll be absolute chaos, tyranny of the very worst sort imaginable. Is that the kind of galaxy your people want, Skalli?"

"No," she whispered.

"Then tell us." He reached for her again, very gently this time. "Help us."

Her eyes met his and she swallowed hard. "All right," she whispered. She took a deep breath and began.

"You have been told that the Falorians wanted to leave Huan," she said. "That's not true. We—the Huanni—banished them. They had labored for us for centuries as slaves, growing our crops, mining the soil, building our cities. When we had sufficient technology that we no longer needed them, the last thing we wanted was to be reminded of them. So we put them on a ship and put them down on Falor."

Kirk stared at her. Her lip trembled. "It was a lovely planet," she said, defensively. "It had everything they needed to thrive. It wasn't cruel to leave them there!"

Kirk said nothing. The whole room had gone silent, everyone no doubt sensing, as did Kirk, that they were witnessing a powerful revelation.

"They did just fine on Falor," she continued. "None of us held grudges. We were happy in their success. We even extended the hand of friendship to them, but we were refused. They hate us, Captain. You can't imagine how much they hate us. That's why I wanted to become an ambassador, and why I was so excited about getting to meet a Falorian. I wanted to be a part of a new chapter in history, to help Falorians and Huanni be allies, even friends. We're the same people, we ought not to let something that happened hundreds of years ago stand between us!"

"But Skalli," Kirk said quietly, "no one ever told us that you had enslaved the Falorians."

"We were ashamed," she whispered, tears pouring unheeded down her face. "Wouldn't you be?"

"You know my planet's history. Until very recently, slavery, unfortunately, wasn't at all uncommon. We were able to see that it was wrong, admit it, and move on," Kirk said. "We didn't pretend it didn't happen. You can't heal what you don't acknowledge, Skalli."

"We were afraid the Federation wouldn't take us, that if they found out, they'd ask us to leave."

Kirk had nothing to say to this. Skalli was right, but for all the wrong reasons. It wasn't the fact that Huan had enslaved and then abandoned half its population centuries ago that was the problem. There were many Federation member planets that had a far nastier and bloodier history. What mattered was who those people were now. The problem was, the Huanni had lied about their past to the Federation. That was more than sufficient grounds for expulsion if such drastic action was desired.

"What does this have to do with the dilithium?" he said at last, hoping the change of subject would help.

"I'm not sure, but there used to be stories. They're now— what was the human term for them—folk stories, fairy tales. Tales about beautiful, powerful gems deep in the earth. You know the sort of stories, where the hero finds them and all kinds of good things happen. You wanted to know if the Falorians had access to dilithium. Maybe they don't have any on their planet, but maybe we do. Huan. Maybe those folk tales are real, and the Falorians, who used to dig in the earth, knew it. And it's a perfect excuse to attack *us*, to hurt *us,* as they feel we hurt them. They'd become very wealthy and exact revenge at the same time."

Kirk's thoughts churned. At first, he wondered—how could the Huanni not know that they had dilithium deposits? As he had just said a moment ago, it was easy enough to scan for, and the Huanni weren't foolish. They'd have scanned for it.

But what if something prevented the scan from reading correctly? Such things happened. Radiation, soil composition—there were more than a few things that could make a scan inaccurate. It wasn't beyond the realm of possibility.

It all made sense now. If the Falorians did indeed have ancient knowledge about hidden deposits of dilithium buried deep within Huan's soil—knowledge of which even the Huanni themselves were ignorant—then of course they would want to control the dilithium trade. Destroying the efficacy of dilithium across the quadrant would make what few unaffected deposits there were fabulously rare. Thanks to the weapons and technology provided by first Julius and then the Orion Syndicate, the Falorians would easily be able to take Huan while the Federation limped along, crippled to the core. Eventually, of course, this "gold rush" of dilithium would fade. They already had the technology to recrystalize dilithium, but as Skalli had stated, they were still working on it. It would happen, yes, but it would take time. Perhaps years.

And in the meantime, the Falorians and all who associated with them would become wealthy and powerful beyond their wildest dreams.

He was so lost in the dire scenario that he didn't hear Scott's comments. "Sorry, Scotty, what was that?"

"I said, I'll want to run some more computer scenarios."
Scott frowned darkly. "Something's bothering me, Captain. I
don't know what it is, but I'll not be happy until I've figured it
out."

"In the meantime, what do we do?" asked Alex. "We're
stranded, we've got no way to warn anybody—"

"It looks bad, yes," Chekov spoke up. "But Captain Kirk has
gotten us out of worse situations." He turned to give what he
doubtless thought was a reassuring smile of utter confidence to
his captain. But to Kirk, it was only a mocking grimace.

It didn't just look bad, it *was* bad. And he didn't have the
faintest idea what they were going to do about it.

Kirk lay awake in bed, thinking furiously. It had been
almost two full Sanctuary days since he'd broken into the facility. At any moment, the Falorians could come for them. Right
now, everyone was very carefully entertaining the fantasy that
nothing was really wrong. But after seeing the research facility
and learning about the truly diabolical plan the Falorians had
come up with, Kirk was not about to make the mistake of under-
estimating Lissan. Lissan knew very well that they were
hostages; he just hadn't made the situation formal yet.

Chekov and Harper were frantically doing everything they
could to try to get a message out, but Kirk knew in his heart that
it was just a way to keep spirits up. Scott was running his additional scenarios, for whatever good that might do. Conceivably,
he could come up with some way to reprogram the nanoprobe
virus, but even miracle worker Scotty needed time and
resources to perform his special engineering magic. And those
were two things that were in very short supply.

His door chimed. He glanced at the chronometer. It was
0214. He reached for a robe and donned it. "Enter," he called.

The door hissed open and Skalli stood there. She looked terrible. "Captain Kirk? I'm so sorry to bother you."

"It's no bother," he said, and it wasn't a lie. Anything was preferable to being alone with his dark thoughts right now. "What's the matter?"

"You know!" And she put her head in her hands and sobbed. "I'm so ashamed . . . of my people, of myself . . . Captain, I've been less than useless to you. I'm sure you regret the day we met."

"That's not true." Again, the comment was no lie, and it slightly surprised Kirk. He'd gotten more used to Skalli's highs and lows, and they didn't bother him nearly as much as they used to. "You have been invaluable. We'd still be stuck wondering what the Falorians were up to without your code-cracking skills."

She waved a hand in angry dismissal. "Any Huanni could have done that."

"I doubt that, but even so, no one else here could have." He sat down next to her in the chair. They were both facing straight forward, and Skalli determinedly avoided his gaze and wiped at her wet face. "And as for your ancestors' treatment of the Falorians, that's hardly your fault. I bet you've never enslaved a single Falorian in your entire life."

He said it lightly, but her eyes again filled with tears. "But we should have taken responsibility for what our ancestors did. You were right. We shouldn't have pretended it didn't happen, even if we did want to be friends. Especially if we wanted to be friends. Friends apologize wh-when they're wrong."

She couldn't know it, but her words stung. Kirk had been very wrong about Skalli. While she was still terribly emotional, she was intelligent, competent, and capable. She'd been the one to keep her wits about her and find shelter during what could have been a fatal sandstorm. She'd been the one to lock herself away with only sandwiches and Vulcan spice tea until she'd cracked a completely new code. And as for her outbursts, well, Kirk knew more than a few humans of her age who were that emotional.

"Well, then, let me be a friend," he said, gently. "I misjudged you, and that was both wrong and foolish of me. You're doing a marvelous job in a very stressful situation, and you have been a great asset to this colony."

Now she did look at him. She swallowed hard. "R-really? You're not just saying that?"

"Not at all. I mean every word." He punctuated the comment with gentle pokes on her shoulder until she smiled and ducked her head. Her long ears crept upward from where they had been plastered against her head. Then she sobered.

"If we do get out of this alive," she said, "then I will have been responsible for Huan being asked to leave the Federation, won't I?"

"No. The Huan Council of Elders, who made the decision to lie about their past to the Federation advisory board, will be responsible, if that even happens. What you will be responsible for is helping us figure out how to stop the Falorians from essentially taking over the quadrant."

Now her ears were fully erect, and she beamed at him. He squeezed her shoulder affectionately. "Feel better?" he asked.

"Oh, very much!" She hugged him vigorously. He supposed he should have expected it. He endured the embrace, and smiled at her as she rose and left.

He went back to bed, feeling oddly better, and was just drifting off to sleep when his communicator chirped. Groaning, he flipped it open. "Kirk here."

"It's Scott. You'd best get here right away."

The clipped, tight sound of Scott's voice put Kirk on red alert. He hurried into his clothes and fairly ran.

Alex, Julius, Talbot, and Gallagher turned to him when he entered, their faces pale and drawn. He imagined he could smell the fear.

"It's bad, Captain. It's very, very bad."

"Show me."

Scott swiveled the computer screen so Kirk could see it. "What am I looking at?" he asked.

"Remember when I told you that all the testing the Falorians did was with an incredibly pure chunk o' dilithium?" Kirk nodded. "That got me to thinking. You and I know that most of the dilithium crystals in operation out there are much less pure. When it comes right down to it, all dilithium crystals really are are hunks of stone. They therefore can be expected to have varying degrees of impurities in them—other minerals and so on. Processing can clean them up a bit, but most of the crystals we use have a certain amount of impurity to them."

Kirk nodded. "Go on."

"This is the test scenario utilizing a crystal of the purity that the Falorians used, over ninety-nine percent pure." Kirk watched as the animated nanoprobes descended. He saw the molecular structure of the crystal altered. The image shrank, pulling back until Kirk was looking at a crystal about the size of his hand inside a warp core. Nothing happened.

"When the virus alters the molecular structure of the crystal, it's as if you put a diamond in the matter-antimatter chamber," Scott said. "Nothing happens. But watch what happens with a crystal that's not quite so pure."

He tapped the keys and the simulation played again. A second time, Kirk watched as the virus went to work and the image pulled back.

The light from the explosion was so bright that he had to close his eyes. "What the—"

"The virus weakened the molecular structure so much that the crystal shattered," Scott explained. He looked ten years older. "The fusion of matter and antimatter without the intervention of the crystal resulted in a warp core breach."

Kirk stared at the screen, which had reset and was replaying the deadly scenario. "How impure was the crystal?"

"About eighty-seven percent. We ran a few more scenarios. If you want to avoid a warp core breach as a result of this virus attacking the crystal, you'd need at least a ninety-two percent purity."

Kirk didn't want to hear the answer, but he had to ask. "I know you don't know exactly, but give me your best estimate. How many starships out there have crystals that will fracture if they're infected with this virus?"

"About nine out of every ten, if we're lucky," Scott replied, grimly.

"So if this virus is released—"

"Nine out of ten starships, of every make and model, of every fleet in the quadrant, will be destroyed," Scott replied grimly.

Kirk's mind reeled. The Falorians weren't just going to invade Huan and dominate the dilithium trade.

They were going to kill billions of innocent people while doing it.

Chapter Sixteen

For a long, dreadful moment, no one spoke. What words could there be, to voice one's horror? Finally, Julius broke the silence.

"I can't believe it," he said, his voice soft.

"You're not calling my scenarios into question, now, are you, lad?" said Scotty softly, with a warning in his rich Scottish burr.

"No, no, I'm sure they're correct, but. . . ." Julius ran a hand through his sandy blond hair. "I'm just having a hard time believing that the Falorians are going to commit mass murder. I thought I knew—"

"We don't know anything about them!" cried Alex, speaking directly to his brother for the first time since Julius revealed his treachery. "*You* don't know anything about them! They're probably reveling in the knowledge of what they're about to do. You think you know someone, and then they go and do things. . . ." His voice trailed off.

"It's one thing to steal something, to hatch a plot to make

yourself rich," Kirk said. "It's quite another to cold-bloodedly set about the murder of billions of innocent people who have never done you harm."

Julius physically shrank from Kirk's words. Kirk knew what he was thinking, because he was thinking it too: *Julius began this. If he hadn't introduced them to the Syndicate, they would never have been able to put this plan into action.*

But attacking Julius wouldn't solve anything. Kirk took a deep breath and changed the subject slightly. "Is the virus presently active?" he asked Scott.

"No, and that's a blessing for sure, at least for the moment," Scott replied. "I can't be certain without more information, but I'm betting that each probe will be remotely activated at some point, probably simultaneously. Whenever the Falorians decide the time is right."

"That makes sense," Chekov said. "They don't want a single probe to be detected until they're ready to wreak havoc with all of them at once."

"Thank heaven for small favors," Kirk said dryly. The disaster had not yet struck, and might yet be averted. The question was, what could they do? How did they go about warning the Federation, and incidentally, saving their own hides?

"Scotty, I don't suppose you could adjust the *Drake* so that it could leave the atmosphere?"

"Not without a lot of parts we don't have, and probably not even then," Scott answered grumpily. "She's a remarkable little atmospheric vessel, but she's not designed for space flight."

"The only ones able to get information out are the Falorians," Kirk said. "You were able to piggyback onto their signal once, to raise their shield and shut down their security systems. Do you think we could get a signal to Starfleet the same way?"

Scott looked thoughtful. "It's possible, but I doubt I could do it without actually being inside the complex."

"Then it sounds like we'll have to get you inside."

"Why haven't they attacked yet?" Gallagher wanted to know as Kirk gathered them together for their final round of instructions. For someone who advocated peace so strenuously, Gallagher always seemed to be itching for a fight.

"On Earth, we have an old saying: don't look a gift horse in the mouth," Kirk answered. "The Falorians may feel that we didn't escape with anything significant, or assumed we'd never be able to decode the information even if it was important. Under normal conditions, they'd be right, but they hadn't counted on Skalli."

From where she sat in the front row, Skalli beamed.

"We've been very careful about where we've discussed our plans," Kirk said. "Or at least, I hope we've all been careful. The Falorians have seen to it that we can't communicate with the outside, and that we can't leave. Whatever it is we do know, we can't spill the beans to anyone. There's no need for them to attack us quite yet. Which is completely to our advantage."

He outlined his plan while they listened attentively.

The weather cooperated, and over the course of the next nine hours, small groups of threes and fours left the perimeter of the colony. They carried testing equipment and food, and moved without haste toward the areas they were studying. Mattkah and his crew went to their flower field and began running tests. Veta went to a cave he'd been mapping. Gallagher went to a forested area, where she'd been conducting tests on the wildlife. Others went to different areas. There were several shuttle runs that dropped off research teams.

In short, the colonists all appeared to simply be going about their business of research and study. Three times, Falorian ships flew over, and Kirk knew they were all being carefully watched. It was perhaps the hardest thing he had asked yet of the Sanctuarians—to pretend that everything was normal when it wasn't. A few of them were tense and harried-looking, and their "conversations" were designed to be overheard. But Kirk was counting on the Falorians doing a quick sweep, not moving in tightly to get facial expressions and overhear words. He only hoped that they wouldn't notice that instead of the usual groups of about three or four, every single colonist was now casually departing the base allegedly to do research.

Each team of "researchers" carried with them emergency ration packs and as many useful tools as possible. The one piece of equipment they didn't have were communicators. Mark Veta's careful, meticulous mapping of the caves over the last few weeks was now invaluable. Everyone had a map of the cave system thanks to his diligence, and that meant a place to literally go to ground and hide. Veta's work could help save lives.

Kate Gallagher had worked with Scotty on refining her "Masker." They had identified the frequency at which it worked to block Falorian tricorder readings. What had been created as a way to protect endangered species from poachers was now being turned to protect endangered colonists from kidnappers. The Masker worked in the lab, but they had no idea just how effective they would be in the field.

"Humanoids are the ultimate predators," Gallagher had said as she was the first to be injected with the subcutaneous chip. "How ironic that we're the hunted now." She had rubbed her sore arm and glared at Dr. Sherman. "You need a better bedside manner, Ted."

The entire plan was a huge gamble, but it was the only way to get people out of harm's way as quickly as possible.

"I want you to go too," Kirk said to Alex, as the last team was getting ready for departure.

"No way," Alex said. "I'm coming with you."

"I don't think that would be a good idea."

Alex flushed. "Why not? Because I'm incompetent? Because I'm not a leader like you? I saw him watching me," he said, jerking his head in Scott's direction. "I know he saw me crack, during the sandstorm. But I've learned so much, Uncle Jim. I could help you."

Kirk put his hands on his nephew's shoulder and looked him right in the eye. "I know you could help me. But they need your help more than I do. The fewer people who try to break into that complex, the greater the likelihood that we'll succeed."

Anguished, Alex cried, "You're taking *him* with you, and he's the one who got us into this mess!"

Julius paled. "You know why Julius is going," Kirk said before tempers could flare further. "He knows the Falorians better than any of us, and he's more familiar with their equipment. We'll need his knowledge when we get inside."

Alex stubbornly refused to reply. Kirk tried again. "Alex, you're not Starfleet. You're not trained in the sort of things you'll be required to do. What you are, is head of this colony. These people trusted you enough to uproot themselves and follow you halfway across the galaxy in pursuit of a dream. That dream is in danger. You owe it to them to be with them. You promised to protect them. Keep that promise."

Alex looked over at the group slipping on backpacks and checking their equipment. They looked back at him intently. Kirk hoped Alex could read their body language as he could: *Come with us, Alex. We need you. We're afraid.*

Kirk removed his phaser and extended it to Alex. The younger man recoiled as if Kirk had offered him a cobra. "I don't want it."

"You might need it," Kirk pressed. "Take it."

"No," Alex said firmly, straightening. For the first time in days, he seemed to have his old sense of confidence back. He was again the intense, persuasive dreamer. "Things have fallen apart, Uncle Jim. A lot of things have spiraled out of our control. But the one thing I can control is how I behave in this crisis. Sanctuary was founded on high principles, foremost among them being a desire not to harm anyone. You're right, the Falorians do need to be stopped. But the minute I take that phaser and fire it at one of them, I become just like them. Don't you see?"

"No," Kirk said, honestly. "I've never seen anything wrong with defending yourself, and the phasers can be set to stun." He smiled. "But this is your colony, Alex. Your people. You have to do what you think is best to protect them in a way that honors all your beliefs."

Alex looked back at the group, as if for confirmation. They were all smiling and nodding. Kirk admired their resolve to adhere to what they felt was right, even in the face of injury or death. Personally, he always felt more comfortable with a phaser in his hand, but one of the reasons he'd used a phaser as often as he had in his life was to protect just such ideals as Alex and the other colonists fervently believed in. He wouldn't force Alex to take a weapon if he didn't want to.

"Besides," Alex said, forcing a smile, "We're just quietly hiding. You five are going into the tiger's lair. You'll probably need all the phasers you've got."

Kirk agreed with him. Frankly, he wished they had more. But three would have to suffice.

Alex's group was the last one to depart. As he had done with each of the others, Kirk shook everyone's hand. Leah Cohen actually pulled him into a quick hug, while Mattkah did little to hide his continuing dislike. Kate Gallagher grasped Kirk's hand firmly, as was her wont, and he hesitated.

"Your Masker is going to save lives today," he told her. "Perhaps not the way you envisioned, but it won't be abused." That, he knew, had been her biggest worry: that somehow her talents would one day be put to destructive use.

She smiled, and her face softened. "Thanks," she said. She didn't let go of his hand for a moment. Then she said, "Hey, Jim, if we ever get out of here, I'd like to show you my thesis one day." Gallagher squeezed his hand and let it drop.

When this last group departed Sanctuary, Kirk nodded to Skalli, Julius, Scott, and Chekov.

"Let's go," he said, and they climbed into the *Drake*.

In the end, Lissan knew that he was glad that 858 had forced the timetable up. Like the Orion, Lissan too was growing impatient. The scientists had had their day. Now, it was the time of those who would act.

Lissan was a direct descendent of Takarik. On a planet where there had been no indigenous peoples, it was fairly easy to keep track of one's ancestry from the hour that the Huanni had abandoned them. While the Falorians did not believe in royalty per se, one's ancestral lineage was considered to be important. So when Lissan had decided to follow politics and eventually become one of the Kal-Toreshi, the governing body of Falor, no one was too surprised. For years, he had been aware of the plan, and despite the warnings of the scientists clamoring for more time to do more thorough testing, he was ready, even eager, to plunge forward.

The Falorians and the Huanni had long been silent enemies.

When forced to interact, both sides had been unfailingly polite, but the Falorians had never bothered to disguise their hatred. And why should they? They had been the wronged, the innocent, forced into harsh physical labor for centuries and then discarded as inconvenient and unwanted. And the arrogance of the Huanni! No mention of what they had done, no offers of regret or apology, nothing.

It had been a racial triumph for the Falorians to have kept the precious secret for as long as they had. It was hard to keep from gloating, but they had managed. Centuries ago, when the Huanni had almost offhandedly deposited their own brethren on Falor, Lissan's ancestor had stolen a single precious crystal— one of uncountable millions yet to be mined. Physical labor had uncovered them, and to this day, the Huanni remained cheerily ignorant of the riches upon which they were squatting. Deep mineral layers under the soil prevented scanners from discovering the unbelievably pure deposits. Technology would not reveal them; only the difficult digging of generations of slaves had done so.

It had been a terrible irony: the Huanni had the means to mine the dilithium, but no knowledge that it was even there, whereas the banished Falorians knew of its presence, but had no means to recover it.

Until now.

Now, the Falorians had weapons, allies, and technology. They could descend upon Huan and quickly, efficiently subdue it with a minimum loss of life. Life was precious to the Falorians, even Huan life; the fewer who died in the coming conflict, the better. Lissan was not after blood, he was after riches, power and acknowledgment, curse them, *acknowledgment* of the wrongs the Huanni had perpetrated upon his people.

Once he had that, the Falorians would move in and harvest

every kilo of the precious crystals, sharing, of course, with their good friends and comrades the Orion Syndicate.

Lissan couldn't resist a smile. This was the sweetest part of a delicious, infallible plan.

Oh, yes, the Orion Syndicate would help them subdue Huan and mine the dilithium. They would even take almost half of the staggeringly pure crystals. Then they would go away, the deal completed to everyone's satisfaction.

And then, Lissan would order the nanoprobe virus activated. The precious dilithium the Syndicate thought they had all but stolen from seemingly gullible Falorians would be worth nothing more than any other rock. Nearly every ship in the quadrant, including Syndicate ships, would be hanging dead in space.

No Syndicate, to come looking for revenge. No Huanni to attempt a retaliatory strike on Falor. And probably no Federation to send their mighty starships, to protect their newest member planet of Huan.

And even if they did, mused Lissan, he had—oh, what did the humans call it—the trump card.

One James T. Kirk.

He was glad of 858's suggestion, now. From what his infiltrators had told him of humans, they regarded the lives of their own as highly as Falorians did. They would do anything to protect their colonists, especially when among that number was a man as honored and revered as Kirk apparently was. Soon, it would be time to—

"Kal-Tor!"

Jarred by the intrusion, Lissan whirled angrily on the youngster who had dared enter in so unseemly a fashion. "What do—"

But Jasslor didn't even let him finish. "Kal-Tor, they've fled!"

"What—who has fled?"

"The colonists! Look!" Completely tossing aside any semblance of protocol, the underling rushed past his Kal-Tor and quickly activated Lissan's monitor. Jasslor called up several cameras, and each one showed the same dreadful image: an empty room. Empty mess hall, empty labs, empty research stations, empty fields.

Empty, empty, empty. . . .

"The pilot conducting the fourth daily flyover reported that he hadn't seen anyone. That aroused our suspicions, so we activated the cameras and . . . and saw what you see. What you don't see." Jasslor looked confused and frightened, as well he should be.

"Right out from under us," muttered Lissan. "They slipped out from right under us like. . . ."

Kirk. This reeked of him. A growl formed deep in the back of Lissan's throat and erupted as a roar of shame and fury. He curled his fingers into a fist and slammed it down on the console. Sparks flew.

"Find them!" he shrieked. *"Find them now!"*

Chapter Seventeen

There were not many Falorians on Sanctuary who could be spared for the search, but Lissan called up every last one of them. He had thought it would be simple, but again, the unexpected cleverness of these humans foiled his plans.

He went over the recordings that the flyover ships had made. Even in his anger and frustration, Lissan felt a certain amount of compassion for the pilots. No one was rushing to safety; the colonists were all walking, carrying their equipment and chatting, as they had done every single day since their arrival. There was nothing to alert any pilot that there was anything amiss.

The only indication as to what was really going on—a mass exodus—was that each of the flyovers saw the same thing: four to five groups of five to ten people going out to do research. Had they compared their recordings, they would have been on to the ruse much earlier, but there was no reason to take that time-consuming step. Alone, each recording looked innocent. Together, they spelled trouble.

Precious time was wasted in simply trying to track them

down. Lissan had thought it would be easy. The signatures of all the colonists, even the nonhuman ones, were greatly different than that of the Falorians. Eventually he realized that the colonists had hidden in the not inconsiderable cave systems that ran through the planet. Further, the trackers were reporting that they weren't picking up any humanoid lifesigns at all. Lissan closed his eyes against the wave of fury that rushed through him. This search would have to be done on foot, and they had utilized the *Drake*.

But he had no choice. He had to get those colonists back. Each life was another reason for Starfleet to refrain from attacking.

He gave the order, and the search began.

"They'll find us," Mattkah said morosely. "You heard what Kirk and them said about the level of their technology. These things under our skins aren't going to throw them off."

Gallagher bridled and opened her mouth to report.

"We don't know that," Alex said swiftly, trying to prevent a fight. "I prefer to hope."

"Of course you do," Mattkah said, in a voice that dripped contempt. "Live in hope, die in despair, isn't that the Earth quote? 'Come with me, we will build a place called Sanctuary, and we'll all live happily ever after.'" Mattkah made an appalling sound and hawked up a huge gobbet of spit and expelled it in Alex's direction.

Alex was on his feet at once. Adrenaline pumped through him and his face was red with a dangerous combination of embarrassment and anger. Mattkah laughed harshly.

"And I've got you all riled now, haven't I? You're just like your brother underneath that complacent surface. All you humans are hotheads."

Alex took a long, deep, slow breath, forcing his pumping

heart to slow. "Yes, you did get me riled. And that's my fault, for rising to the bait like that." He was still edgy, nervous, and began to pace.

"Alex," said Leah Cohen, staring at her fingers, "are they going to find us?"

"I don't know," he said honestly. "But I do know that we are doing all we can. We knew there would be dangers on this journey. We knew we'd be far away from anything safe." He laughed, sadly. "What we didn't know was that the danger would be coming from the one group of people we thought we could rely on for help."

"I hope Kirk gets that message out," Mattkah said, "and after they've done that, I hope one of the Falorians rips Julius's head off. Damned betrayer."

Alex paled. "What do you mean?"

Gallagher sighed. "It's a small colony, and it's hard to keep secrets, Alex. We know about Julius."

She didn't seem particularly angry, nor did any of the other colonists. Save for Mattkah, they all appeared to have forgiven Alex's wayward brother. If only Alex could, too.

Alex warred with conflicting emotions. He was furious at Julius, and terribly, terribly hurt. But no matter what his brother had done, Alex still loved him. He would always be little Juley to him, frightened and clingy and seeking reassurance. Even seeing Julius confess had not changed that.

Once, Alex had lived for Julius. If he now had to die for that, so be it.

"Perhaps Julius made it easier for the Falorians," Alex acknowledged. "But they would have found someone else if it hadn't been him."

"Yeah, but maybe then we wouldn't be stuck hiding in these caves and fearing for our lives," Mattkah said.

"Maybe. But don't blame Julius for that. Blame me. You're my responsibility."

"All right," Mattkah said with an evil cheeriness. "I will."

At that moment, they heard a sudden noise as of dozens of running feet. A powerful bright light blinded them.

Unable to see, Alex still rushed toward the sound. "My responsibility," he cried, and then fell backward as a blast caught him in the chest.

It had been a particularly long day for Laura Standing Crane. She had processed two more requests for Federation membership, joined together in a remote conference with Chancellor Azetbur to come up with a . . . well . . . *creative* reason as to why their chief negotiator was unable to continue with the conference, and heard about sixteen more annoying incidents with the Falorian delegates on no fewer than twelve Federation planets.

She stood for a long time in the shower, letting the hot water beat down on her hair and breathing in the steam. Too bad she couldn't spare an hour for a massage; she could certainly use it. Standing Crane got out of the shower and toweled herself dry, lighting a smudge bundle to help purify the environment of her small apartment in which she barely spent five hours a night, if she was lucky.

The pungent, calming scent soothed her somewhat, but not completely. She extinguished the smoldering bundle in an abalone shell and let the smoke curl around her. Her thoughts were on Jim. She combed out her long, thick, silver-shot black hair, not seeing her own reflection as she stood in front of the mirror.

Spock was not the sort of person to overreact, even given his love—yes, love, though he'd die before using the word—for his former captain and friend. And Azetbur was hardly one to put herself out for a human. Despite what she had said to Spock, Standing Crane completely believed everything he had told her. There was no doubt in her mind and heart that Jim, beloved friend for so many years, was in danger.

But she had responsibilities that extended beyond her own personal thoughts, fears and affections. She had told Spock the only thing she could—that she couldn't authorize the use of a starship based on rumors and innuendos. Azetbur had sent her a brief, mysteriously worded note that had convinced Standing Crane that the chancellor herself had arranged for a ship. Standing Crane was glad of it. She hoped to hear at any minute that Spock had found out that the whole thing was a mistake and there was no trouble at all. Failing that, that he'd gotten proof that the colony was in actual danger, because she would like nothing more than to get a starship out there, pronto.

Her computer made a soft beeping noise. Spock? Standing Crane wrapped a towel around herself and sat down in front of the message.

The image of the president of the Federation, not Spock's impassive visage, filled the screen. Great Spirit, more work, then. She smiled tiredly. "What's the trouble now, sir?"

Standing Crane had always thought that the president looked more than a bit like the famous author of several centuries ago, the humorist Mark Twain. But there was nothing light about his expression. He looked as strained as she had ever seen him, and worry shot through her.

"Get dressed and prepare for transport *now*," was all he said.

Four minutes later, a four-star admiral stood clad in a hastily donned uniform with dripping hair in the president's office in

Paris. She felt the wetness along her back spread with each second, but paid it little heed.

"We've got a message from one of the Falorian Kal-Toreshi. Calls himself Lissan. He particularly asked for you, Laura," the president said.

Standing Crane nodded once. She took her place alongside four other admirals and various high-ranking Federation civilians as the president signaled the screen to be activated.

The face of Kal-Tor Lissan smiled pleasantly. "Thank you for attending. It is my understanding that the hour is late on your planet. I apologize."

"Kal-Tor," said the president, "you didn't roust us all out of bed to exchange pleasantries. I gather your message is of some import. Do you have concerns about the way your delegates were treated? Because we were just about to offer you membership upon certain—"

Lissan interrupted him with a hearty laugh. "Oh, the timing is too amusing. We have no desire to join your little club, Mr. President."

Standing Crane felt heat rise in her face. What game was this arrogant creature playing?

The president stiffened beside her, but he kept his voice calm. "If you no longer desire membership in the Federation, rest assured, we will not pursue you. But if that's not the reason for your contacting us, then may I inquire as to what is?"

"I must admit, that from everything I have heard from our delegations, the planets of the Federation have shown us great hospitality. And for that, we thank you. Soon I will tell you how valuable those gestures were to us. But first, out of gratitude for the kindness you have shown us, I am going to give you a warning."

Lissan leaned forward until his face filled the screen. "We

are poised to take Huan. Our vessels and those of our . . . allies . . . are moving even as I speak to you. This is a quarrel that goes very deep, its dark roots extending into the shadows of the past. It has nothing to do with you, and you will be well advised to stay out of it."

"Huan is a Federation planet!" snapped the president. "We will come to the aid of one of our own!"

"A noble sentiment, but quite misplaced," Lissan continued maddeningly. "I will say this once, as clearly as I can, out of respect for the lives and safety of your people. Listen well. We have set up buoys around Huan. If any vessel, Federation or otherwise, violates that perimeter, then we will activate a virus that will leave every ship you possess hanging dead in space. No Federation vessel will be able to engage warp drive. Think about that, Mr. President. Think about all the ships on deep-space missions far away from any hospitable planet or starbase. It would take them years to get anywhere under impulse power. Some ships would do just fine, but others wouldn't. Even if they did get home, the crews of many ships would be old and gray before they ever again saw their loved ones. This is not something I would see happen to innocent people. Do *you* want that to happen, Mr. President? For the sake of a few million worthless Huanni?"

A young man named Parkan had been listening intently to the conversation, and out of the corner of her eye, Standing Crane had been watching him just as intently. Now she saw the color drain from his face, his breath catch, and his eyes widen slightly. Standing Crane closed her dark eyes briefly. She thought she knew what Parkan's reaction meant, and she prayed she was wrong.

Instead of firing more questions about the threat, the president chose a different tactic. "It is clear to me that you have a great enmity toward the Huanni."

"You choose pallid words, Mr. President."

"The Federation has long been known for its ability to fold in different cultures and create harmony," said the president. He looked over at Standing Crane.

"Even now, we are making peace with a people who have historically been our worst enemies," Standing Crane said, picking up her cue. "It has been a hard road, but when they were in need, we came to their aid. We are helping preserve the Klingons as the proud, powerful people they are. We are not trying to make them just like us. Perhaps we could help you initiate negotiations that could lead to peace between both your peoples. War may not be the only option."

Lissan looked at her searchingly. "Tell me, Admiral, have you ever been owned?"

"What?"

"Have you ever been owned," he repeated. "Has anyone ever owned your ancestor, made him work hard labor, and then tossed him away like so much trash when his usefulness was done? Has anyone—"

"I have such a history," spoke up Admiral Thomas Mason. He stood tall, proud, and handsome, his dark brown skin slightly shiny with beads of perspiration induced by the incredible tension in the room.

"A few hundred years ago, I would have been her property," he said, nodding in the direction of Admiral Anastacia Cannon. The younger woman met Mason's gaze evenly. They stood side by side, her short blond hair and pink complexion a contrast with his dark brown skin, hair and eyes. "And Standing Crane— her people were once herded like cattle onto reserved chunks of land, their histories diminished, their language all but destroyed. So you aren't telling us anything that we haven't experienced and overcome right here on this single planet."

He reached and grasped Cannon's hand, and their fingers entwined, the dark and light merging into a single strong unit, yet retaining their individual differences. Together they raised their joined hands.

"This is what we are all about now," said Cannon. She looked deceptively delicate, but Standing Crane knew there was fire in her heart. "Unity. Working together. The past is the past. We learn from it, and then we move on. The Falorians and the Huanni can do the same."

Lissan seemed stunned. Clearly, whatever research he had done on human history hadn't included checking for such disharmony. He'd have found it easily enough; nothing was covered up. But neither was it anything that anyone thought of on a day-to-day basis anymore. There were too many other important things going on for long-gone racial conflicts to be an issue.

"I . . . I would I had learned of this sooner," Lissan said. Then he shook himself slightly and his old demeanor returned. "But now it is too late. You have my warning. Perhaps you need another."

He turned and gestured to someone off screen. Another Falorian moved into view, roughly pushing a bound human who was obviously a prisoner in front of him. The Falorian spun the human around to face the screen.

"Alex," breathed Standing Crane.

Alexander Kirk stared at her, his face puffy and bruised and bleeding. His blue eyes were large and despairing.

"Tell them," Lissan said.

"I . . . won't. . . ." Alex growled between clenched teeth.

Lissan sighed and nodded to the guard, who curled his fingers into a fist and landed a solid punch to Alex's abdomen. As one, every person in the president's office instinctively moved forward.

"Tell them," Lissan repeated.

"The *Mayflower II* has been destroyed," whispered Alex, struggling for breath. "They've captured some of us, of the colonists. They say they have Uncle Jim, too, but—"

The guard moved forward menacingly, but Lissan raised a hand. "I do not enjoy cruelty," he said, "and I would much rather not have to hurt my hostages further. If you stay away from Huan space, your ships and your people will be safe. This is my warning to you. Heed it, or face the consequences."

He abruptly terminated the conversation. When the screen went dark, everyone in the room sagged a little.

The president turned to Parkan. "Tell me he's bluffing," he almost pleaded.

Parkan turned a stricken face to the president. "He's not. At least, not about most of it. They are indeed moving toward Huan, and the desire for revenge is very powerful in him. There's a tremendous sense of righteousness about him. He's telling the truth about what this virus can do as he knows it, I'm certain of that. He also isn't comfortable with hurting the hostages. But he's hiding something. He hasn't told us everything yet. What is your human phrase . . . something about waiting for a dropping shoe? That's what I'm sensing here."

There was no doubting Parkan's conclusions. His people had a proven ability to accurately sense such things as emotions and falsehoods. The only hope lay in the slim chance that Lissan himself had been misled.

"There's so much about this I don't understand," said the president, shaking his white head. "How is it they were able to plant this thing so well? And who was that young man, and who is this Uncle Jim he spoke of? You seemed to recognize him, Admiral."

Standing Crane swallowed hard. She straightened and

turned to face the president. "I claim responsibility, sir," she said in a formal voice. "I am the one who gave permission for the Falorian delegations to have the access they did."

"Standing Crane," the president said softly. "You must have had a reason."

"They seemed so harmless, sir," Standing Crane continued, knowing how pathetic the words sounded. "We did our research. We never heard anything from either the Falorians or the Huanni about this history of slavery. Neither species seems inclined to violence, and it appeared as though the delegates were merely curious. Of course, I never let them into classified areas," she hastened to add. "They were only permitted in areas that are generally available to all promising candidates for membership. The trouble is, they were insistent about visiting *every* permitted area, not just some."

"Tell me," said the president.

In an emotionless voice, but feeling misery and fear roiling inside her, Standing Crane recited the lengthy list. It included starbases, Starfleet and Federation headquarters, large ships, small ships, planet capitals, and research centers. With every word, it seemed to Standing Crane that the mood in the room dropped lower and lower.

"No one suspected," she said. "I discussed this with the Vulcans, the Makorish, the Andorians—all of us were *amused* by their curiosity."

The president merely nodded. "And the young hostage?"

"His name is Alexander Kirk," Standing Crane answered. "He is the nephew of James T. Kirk, the former captain of the *Enterprise* who—"

"—saved my life a few months ago," the president finished. "This is a damn bad business we've got here. Parkan, Alexander seemed to indicate that they might not have Kirk. Your opinion?"

"The mention of the name roused a great deal of anger in Lissan, but I couldn't tell whether or not they had captured him."

"We must proceed as if they have," the president said grimly.

"One thing in our favor," Standing Crane said. "If they do have Jim Kirk, he's giving them hell. And if they don't, he's doing everything he can at this very moment to contact us and free those hostages. I'd bet my life on it."

"Let us hope you're right. Now, can anyone—"

"Sir," Standing Crane said, "there's more. A few days ago, Captain Spock came to me with rumors that the colonists might be in trouble. I said I couldn't authorize a starship on nothing more than rumors, but I did give him permission to investigate on his own if he could find a ship to take him to Sanctuary."

"Sanctuary? Is that the name of this colony?" When Standing Crane nodded, the president blew angrily through his dangling mustache. "We didn't need that irony on top of everything else. Anything more you wish to tell me, Admiral?"

Standing Crane licked her lips. "No, sir. I think that's about all."

"It's enough." At her barely perceptible wince, the president added, "You couldn't have been expected to guess that all this would unfold the way it has, Admiral. No one could." He turned to face the rest of the group. "We've got work to do. Send out orders to every civilian and Starfleet vessel to head for the nearest habitable planet or starbase at top speed, and wait there for further instructions. I won't have our people stranded in the cold of space. We'll have to think of some other way to help Huan. About this virus . . . I want everyone who. . . ."

He continued speaking, but Standing Crane didn't hear him.

I should have trusted Spock, she thought, with an anguish that she would never let show on her dark face. *He wouldn't have come to me if he didn't think there was a good reason. Damn it, Jim, I just hope I was right about you being able to handle yourself. If I never see you again, how will I sleep, knowing I might have saved you?*

Chapter Eighteen

Scott knew exactly how high the *Drake* needed to fly in order to evade Falorian scanners. Visual contact was still a possibility, of course, but they had to hope that if they were indeed spotted, the Falorians would merely think them colonists out on another research mission.

"I wish there were some way to find out if they were on to us yet," Kirk said, thinking aloud. "I'd feel better if I knew the colonists were still safe."

Scott craned his neck and looked back at his captain. "Och, we can do that. I'd have done it before but there's a slight risk it'd be detected."

Kirk leaned forward. "I'll take that risk, Scotty. How did you manage that?"

"Well, it was a wee bit tricky getting into their communication system once," Scott said. "I didn't want to have to do it all over again if we needed to, so I installed a back door while I was waiting for you and Mr. Chekov. Kept me from getting bored." There was a slight twinkle in his eye as he spoke.

"Back door?" Chekov said, confused.

"Oh, aye. It's an old computer term. It means I've got a way back in. Half a moment. . . ." Scott fiddled with the panel as only he could, and then the small screen on the console sprang to life and Lissan's arrogant voice filled the shuttle.

"—to take Huan," he was saying.

"No," whispered Skalli fiercely, and crammed her knuckles into her mouth in order to keep from sobbing aloud.

"Our vessels and that of our . . . allies . . . are moving even as I speak to you," Lissan continued. The five watched intently. "This is a quarrel that goes very deep, its dark roots extending into the shadows of the past. It has nothing to do with you, and you will be well advised to stay out of it."

"Scotty," Kirk said urgently, "can we get a message out ourselves?"

"Huan is a Federation planet!" It was the president of the Federation. Kirk knew the voice, although he could not see the President's visage. "We will come to the aid of one of our own!"

"We'd definitely be detected," Scott warned.

"A noble sentiment, but quite misplaced," Lissan smirked. "I will say this once, as clearly as I can, out of respect for the lives and safety of your people. Listen well. We have set up buoys around Huan. If any vessel, Federation or otherwise, violates that perimeter, then we will activate a virus that will leave every ship you possess hanging dead in space. No Federation vessel will be able to engage warp drive. Think about that, Mr. President. Think about all the ships on deep-space missions far away from any hospitable planet or starbase. It would take them years to get anywhere under impulse power. Some ships would do just fine, but others wouldn't. Even if they did get home, the crews of many ships would be old and gray before they ever again saw their loved ones. This is not something I would see happen to innocent people. Do *you* want that to happen, Mr. President? For the sake of a few million worthless Huanni?"

"I don't understand," Chekov said. "They would be more likely to comply if they knew they would die otherwise. What's this nonsense about being old and gray?"

Kirk waved him to silence. "Do it, Mr. Scott. If we can get a warning out it'll be worth it."

The president was speaking again. "—that you have a great enmity toward the Huanni," he was saying.

Lissan's eyes flashed. "You choose pallid words, Mr. President."

"The Federation has long been known for its ability to fold in different cultures and create harmony."

"Scotty. . . ." Kirk said, his voice tense.

"I'm trying, Captain, but it's not as easy as you might think!" Scott retorted, his fingers flying over the console.

"Even now, we are making peace with a people who have historically been our worst enemies," came a new voice. Kirk instantly recognized it as Standing Crane. "It has been a hard road, but when they were in need, we came to their aid. We are helping preserve the Klingons as the proud, powerful people they are. We are not trying to make them just like us. Perhaps we could help you initiate negotiations that could lead to peace between both your peoples. War may not be the only option."

"Pray God he listens to you, Admiral," Scott muttered.

Lissan's reply shouldn't have been unexpected, but it was, and Kirk felt a stab of pain at the Falorian's words. "Tell me, Admiral, have you ever been owned?"

"What?"

"Have you ever been owned," he repeated. "Has anyone

ever owned your ancestor, made him work hard labor, and then tossed him away like so much trash when his usefulness was done? Has anyone—"

"I have such a history," came yet another voice.

"Who's that?" Chekov asked.

"Admiral Thomas Mason," Kirk said. They listened intently as Mason described the institution of slavery that had once haunted humanity, and spoke eloquently of the shameful acts perpetrated on indigenous populations all over the planet.

"I've almost got it," muttered Scott. "A few more minutes. . . ."

"Listen to him," said Skalli, as if Lissan could hear her. "Please, listen."

"The past is the past," Mason was saying now. "We learn from it, and then we move on. The Falorians and the Huanni can do the same."

Lissan stared, his mouth slightly opened. For a moment, he was silent.

"That shook him," Kirk said. "He doesn't realize that the Falorians aren't the only species to have endured slavery."

Beside him, Skalli sniffled loudly and wiped her nose on her sleeve.

"I . . . I would I had learned of this sooner," Lissan said. Then he shook himself slightly and his old demeanor returned. "But now it is too late. You have my warning. Perhaps you need another."

Kirk suddenly felt a knot of apprehension in his gut. When Lissan turned and motioned to someone off screen, Kirk knew what was going to happen next.

"Alex! God, no. . . ." Julius turned his face away from the screen and wiped at his eyes.

Kirk kept watching with narrowed eyes, taking it in swiftly.

Alex had been roughed up some, but he didn't appear to be seriously injured. He had a few shallow, superficial cuts and some bruising, but that was it. Kirk had a sudden, swift realization: *This is for show.*

"Tell them," ordered Lissan.

"I . . . won't. . . ."

Kirk winced as the guard punched Alex. Maybe that was for show, too, but it clearly hurt.

"Scotty. . . ."

"I'm going as fast as I can, Captain!"

"Tell them," Lissan repeated.

"The *Mayflower II* has been destroyed," whispered Alex, gasping for air. "They've captured some of us, of the colonists. They say they have Uncle Jim, too, but—"

Lissan intervened before the guard could land a second punch. "I do not enjoy cruelty," he said, "and I would much rather not have to hurt my hostages further. If you stay away from Huan space, your ships and your people will be safe. This is my warning to you. Heed it, or face the consequences."

His image disappeared. Scott uttered a blistering oath.

For a long moment, there was silence in the shuttle.

"Another second or two and I'd have had it," Scott said bitterly. "We could have gotten a signal out on their signal, but now they've terminated communication, the only way we'll be able to talk to the Federation is to get into the Falorian stronghold and sit ourselves right down at the console."

"It's all right, Scotty. We'll just continue with our first plan. Keep monitoring their communications," Kirk said calmly. "Let me know if you learn anything significant."

"Aye, sir," Scott said, subdued.

Suddenly Julius uttered an incoherent cry and slammed his fist against the ship's console.

"Hey, that's delicate equipment!" Scott snapped angrily.

"I don't give a damn," snarled Julius. "I want Lissan! That son of a bitch hurt my brother, and damn it all, it's my fault. Alex," he said, and fell silent.

Thoughts were racing through Kirk's brain at a kilometer a second. "Something's just not adding up," he said. "Lissan warned the Federation not to intervene or else they would activate the virus and strand millions."

"But that's a lie!" Skalli's voice was thick with unshed tears. "They know that once the virus is activated that all the warp cores involved will breach!"

"I'm not so sure they *do* know," Kirk continued. "They warned the Federation about the virus instead of just going ahead and activating it, so we could bring our people to safety. Did you see how shaken Lissan was to learn that other species had dealt with being enslaved? And the cuts on Alex's face—he wasn't tortured. All the injury was to his face—where it would be visible, where we'd be sure to see it. Lissan didn't even let the guard punch him again. Does all this sound like the behavior of a butcher who's knowingly planning on cold-bloodedly murdering billions of innocent people?

There was silence in the shuttle. No one spoke.

"Lissan doesn't know," Kirk said firmly. "I'm sure of it."

"Doesn't know what?" snapped Julius.

"He doesn't know what the virus can do."

"Oh, come on, Uncle Jim, his people *created* the damn thing!"

Kirk ignored his nephew's outburst. "Scotty, what was it you were saying—that the dilithium the Falorians used for testing was incredibly pure?"

"Aye," said Scott. "Over ninety-nine percent pure. I've never seen the like."

"And you saw no indication that they ever used a crystal that was less pure."

"None at all. It looked as if all the tests were run with samples from the same crystal. They all had the exact same level of purity." Scott glanced back at him, his brown eyes curious. He was wondering what Kirk was getting at.

"Is it possible, in theory," Kirk continued, reaching for the thread, "that the Falorians really believe that all this nanoprobe virus is going to do is render the crystals inert? That they have no idea that it could cause a warp core breach?"

Scott's eyes brightened. "All the tests they ran on that one crystal would verify their theory that the virus would make the dilithium useless, but not dangerous."

"They'd be taking advantage of the whole quadrant, but they don't think they'd be killing anyone," Chekov said.

"Oh, they'll be killing people, all right," Skalli said with a harshness that surprised Kirk. "They're getting ready to kill *my* people so they can take Huan's dilithium."

"Skalli's right," Julius said. "And part of that blood is going to be on my hands."

"I'm not saying that the Falorians have suddenly become the good guys," replied Kirk. "And I'm certainly not trying to pretend that an attack on Huan is trivial. What I'm saying is it sounds to me as if they don't know that their virus is lethal. We have to tell them that."

"Somehow I don't think Lissan is going to sit down over a nice cup of tea and let you talk to him about his virus," said Julius.

"I'm certain he won't," Kirk said. "We've got a job to do, but informing Lissan about the virus is part of that. Scotty, take us in."

* * *

Standing Crane didn't think she'd ever seen so many famous dignitaries gathered together in one place. Many of these people she'd never even met, and wished that they were mingling at a banquet over drinks and not around a table discussing the possibility of the entire galaxy being plunged back into the dark ages.

The president called the meeting to order. The assembled group watched as the conversation between the president and Lissan was replayed. There was utter silence in the room. When the lights went back up, the president continued.

"We have had the best scientists in the Federation working on this," he said. "Samples have been obtained from every known area in which the delegates from Falor were present. Unfortunately, it appears that Kal-Tor Lissan was telling the truth. We have discovered a nanoprobe virus at every site."

Soft groans and winces went around the table. The president pressed on.

"Even worse, the technology involved is quite beyond our present understanding. We're not sure if we could deactivate even the samples we have, which are but a fraction of what's out there. As I understand it, this is a true virus, even though it's comprised of tiny machines. If you shook hands with a Falorian delegate, if he was on your ship, at your space station, visiting your capital or being entertained in your banquet halls, he left the virus. Then anyone who walked through that banquet hall, or brushed up against you, or stopped at that space station—they, too, would have the virus. It's on your clothes, your hands, in your body."

"Have any of our esteemed scientists learned what this virus will actually do?" The question was asked by Sarek, his face as calm as ever.

"Lissan said it would render all our ships dead in space,

unable to engage in warp drive, and Parkan has told me that on this, he did not lie," the president answered. "Of course we'll have to confirm that independently. There's a chance Lissan might have been lied to, but I personally doubt it. Our next concern is to determine if other machinery will be affected, and how. Preliminary investigation into the nature of the nanoprobe reveals that it is harmless to organic beings, which is a small blessing."

"I have been doing my best to be constructive," the Huanni ambassador, Ullak, said. His expressive face worked as he clearly tried to get a handle on his emotions. "But I cannot sit quietly by while we discuss the virus without voicing the needs and fears of my people! Huan is a Federation member in good standing. What is the Federation going to do to prevent this undeserved attack?"

"Ambassador," the president said quietly, "your planet is currently not in good standing, as you must know. You have admitted that you lied to us regarding Falor. Had we known of your . . . past relationship . . . with the Falorians, steps might have been taken to bring you both to the negotiating table at that time. This whole tragedy might have been averted."

"Whatever we did in the past," Ullak cried, "surely you cannot sit here and tell me that the living Huanni deserve to die for it!"

"Of course not," replied the president. "But neither can we move to stop the Falorians until we know exactly what their virus will do to us. It's not just Huanni lives at stake here, Ambassador. It's the lives of people on ships throughout the quadrant."

He looked suddenly weary, and nodded to Standing Crane that she take over at this point. She cleared her throat.

"Lissan's threat was very specific: If we violated the space that they had designated with the buoys, they would activate the virus. What we can therefore do is bring at least a few ships right up to that point and have them wait there for further instructions. Every other ship is to be recalled to the nearest starbase or planet, just in case this thing does go off. At the present time, the closest vessel capable of defending the Huanni is the *Excelsior.* I've notified Captain Sulu about the situation and he's en route at this very moment."

"Good," the president approved. "In the meantime, we wait . . . and hope the scientists will learn something useful."

From the expressions on the faces of those seated around the table, this was an unsatisfactory resolution. She shared their sentiments, but at the moment, there was nothing else to do.

She envied Spock and Sulu at the moment. At least they were getting to do something.

Chapter Nineteen

McCoy was frustrated at being unable to do anything except sit back and twiddle his thumbs. Why in God's name had Kirk's nephews ("Alexander" and "Julius" indeed, factor in "Tiberius" and it was clear that the whole Kirk clan had an unhealthy obsession with ancient empires) gone gallivanting halfway across the galaxy for this Sanctuary? Was it that hard to find a nice little planet closer to home?

They had only been able to acquire a handful of rations, and those were now gone. Spock had said coolly that they would be able to survive on what the Klingon crew ate; the digestive systems of human and Klingon were sufficiently similar. Those were his exact words—"sufficiently similar." However, the writhing mass of worms on the plate in front of him was not "sufficiently similar" to spaghetti or indeed *anything* McCoy had encountered and recognized as an edible foodstuff for him to want to pop it into his mouth.

"I'd sell my soul for a nice, thick steak along about now," he muttered.

"Heck, I'd swap mine for a ham sandwich," Uhura said. She poked and prodded at the squiggly mess, an expression of distaste on her lovely face. Finally she put her fork down and delicately pushed the plate away. "You know, a water fast is great for slimming down," she said, "and I've got a performance in a week or two. Provided we get home by then."

McCoy was in high dudgeon now, though, and simply pushing the plate away was not a "sufficiently similar" option to complaining loudly.

"And why is everything always red or black with these characters?" He gestured theatrically. "Red lighting, black walls, blood wine, black armor. Damn boring color scheme if you ask me."

"I do not recall anyone aboard this ship asking your opinion on their decorating choices," Spock interjected mildly as he joined them in the mess hall.

"So what are you going to have?" McCoy asked, scooting on the bench to make room for the Vulcan captain. "Some red and black, spiky, dangerous-looking Klingon version of rutabagas?"

"I am joining Commander Uhura in her fast," Spock said. "The Klingons do not eat vegetables."

"Well," McCoy said, "Aren't we going to be the lean, mean fighting machine when we reach Sanctuary."

"Take heart, Doctor," Spock said. "We should be there shortly."

"You must eat!" bellowed a jovial voice. McCoy tried and failed not to roll his eyes as Karglak entered, carrying a tray loaded to the gills with slimy, purple-black, moving items that the Klingons called "food." He caught Uhura's gaze and stifled a laugh. Poor thing. She sure hadn't asked for this.

When Uhura had informed Karglak and Lamork that she

had been called up on an emergency mission and the concert might have to be postponed, Karglak had been horrified. He had insisted that he be allowed to accompany her. Apparently, opera singers had a lot of clout, for sure enough he'd been in the transporter room ready to depart with the rest of them. The Klingons on the ship treated him like a sort of deity. When McCoy had pressed for something resembling a logical reason as to why, Captain Q'allock had replied, "Why, his honor is double. He is a warrior and a performer. Therefore, he can perform glorious deeds *and* sing about them."

It was an answer, McCoy supposed, but it didn't clear up a damn thing for him. Uhura had been doing her best to duck him, but the fellow clung to her like a burr. Karglak hadn't declared his feelings openly, but it was obvious to anyone that he had a bit of a crush on the lovely human woman who, like Karglak, could hold her own in a battle *and* sing about it afterward.

"Captain Q'allock to Captain Spock."

"Go ahead, Captain."

"Chancellor Azetbur would speak with you." McCoy thought Uhura looked relieved.

"Patch it through to the mess hall," Spock said, turning to the wall where the large screen was located. It came to life, and Azetbur's face, tense and angry-looking, filled the screen.

"Captain Spock," she said. "Your errand has taken on a new urgency. Stand by to receive a transmission. This is what we recently heard from Kal-Tor Lissan."

All thoughts of food—even of fresh-baked chocolate chip cookies and deep-fried chicken—fled McCoy's mind as he and Uhura rose to stand beside Spock. Not to be left out, Karglak left his tray of quivering foodstuffs and hastened to Uhura's side. They all listened to the conversation in utter silence, absorbing the sobering message. When it was over, Azetbur's face reappeared.

"I see your point," Spock said.

"The *Kol'Targh* has been in space for several months," Azetbur said, "so the chances that it has been infected with this virus are practically nonexistent. You can probably assume that you are safe."

"Now there's a comfort," McCoy said. Spock said nothing.

"The captain of the *K'Rator* assures me that James Kirk has not yet been captured," she continued. "We have been able to monitor his unique signal throughout this entire ordeal. We should yet be able to fulfill the *DIS jaj je.*"

McCoy brightened, and gently squeezed Uhura's shoulder. Karglak grunted, but it sounded like a happy grunt. "It is good to satisfy honor," he growled.

"It seems your suspicions that Captain Kirk and the colonists were in danger were completely validated, Chancellor," said Spock. "But the nature of our mission has now changed, I would think. The reason we are all here is to ensure Captain Kirk's safety, but now it appears the stakes are higher. May I ask how you wish us to proceed?"

Azetbur's eyes flashed, and McCoy almost took a step backward. Damn, Klingons could be intimidating, even the best of them.

"Planting a virus to cripple a foe's fleet is a coward's way of fighting," she said, contempt dripping from every syllable. "Some of the Federation members are happy, pleased that Lissan was thoughtful enough to warn us. He may indeed not activate the virus if we don't violate his space and give up Huan without a fight. He may keep to his word. Or, he may do it anyway, now or at any time. The Federation is proceeding with caution and much wringing of hands."

"You have not answered my question," Spock said. "Perhaps I should ask another. How would a Klingon proceed?"

A predatory smile curved her lips, revealing pointed teeth. "We would find the laboratories that created and controlled such a virus, blast any guard ships out of the stars, free our people, and bombard the base until nothing but the barest specks remain."

"It is therefore unfortunate that the incident is not your problem," Spock said.

"If the virus is as widespread as Lissan claims, then it is everybody's problem," Azetbur retorted. "Do what you will."

Spock raised an eyebrow. "There is an old Earth saying: When in Rome, do as the Romans do." He looked around. After so many years together, McCoy could read the Vulcan's mind. Spock was looking at the Klingon ship, sponsored by the Klingon government, operated by a Klingon captain.

And he was doubtless thinking, *when on a Klingon ship. . . .*

The battle cruiser approached the badly misnamed Sanctuary under full cloak. Spock settled into the command chair, which was quickly vacated by Captain Q'allock.

"Report," Spock asked. McCoy and Uhura had accompanied him to the bridge. And, of course, where Uhura went, there went Karglak also. Spock wished he had been able to dissuade the singer from accompanying them, for many reasons. The mission was likely to be dangerous, and if the best-loved opera star of his generation were slain, it would seriously affect the peace negotiations.

Or would it? Perhaps it might buy them yet more honor. With Klingons, such things were hard to predict.

McCoy came to stand by his chair, as he had so often done with Kirk, and Uhura moved almost without thinking to the equivalent position of her old post, Karglak following as unobtrusively as it was possible for an enormous Klingon to do. Spock was glad his former *Enterprise* colleagues had accompanied him, for reasons other than their excellence at their duties.

"We are still several parsecs away," the navigator informed him. "The *K'Rator* has informed us that the Falorians have constructed a spacedock."

"What ships are currently docked there?"

"Seven—no, eight small attack ships. They are built for speed, not for lengthy battles."

"Weapons?"

"Phasers only."

Spock nodded. Although he did not know the specific ship, he knew its type. It was designed for surprise attacks rather than sustained battle. Eight of these small vessels posed little threat to a Klingon battle cruiser and bird-of-prey.

"Any sign of any larger vessels on the long range scanners?"

"Negative, sir."

"From what Azetbur told us, I'd guess that all their battleships are either at Huan or en route," Uhura said.

"Brilliant!" exclaimed Karglak, gazing fondly at her.

"A logical conclusion, Commander," Spock said. "Obviously, we were not expected here at Sanctuary. They do not think this is where the conflict is. They are mistaken."

He felt McCoy's surprised gaze on him, but did not turn to look the doctor in the eye. If McCoy chose to infuse the statement with emotion, that was his interpretation. Spock was merely stating a fact.

As far as he was concerned, this was where the real fight would be.

* * *

"It won't be as easy as it was the last time," Scott said. "They'll be watching for us for sure."

"Especially if they've gotten all the other colonists and we're the only ones missing," Julius said.

Kirk laughed a little. "Easy, Mr. Scott? I didn't think it was easy the last time." He sobered. They were within a few hundred kilometers of the base.

"All right then," Scott said, more to himself than the others. "They still could take a few lessons on how to watch for intruders. There are no ships or guards at the base."

Julius made a small, happy sound in the back of his throat. "They're probably scattered, chasing the rest of us."

"Long-range scanners would seem to indicate that," said Scott.

"There were never very many Falorians here to begin with," Julius said. "Even considering Lissan was lying to me about a lot."

"Most of them are probably in their warships attacking Huan right now," Skalli said morosely.

Kirk said nothing, but he assumed that Skalli was correct. Most of the Falorians here on Sanctuary would be the researchers who had created the virus. There would be a few guards, but considering that Kirk and company by all rights ought to have been met with everything Lissan had, their tactic of having the colonists scatter was proving to be a boon. He was deeply sorry Lissan had found Alex, but oddly reassured by the targeted beating. Kirk had witnessed, and even experienced, real torture; compared to what brutalities could be inflicted upon the fragile human body, Alex had gotten little more than a slap on the wrist.

"It would seem that Lady Luck is with us," he said. "Let's do our best not to offend her."

But Lady Luck was a fickle date, and Kirk wondered how

much longer she'd hang around them before seeking entertainment elsewhere. The small group of five grew silent as they approached the base.

"Still no sign that we've been noticed," Scott said, his eyes on the screen. "I'm sorry I couldn't tap into the conversation in time for us to contact the president while we had him, but there's an up side. We'd have given ourselves away and they'd be on us like a duck on a June bug."

"That's hardly a Scottish saying," Kirk said.

"No, I got it from Dr. McCoy."

Kirk felt an unexpected, quick pang. He'd been so engrossed with first his nephews, then the colony, then the disaster that was threatening to descend that he hadn't realized how much he missed his old friends.

Bones. Spock. Uhura. Sulu. He permitted himself a brief moment of nostalgia, and wondered what they were doing now. Spock, Uhura, and McCoy, he knew, were involved with the Klingons. He had heard something about a medical forum, and hadn't Spock hinted at a musical program? And Sulu, lucky Hikaru Sulu. Captain of his own ship, off having adventures like he, Kirk, used to have.

And just what is this, Jim? he thought. *Breaking and entering a secret enemy facility in an effort to save a few billion lives is hardly a walk in the park.*

But anyone could do this. Even Alex, if he had to. Kirk desperately yearned to be on the bridge of a starship again, to be in charge, to make the decisions that could help bring peace to the galaxy. And, yes, to give the order to fire when all avenues had been exhausted in the name of that peace.

Along about this moment, Lady Luck decided she'd had enough.

"Three small ships approaching, Captain," said Scott.

Chekov muttered something vicious-sounding under his breath.

"Hang on," Scott grunted.

And with no more warning than that, Scott pulled the little atmosphere shuttle up at top speed. The Falorian ships followed, keeping close on the *Drake*'s tail. Scott frowned and the ship veered down and to port. Beside Kirk, Skalli gasped and dug her fingers into the seat.

"I'm . . . not very good with rapid movement like this. . . ." she said, gasping a little and turning an odd lavender color.

"This would be a particularly bad time to get sick, Skalli," Kirk said as noncommittally as he could. She nodded, and began trying to breathe slowly and deeply.

The shuttle now lurched violently to starboard and then seemed to go straight up. Kirk was slammed against the back of his chair and saw only sky in the windows.

"Clumsy big things," Scott sniffed. "Can't outrun my sleek wee bairn." He patted the console affectionately. "I like her better than the boat, I think. Maybe I'll get one when we get back to Earth."

"I'll help you pick one out myself if you can get us through this," Kirk said.

Scott didn't reply. He was too busy doing a complete loop and heading back the way they had come. Kirk looked out the window to see two smoking wrecks on the ground. Even as he watched, the doors to one opened and an obviously shaken Falorian crew emerged.

He breathed a little easier. The fewer casualties on any side in this strange battle, the better.

The ship rocked suddenly. Kirk remembered belatedly that there were three ships, not two, and apparently one had managed to stay aloft sufficiently to fire on them.

"Julius, this thing have any weapons?" Scott asked.

"No," Julius said, sounding a little disgusted. "Alex ordered the weapons system disengaged when we arrived. Said we'd have no need for it."

"You know, I respect Alexander's pacifism," Chekov said, "but I really wish that he'd forgotten about disabling the *Drake*."

"That makes two of us," Scott said grimly, again performing evasive maneuvers that made Kirk just as glad he hadn't eaten for several hours. Beside him, Skalli whimpered, just a little.

Whoever was on their tail was good, Kirk had to give them that. The Falorian vessel refused to be shaken.

"Mr. Scott," Chekov said, "would you be willing to let an old navigator have a try?"

Scott's strength was technical, and everyone knew and respected it. Kirk had him at the helm so that he'd be in a ready position to counter any attempts by the Falorians to fix on their position, and also so they wouldn't waste a moment trying to break into the facility.

But Chekov had spent years, together with Sulu, in handling the *Enterprise*. Scott looked at Chekov's still-healing hands even as the *Drake* shuddered again from a glancing blow.

"Your hands, lad," Scott said softly.

"Don't worry about that. Let me try," Chekov said. Scott glanced back at Kirk, who nodded.

Chekov swiveled his chair to reach for the console as Scott leaned back to give him room. Kirk saw the muscles of his face twitch in pain as his injured fingers moved across the lighted buttons, but Chekov didn't slow down. With amazing speed he programmed a sequence of movements.

"Now!" Chekov cried.

The shuttle seemed to take on a life of its own. It shot upward, then sped downward so close that Kirk could see each individual petal on a single flower. It then swung violently to the left, then right, then up, then down again. Beside Kirk, Skalli clapped one hand to her mouth. With the other, she clutched the chair as if for dear life.

Kirk heard the sound of the ship that was in pursuit plowing into the ground behind them. Smoke billowed past them as the *Drake* began again to gain altitude.

"Good job, lad!" Scott enthused, again taking the controls as Chekov leaned back in his seat. He permitted himself a grimace as he placed his bandaged hands gingerly in his lap.

"Well done, Mr. Chekov," Kirk said. Chekov gave him a faint smile.

"Now we just come a'calling as we planned," Scott said. "There's no sign of any more pursuit. Let's get this thing open and us inside."

"Captain Spock," the Klingon helmsman said. "I am detecting explosions and several moving craft around the Falorian base."

"Onscreen."

The pleasant image of the slowly turning blue and green planet was replaced by that of a glowing hemisphere of softly radiating blue light. The research that Commander T'SroH had done had provided some information about what was inside the facility. It was little enough—indications of labs, some weaponry, advanced technology. But with what Spock knew now, it became clear to him that the Falorians had chosen Sanctuary to be the place where their nanoprobe virus would be developed and honed.

Even as Spock watched, a small atmosphere shuttle approached. With no warning, the shield went down and the shuttle landed.

"Now who in blazes would—oh." McCoy's question was

immediately answered when Kirk, Scotty, Chekov, a younger man that McCoy didn't recognize, and a Huanni female clambered out of the shuttle and high-tailed it for a large entrance that obviously led to a subterranean shelter. Of course it was Jim. Who else would fly right into the lion's den to rescue over a hundred Daniels?

"Such courage!" exclaimed Karglak. "When we return, I will commission an opera about this adventure." He straightened. "And I shall play the intrepid Captain Kirk."

At any other time, Spock would have been pleased at the honor Karglak was offering to a human, but right now, more immediate problems pressed.

"Closer on the captain," Spock said. Jim's image filled the screen. Spock nodded. "Hail Captain Kirk," Spock said. "I see he still has his communicator."

"Captain, with respect," Q'allock growled, "that would give away our position!"

Spock swiveled in the chair and, McCoy would later swear, *glared* at Q'allock. "Hail him," he repeated, his voice as cold and hard as the doctor had ever heard it.

When the Klingon at the communications console still seemed to hesitate, Uhura stepped in. Brusquely and with the efficiency of one who'd been doing this for years, as indeed she had, her long, sure fingers flew over the console. "Cap—"

She wasn't even able to finish the first word. The security field had sprung back up and any attempt to speak with Kirk or anyone else inside was now impossible.

Uhura and McCoy's eyes met, and though Uhura conducted herself like the professional she was, McCoy felt a surge of sympathy at the expression of anguish in those beautiful brown eyes. Karglak, standing by her side, reached to pat her shoulder reassuringly.

A sharp whistle shattered the moment. "Captain Spock," Uhura and the Klingon communications officer said at the same time. Glowering, the Klingon sank back in his chair and crossed his arms across his broad chest.

"Captain Spock," Uhura said, "we're being hailed."

"I told you!" the Klingon captain bellowed. "You've thrown away any element of surprise we possessed—our best weapon!"

"Captain Q'allock," Spock said, "your silence will serve us all best now. Uhura, onscreen."

The visage of the Falorian Kal-Tor known as Lissan appeared, and he grinned malevolently.

"Captain Spock, I presume?"

Chapter Twenty

"**K**al-Tor Lissan," Spock replied.

"I have done my research," Lissan said. "I know of you, Captain. And Dr. McCoy and Commander Uhura, as well. How touching, that you rush so eagerly to the rescue of a friend. But am I not correct in assuming that this is hardly a Starfleet-issue vessel?"

"What this vessel is or is not is not under discussion," Spock said.

"And what precisely *is* under discussion?" Lissan asked. "What do you want from me, Captain Spock?"

"These games do not become the representative of such an intelligent species," Spock said. "We have knowledge of your recent communication with the president of the Federation and your threat. We have come for the hostages, as you must know."

"We have them all, you know," Lissan said. "Including Scott, Chekov, and James T. Kirk. Surely you can't imagine that we'd turn them over simply because you asked nicely?"

"My Starfleet training compels me to pursue the diplomatic option first," Spock said.

The words seemed to anger Lissan. Before, he had been lounging in his chair, sneering. Now he bolted forward, his hands on the desk in front of him.

"Always the diplomats, you Starfleet and Federation types. Well, my people are at war, Mr. Spock, and frankly, as we both know, the fleet presently on its way to Huan is no match for your powerful vessels over the long term. However, I have two safeguards—the virus, about which you already know, and the hostages. I won't hand them over, and if you don't depart Sanctuary space within ten of your Earth minutes, I will begin killing them one by one. I know your kind, Mr. Spock. You Federation types are soft. As long as I hold the hostages, I have the upper hand. You'll back down."

Desperately McCoy tried to read the face on the screen. He didn't know Lissan or his people from a hole in the ground. Some species would indeed start killing the hostages without a care in the world. Others would be bluffing, preying on the human respect for life in order to get what they wanted, but also sharing that respect. Which one was Lissan? A killer, or a good poker player?

"You have made an error in judgment, Kal-Tor," Spock replied. "While a professional Federation negotiator might indeed back down, as you put it, I will point out that I am a Vulcan. Under these circumstances, I find backing down illogical. I am aboard a Klingon ship. Klingons find backing down dishonorable. Commander Q'allock, fire at will."

Kirk's communicator sounded. Even as he ran, phaser in hand, firing as he went, he fished for it and flipped it open. It crackled, and a sound that might have been a voice and might have been a high-pitched squeal of static issued forth. Then, dead silence.

A phaser blast whizzed past, almost hitting him. Kirk whirled, communicator still in his left hand, and fired in the direction from which the shot had come. The five of them kept running, in a close-knit group, all three phasers being put to good use.

Even as he defended himself, Kirk's mind raced. What had just happened? Had some of the colonists disobeyed orders and taken communicators? They had discussed this and decided it was too risky. If Lissan had been able to get a hold of even one communicator and had had his wits about him, he could have tricked any of the colonists into revealing themselves. But Kirk knew that these independent idealists couldn't always be trusted to obey orders to the letter. It wouldn't have surprised him if someone thought they knew better than James T. Kirk and was now trying to contact him.

Or was it just a burst of static, an accident? Given all the signals being broadcast here, it wouldn't surprise him in the least if his communicator had inadvertently gone off.

Regardless, it was irrelevant. There would be no way to talk to anybody until they got to the precise console and could send a message out. Still running, he smoothly returned his communicator to its holster. Looming ahead was the entrance.

The Klingon crew currently under Spock's command had clearly been itching for just such orders. Barely had the words left Spock's mouth than the weapons officer, uttering a cry that made the humans' hair stand on end, fired phasers.

The eight small attack ships had their shields up, but even so they took damage. They zoomed from the spacedock with startling speed, their quickness an advantage over the larger, but more heavily armed, battle cruiser. As they zipped past, they fired. The ship rocked.

"Report," Spock ordered.

"Slight damage to the port nacelle," the Klingon bridge officer cried. "Decks one and three are staunchly carrying on."

Spock and McCoy exchanged glances. While McCoy's expression remained appropriately serious, there was a twinkle in his eye at the words the Klingon chose to describe the ship's damage.

"Lock phasers on their weapons and fire again," Spock said.

The Klingon gleefully did so. He struck one of them a good blow. It slowed and stopped, dead in space.

The ship rocked again. "Target weapons systems and engines of all vessels and fire at will. Helm, maneuver as necessary. I suggest everyone grasp a secure hold of a railing or chair."

Shrieks of victory filled the bridge as the Klingons obeyed. One voice rose over all the others, and Spock recognized the famous aria "Bathed in Blood, I Stand Victorious."

Red phaser fire screamed across space, hitting target after target. For a moment, the ship pretended it was a little skiff, moving so rapidly that even Spock became slightly disoriented. There was a half roll and a dive. Ship after ship took damage. Despite Spock's orders, he suspected that the Klingons were not being terribly scrupulous in their targeting. He supposed he could not blame them.

After what seemed an eternity of Klingon curses and song, a rolling ship, and the yellow light of fire filling the screen, the ship steadied.

"We have Kahless's own luck," Q'allock announced. "All ships have either been destroyed or disabled."

Spock sat back in his chair, thinking. If there had been any weapons on the planet, Lissan would have put them to use by now. It was indeed too bad that Vulcans did not believe in luck.

"I believe we are safe for the moment," he said. "We must now focus on destroying the force field and retrieving Captain Kirk and the others."

Standing Crane was halfway through the list of people she had to contact when she received a top-priority incoming message. Her gut clenched. What now?

"Yes, Mr. President?" she said as his visage filled her screen.

"We've gotten some preliminary results back from the first round of tests," he said. "Lissan was correct. This virus will indeed prevent any infected vessels from going to warp."

She could tell by his expression that there was more, and her heart began to thud rapidly. "And?"

"The virus targets the dilithium crystals. Any attempt to introduce matter and antimatter causes them to shatter."

"Great Spirit," Standing Crane breathed, her hand coming to her mouth. Shattered crystals meant a warp core breach, and that of course meant . . . "H-how many ships would be affected?"

"Our best guess is only an extrapolation. Taking into account all the ships and docks and starbases actually visited by the Falorians, and assuming a certain number of cross contaminations, we're looking at upward of six thousand vessels. Delaney tells me that it's a conservative guess. She thinks it's more likely to be in the tens of thousands. And with each minute that ticks by, the likelihood of further contamination doubles."

Tens of thousands of vessels, not people. Thousands of ships that would try to go to warp and end up as atoms floating in space. Millions of people who'd end up the same way.

For a moment, she couldn't speak. She stared numbly at the

president, knowing that her horror was written plainly on her face.

"I know. It took me several minutes to calm down sufficiently to tell you," the president said, sympathizing. "It appears that most of the planets that are mining dilithium have been infected, too, so it's not a matter of swapping out the crystals. Laura, we're looking at the worst disaster the Federation has ever faced."

"And because of the very nature of that disaster, we can't do a damn thing about it," she finished, nodding her head. She forced herself to breathe deeply and slowly, to regain control. She would not serve well if she broke down. "So, what do we do now?"

"Delaney is trying to figure out how to counter the virus, but she's not making much progress. Most of the ships have docked safely, but there's a lot of them still out there."

"The only way then for us to remain safe is to permit no ships to go to warp until we've figured this out," Standing Crane said. "Lissan and his buddies are going to walk all over Huan, and there's not a thing we can do about it."

"There are some days when it just doesn't pay to get up in the morning," the president said dryly, and Standing Crane forced a smile.

If she didn't laugh, she'd cry. And she knew if she started to cry, she might not stop.

Kirk took back his comments to Scotty about their previous attempt not being easy compared to this second one. Every inch of ground they got was hard won. They tried to keep Julius and Skalli in the center, as there were only three phasers between them. They did a good job, but even so, at one point Kirk heard Skalli cry out and turned to see that she'd taken a hit. She clapped a hand to her smoking, burned shoulder and grimly continued, though her expressive face was contorted in pain.

Once, Julius stumbled and hit the ground hard, facefirst. In one smooth motion, Kirk leaned down, hauled his nephew up by the arm, and pushed him forward. They had to keep moving. Julius's face was a mask of blood. It looked as though he'd broken his nose and knocked out a few teeth, but they were almost there.

Ahead, looming over all, was the Starfleet-issue subspace relay tower, the source of the carrier wave. Kirk knew that the controls were inside, deep underground. Briefly, Kirk wondered if this was part of the black market equipment Julius had helped the Falorians smuggle in, or if this was something they'd obtained on their own. Angrily he cut off that line of thinking. Whatever Julius had done was in the past, and now that the Falorians had shown their true colors, Kirk felt certain his nephew would do everything he could to help them. It was the reason he'd brought the boy along.

Under heavy fire, they kept going, until they were at the entrance of the tunnel. Skalli, who had been checking her tricorder despite her injury cried out, "Wait! They've got a field up!" The group skidded to a halt and ducked behind one of the small outbuildings. It wasn't much, but it offered temporary shelter while they weren't moving targets.

"Julius, you got them this equipment," Kirk said. He knew how harsh it sounded, but it was the truth, and there wasn't time to dance around Julius's feelings. "What frequencies do they use?"

A phaser blast struck the building. Kirk leaned around the edge, fired quickly, and was rewarded by a harsh cry of pain.

Julius spat out a mouthful of blood. He leaned in close to Skalli and together they adjusted the tricorder to the same frequency as the shield.

"Got it!" cried Skalli.

"Watch out—they'll have guards down there!" Kirk got off a few more shots and then they ran hell for leather for the tunnel entrance. They were greeted by phaser blasts. Kirk, Chekov, and Scott took careful aim and picked their attackers off one by one.

They scrambled down inside, all clinging as best they could to the gantries. "Skalli, change the frequency and get that force field back up," Kirk cried, gasping for breath. It wouldn't last for long, but any second of reprieve would be welcome.

He looked around, phaser at the ready, and was stunned to find they encountered no further resistance. Apparently the guards who had attacked them on the surface, plus the four or five who had fallen defending the entrance, were all the security Lissan could summon. It was a lucky break, and Kirk intended to make the most of it.

"Shield's up, Captain, and the frequency has been reconfigured," Skalli said. "I threw in a few things to make it harder for them to crack it. They'll figure it out eventually, but it should buy us some time."

Kirk paused for a second to regard Skalli with respect. She continued to astonish him. If they got out of this alive, he wouldn't just be her advisor, he'd be her damned sponsor through Starfleet, and count himself lucky to have the privilege.

"Everyone all right?" he asked.

"We can all walk," Scott said grimly. It wasn't exactly a direct answer to the question, nor was it encouraging, but Kirk took it. He nodded, gulped for air, and then they began to descend.

Somewhere down there were the controls to get a message out to Starfleet about the true scope of the disaster they were facing. Kirk would get that message out, or die trying.

Chapter Twenty-one

Lissan was at his wit's end.

It had all been going so well. Everything had unfolded as it should. The Federation had reacted precisely as Lissan had predicted. The Orion vessels were taking up position around Huan, waiting to swoop in on the dilithium like *taggors* on a dead animal once the Falorian fleet had conquered Huan. Although Lissan and the other members of the Kal-Toreshi realized that Huan's fall might take a while, even with the Orion-provided weaponry and ships, early signs were promising. Lissan was sweating every single minute until that longed-for hour when the virus would be activated, and the entire quadrant would be begging for the largest cache of pure, uncorrupted dilithium in the known galaxy. It would all be all right then, but until that time, things could go wrong.

Things like two Klingon vessels showing up here at Sanctuary and blasting all eight of his ships out of the sky. Things like one of those vessels being captained by a famous Starfleet figure known to be Kirk's best friend, somehow allied with a species Lissan knew to be hostile to Vulcans and humans alike. Things like the wiliness of the aforementioned James Kirk.

Lissan and his people were now as stranded on Sanctuary as the colonists were. Once the battle for Huan was over and the Falorians victorious, of course, they would come for him. But until then, he was not pleased about his forced isolation.

Precious resources and time were being squandered in chasing down the scattered colonists. Now that Lissan had moved to take them hostage, he had to do so, or the whole plan could collapse. His troops, what few there were, were all over the planet trying to find them. Only a handful had been captured to date. He knew he had been exceedingly fortunate that Alexander Kirk was among the few they had found. He'd seen the reaction when the youth's bloody face had been presented to the Federation.

The beating had been 858's idea. Actually, killing and mutilating Alexander had been 858's idea—"Nothing convinces someone you mean business like a dead body"—but Lissan had been so appalled by the suggestion that the Orion had backed up a step.

"Verbal threats are good," the green-skinned alien had said, "but physical evidence is better. You can lie about what you might do, but when they see what you've already done, what you're willing to do, well, your threat becomes that much more effective."

They had argued about just what that beating should consist of. 858's dark eyes had brightened when he described cutting off digits, inserting sharp implements in nostrils and ears or under finger- and toenails, or peeling off skin. Lissan fought desperately to conceal his disgust and horror. He seized on what he thought might convince the Orion, which was that Alexander might be of more use to them alive and ambulatory than not. Even so, he had not enjoyed watching Alexander's face get pummeled.

And now word had just reached him that Kirk and a few others, including Julius, were loose in the facility.

His computer made a sound and Lissan sighed. He was certain he did not want to talk to whomever might be trying to contact him, but resolutely tapped a button. When 858's green visage filled the screen, Lissan cringed inwardly but kept his face impassive.

"I understand that there might be a problem. A very, very big problem."

"I don't know what you're talking about," Lissan lied. "We had a deal. You gave us the vessels we needed to attack Huan. We hold off the Federation long enough to access the dilithium, and you get paid. Well paid. You then go away and leave us alone while we handle the wrath of the Federation. How difficult is that for you to comprehend?"

"What kind of idiots do you think we are?" 858 asked. "Did you really think we wouldn't be monitoring your communications? You've got a nice setup, I'll admit, but we finally cracked your conversation with the Federation president, and we are very interested in learning more about this virus of yours."

Lissan made a dismissive gesture. "A lie, a trick," he said.

"You've never been a good liar, especially not to me," 858 said. "And we have found traces of this virus on our own ship."

Desperately, Lissan wondered if half-truths would save him. "All right. There is a virus." True. "And you probably tracked it onto your vessel yourself." Untrue—it had been quite deliberately placed. "It's all over here, too." True. They had a way to ensure the nanoprobes harmlessly self-destructed by transmitting a simple signal accompanied by the correct code. "It's totally inert—the nanoprobes don't do anything." That was as

216

great a lie as anything Lissan had ever uttered. "The Federation will figure this out in the not too distant future, but it won't matter. It will stall them long enough for us to take Huan and you to get paid. Once the Federation realizes that they've been tricked, yes, they will come after us. But we will be entrenched on Huan, thanks to you, and will be fighting from a position of strength."

Please believe this, Lissan thought frantically. *Please believe this.* Surely there was enough truth to it to make it sound plausible. They'd find him out, of course, but maybe he could hold them off just long enough.

858 met Lissan stare for stare. "I should have called this off sooner," 858 finally said, obviously disgusted. "I never believe in advancing credit to begin with, and this—well, I didn't agree to it, just to enforce it. All right, Lissan. I will take what you've told me to my superiors, and do rest assured, we will be testing your so-called inert nanoprobes. And if you have lied to me—if what you told the Federation is true—then rest assured, I will come for you and carry out your execution myself."

He smiled a slow, predatory smile. At any other time, it would have chilled Lissan to the bone. But for a brief, wild moment, the Falorian wanted to laugh. 858 was millions of kilometers away. One push of a button, and his ship would stop dead. It was hard to execute someone when you couldn't get to him. Still, it wouldn't do to gloat.

Not yet. Later, perhaps.

So Lissan looked appropriately serious when he replied, "You'll find that all is as I have said. I only hope you're not so busy checking up on your ally that you miss your window of opportunity. The Federation won't be fooled forever, and I'd hate to see you embroiled in a battle with them without your share of the dilithium."

He heard it, even as he tried to stifle it—that burbling pleasure in his voice. 858 looked at him sharply, then the screen went dark.

Lissan sagged in his seat, the odd burst of pleasure gone. What was he thinking? The Federation had probably already confirmed what Lissan had told them about the virus. The Orion Syndicate didn't put the value on scientific research that the Federation did, true, but it certainly had access to scientists and labs. They, too, would find out in fairly short order what the virus could do. And they would know they had been double-crossed.

With his forefinger he stabbed a button. "Any word on Kirk?" he demanded.

The head of security looked chagrined. "Nothing, sir. They were able to penetrate the force field and are presently unaccounted for."

"You had better account for them soon," Lissan said.

"It's—difficult, sir," Jasslor stammered. "They have some kind of technology that masks their bio signs. It's the reason it's been so hard to find the colonists. The only thing we can tell for certain about their location is where they *have* been—when someone doesn't report in, or a security field is breached. Where they are is another matter."

Lissan summoned patience. "Can you give me your best guess?"

"We think they're still in the upper levels, judging by the activities reported. At least we hope so, because that's where the guards are. If they're not, if they've gotten deeper into the complex, there will be only about five people capable of stopping them. After that, you're going to have to think about arming your scientists—and yourself."

"Where to, Julius?" asked Kirk.

"How should I know? You've been here before, you tell

me." Kirk was mildly amused at the still-rebellious tone Julius used.

"You know the types of equipment they have better than we do," he said.

"Yeah, I know, I know, because I sold it to them. You've made your point." Nonetheless, Julius examined Chekov's tricorder and looked around him. "They're very orderly, very meticulous," he said. "They'd probably have a special section for everything. We wouldn't find communications mixed in with labs. We've already passed the security level. And this entire floor looks like research to me."

It looked familiar to Kirk. "Chekov, do you remember this section?"

"Aye, sir," Chekov replied. "This upper level was where we found the test labs and where we almost ran into the scientists."

"We took a lift down several stories," Kirk said, the details coming back to him. "We saw quite a few storage rooms. About twelve stories down was where we found the padd in that small lab."

Chekov nodded. "I was able to get onto the computer. Perhaps we could try it there again, find out where the main communications area is located."

"Too risky," Scott said. "They didn't know you were here that time. They do now."

"Captain," Chekhov said, trying to keep his voice from sounding too excited, "I'm detecting human life signs."

"Where?" Julius cried.

"About two stories down, halfway across the tunnel," Chekov said.

"Then let's go!" Julius was halfway down a metal ladder when Kirk stopped him with a sentence.

"We can't," Kirk said.

Julius looked up. He looked frightening, his blue eyes blazing against the smear of drying maroon blood on his face.

"You give me one damn good reason why I'm not going to find my brother," he said, his voice deep and intense.

"I'll give you several," Kirk said, refusing to be drawn into Julius's vortex of pain, guilt, and anger. "We wouldn't be able to rescue them, not with just a few phasers. Even if we did manage to free them, we couldn't get them to safety. Attempting to do so would give away our position, and if we get caught, then the Falorians get five more valuable hostages and no one gets warned about the real danger of that virus."

The muscles in Julius's bare arms tensed and his chest moved rapidly. His eyes never left Kirk's. "He's my brother," he finally said, softly.

"I know exactly how you feel."

"How can you—"

"I know what it's like to lose a brother," Kirk said. "I'll never forget beaming down to Deneva and finding his body. I loved your father, just as you love Alexander. I know what I'm asking of you, and I don't ask it lightly. But if we play our cards right we'll all get out of here alive, and we'll be able to save other lives as well. Millions of other lives. Help me, Julius. We need you. You've got a chance to correct the mistakes you've made. Not everyone gets that kind of opportunity."

For a long moment, the two Kirk men locked gazes. Finally Julius uttered a long, quavering sigh.

"Damn it," was all he said. "Damn it." But he climbed back up the ladder.

They continued downward. On their previous reconnaissance of the area, Kirk and Chekhov had discovered that the deeper they went, the more security systems they encountered.

It was a good bet that communications, which was clearly vital to the implementation of the Falorians' plan, would be here, where it could be well protected.

It was harder this time; the Falorians had beefed up their security. Julius was not patient with the time it took to deactivate each force field or break into each area. Kirk sympathized, but he knew where his duty lay.

Although the time seemed long to Julius, Kirk was frankly amazed at the speed with which Scott deactivated seemingly complex systems.

"In another lifetime, Mr. Scott, I'm sure you had a successful career as a safecracker," he said at one point, remembering how Scotty had enabled an escape when they were prisoners at Sybok's hands.

On his hands and knees, tinkering with the tricorder, Scott laughed. "Oh, aye," he said. "But don't you be holding that against me, Captain."

"On the contrary. I'm counting my blessings even as we speak," Kirk replied.

Level by level, door by door, the five wound their way into the heart of the Falorian complex. While Scott worked, Kirk and Julius hung back, keeping an eye out for guards. More than once, they surprised a few; more than once, unconscious Falorian bodies lay sprawled in the corridors.

Finally, Scott uttered a long, happy, satisfied sigh. "Gentlemen," he said, his burr more pronounced with pleasure, "We're in."

Chapter Twenty-two

Approximately twenty-three minutes and thirty-seven seconds had passed since all eight Falorian vessels had been destroyed. Spock had issued orders that the field surrounding the complex be analyzed, the data prepared, and presented.

The Klingons had grumbled. They felt such a dispassionate, measured approach was, if not precisely dishonorable, at the very least not something about which one would boast. But they had obeyed, and now Spock, McCoy, Uhura, and four Klingons, including the ubiquitous Karglak, sat around a table in the captain's ready room.

Spock steepled his fingers and listened intently to the information they had been able to gather. Finally, he nodded.

"I regret that we seem to have but one option," he said, rising and going to the screen that displayed a graphic of the shield. "Although I anticipate that my crew will, on the contrary, be quite pleased with the order I am about to issue." He indicated the glowing blue shield. "This is not a large area. We can see no noticeable generators. From what little information we have been able to obtain about this facility, most of it is located well below ground. It would seem quite secure, perhaps impregnable. We have little knowledge of the Falorians which would enable us to disable the field by manipulating the frequency."

He lifted an eyebrow. "We must therefore take a more Klingon approach to the problem. We have disabled all the adversaries who lay in wait to attack us. We know that it is unlikely that the Falorians will spare any vessels from Huanni space to engage in conflict here. Therefore, as I see it, the only option we have is to fire steadily upon the shield and hope that, eventually, it weakens."

Captain Q'allock let out a roar of approval, and he and the other three banged their fists on the table repeatedly until Spock held up a hand for silence.

"I do not believe it will fall easily, but at the very least we can be an annoyance. A steady attack will busy their computer and people, and with luck cause various outages throughout the complex. It will probably not do any serious damage, but it might provide Captain Kirk with a welcome distraction."

McCoy's craggy face spilt into a grin. "No-see-ums, by God!" he exclaimed.

Both of Spock's eyebrows reached for his hairline. McCoy often uttered colorful phrases that Spock did not quite understand, but this one was truly bizarre.

"I beg your pardon, Dr. McCoy?"

"No-see-ums," McCoy repeated.

"Your answer does not offer clarification," Spock said.

"No-see-ums are these little bugs that plague you in the summer, specially in the warmer climates," McCoy continued. "They were the bane of my existence when I was growing up in Georgia. Gnats, or something, I don't remember exactly what the little devils are properly called, but they travel in a cloud.

They're very tiny, and you don't see them until you're smack dab in the middle of a whole slew of them."

"Hence the name," Spock said, nodding. "No-see-um. One does not see them."

"Knew you'd catch on eventually," McCoy said. "They're not dangerous—no bites or stings—but boy, are they annoying! They get in your eyes, your mouth, your nose, your hair—they'll stop you dead in your tracks and have you dancing around and waving your arms until you're clear of the cloud." He sank back in his chair, satisfaction writ plain on his face.

Spock considered McCoy's words, and then nodded. "It is perhaps an overly enthusiastic, but nonetheless apt, analogy," Spock said. "We shall be like these insects of Dr. McCoy's. We shall have very little bite, but undoubtedly we can do a superlative job of aggravating the Falorians. Also, Commander Uhura, I want you to do everything you can to block any communication that might originate from the facility."

Karglak puffed up with pride on Uhura's behalf, but Uhura herself frowned. "With respect, Mr. Spock, that means that if Captain Kirk tries to contact us, we won't know it."

"If we succeed in forcing them to drop the shield, we will be able to contact the captain via his communicator," Spock said. "If we do not, it is highly possible that the order to activate the virus will be given from this facility, since it is where it was created. I cannot risk—"

The door hissed open. "Captain Spock." It was Captain Q'allock, who had the bridge in Spock's absence. "An urgent message from the Federation president is coming in."

"I will speak with him," Spock said, rising.

"Sir, it's a recorded message, sent to all Federation vessels. And us," he added, clearly feeling a need to distance himself from the "Federation."

"Patch it through to here," Spock said. His curiosity was aroused, and though he would not admit it, he felt apprehension stir as well.

Spock felt a start of surprise, quickly suppressed, at the haggard appearance of the president. His white hair was in disarray and there were hollows under his eyes. His body posture sent a clear message of hopelessness even before his words confirmed it.

"Attention all Federation vessels. Before anything else, let me say that you are not, under any circumstances, to engage warp drive until further notice. Consider this as inviolable an order as you have ever received. You have heard about Kal-Tor Lissan's threatened virus. Our scientists have learned that the Falorians told us only part of the truth. If any infected ship attempts to engage warp drive, the dilithium matrix could destabilize and the crystals may fracture or shatter. An instantaneous warp core breach would occur."

The president paused and took a deep breath. McCoy and Uhura exchanged glances. Spock kept his eyes on the recording.

"Obviously, not every ship is infected, and there are a very few of you who know with certainty that you are not. We ask you few to hold your positions. It may well be that when this is all over, you will be the only vessels in the Federation capable of warp drive, and as such you will be precious indeed to the cause of unity and freedom in the galaxy."

"My God," McCoy breathed. Karglak growled.

"We have the top scientists in the Federation working around the clock to find a way to counter this virus, and we have every hope that they will succeed," said the president, although Spock noted that his body language belied his confident words. "Stand by until further notice."

The screen went dark.

"Captain Q'allock," Spock said, sounding exactly the same as he had before this message had been played, "is this vessel one of the few of which the president spoke?"

"We've been nowhere near the *pahtk* who did this," the captain said, and turned and spat on the carpeting. "We have been in space for many months. You are the only passengers we have taken on."

"Your homeworld was one of the sites visited by the Falorian delegation," Spock said. "We therefore must assume that we, too, have been contaminated."

"Do you mean to tell me," Q'allock said, rising anger in his voice, "that you have brought us out here to strand us in orbit around this pathetic planet for the rest of our lives?"

Karglak sprang to his feet. "You shame yourself with those words! We are here on orders from our Chancellor, to fulfill the Year and the Day!"

"It is my understanding that Klingons are willing to die to see an honor debt satisfied," Spock said calmly. "Are they unwilling to live to see the debt paid?"

The Klingon had no response to that. He folded his arms and glowered.

"We came here to satisfy the *DIS jaj je*," Spock continued. "Let us be about it."

Lissan stood straight and tall as he reported to his fellow Kal-Toreshi. Even as he spoke with an easy confidence, he felt a brief pang inside. Lying had once been something he had abhorred. Now, it seemed to come to him far too easily. The falsehoods rolled glibly off his tongue. No, the Federation would be no trouble at all. Yes, 858 might have gotten wind of the plot, but Lissan had been able to put him off. No, the colonists weren't being any problem, and of course Lissan had been able to capture them all. No, 858 had exaggerated the skirmish with the Klingon vessel. The eight ships suffered minor damage but were victorious. Could they see Kirk? Not at the moment, the pesky human was being interrogated. Soon, Lissan promised. On schedule? Of course everything was on schedule. This had been planned down to the last second, why wouldn't everything be on schedule?

On their end, unless they were lying too, the Kal-Toreshi had very good news to report. Lorall, the aged female who was the head of the small group, fairly radiated pleasure.

"The Huanni are putting up a good fight, but they are no match for our enhanced fleet," she enthused. "The first few hours have gone well. There is no reason to believe that the planet will not eventually fall to our forces."

"That is wonderful and welcome news," Lissan said, and for the first time since the conversation began, knew those words to be the unvarnished truth.

There came a deep rumbling sound, and the image of the Kal-Toreshi was shot through with static. "Lissan?" Lorall's voice was harsh and buzzing, and her image was fuzzy. "We are having trouble—"

Panicked, Lissan turned off the screen and contacted his head of security. "What is going on?" he demanded, his voice high.

"The Klingon vessels are firing on the shield," Jasslor reported.

"What's the damage?"

"Insignificant, sir. We think the shield will hold through several hours, perhaps days, of such bombardment. However, they are also firing into the ground around the shield. There is a great deal of energy rolling off the shield into the surrounding area. The soil and rock is grounding most of it, but we're still getting power spikes and are going to have to take some systems closer to the surface offline." Inwardly, Lissan groaned. Security was located immediately below surface level. The chief hesitated, and then added, "It looks like they are also successfully jamming our communications."

"We are in the final stages of activating the nanoprobe virus," Lissan said, hissing the words. "We need to be able to communicate. We need to transmit the order that will ensure our victory. We need to not lose data. What are you doing about this?"

"Sir, as I've told you, we are very short on security personnel, and with the problems caused by the bombardment—"

"I know, I know, security systems are being taken offline. Then leave the cursed colonists in their hidey-holes. Call all security back in," Lissan ordered. "It looks like we need them here more."

Jasslor hunched his shoulders and managed to look more miserable than he had earlier. Lissan had not thought such a thing possible.

"Sir," he said, "With the communications systems jammed, we can't contact them to have them report back."

Lissan was so horrified at how rapidly and severely the situation had deteriorated that for a moment he didn't even have breath to reply. For the briefest of moments, he felt sheer panic stalking him like a wild beast. No. He would not yield. Wild, uncontrollable emotions were a Huanni trait, not a Falorian.

"Here is what you will do," he said, calmly. He leaned forward into the screen. "You will find a way to get external communications working again. You will contact all personnel currently searching for the colonists and call them back. You will stabilize the field so that these attacks do not disrupt it further, and you will find Captain Kirk and his comrades and bring them to me. Do I make myself clear?"

Jasslor swallowed. "Yes, sir," he said.

The minute they were inside, alarms began to ring shrilly. At once, they slammed the door shut. There was no time to let Scott work his magic and reactivate a scrambled security device; Kirk simply fired at the controls. If anyone wanted to get in, they would have to blow open the door or phaser it open physically.

Unfortunately, if they wanted to get out, they would have to do the same.

"We're in it now for sure," Julius said.

"Were you ever not?" Kirk asked sharply.

Unexpectedly, Julius smiled. "Once," he said, "but not anymore."

Kirk looked around and assessed the situation. They were again in the enormous control center, the very heart of the place. He felt a brief stab of anxiety as he looked at the screen that had once showed the formal reception hall of Starfleet Command. All the screens were blank. No doubt that hall was presently empty, of course; no time for entertainment or festivities now. Here was where Kirk first grasped the vastness of the Falorian plot, although the details had not yet been revealed. Here also was where he had given the order that had caused Chekov's hands to be so badly damaged. He wouldn't make that mistake again.

"Let's find out which of these is the communication console," he told Scott. "And make sure you disable any security precautions. I don't want anyone else injured."

At that moment, they heard sounds from outside. Someone was banging on the doors.

They had been discovered.

"Time's a-wasting, gentlemen," Kirk said. He took up a position at the door, phaser at the ready. The guards might eventually break through, but Kirk was going to stop at least a few of them. Chekov, too, stepped beside him and lifted his phaser.

Scott and Julius went from console to console, trying to find the right one. Skalli trailed behind them, craning her long neck and wringing her hands, but keeping silent.

"I think that's it," Julius said. "Some of the readings look similar to other communications devices I've seen the Falorians using. What do you think?"

The banging stopped. A new sound could be heard faintly over the shrill alarm; the high-pitched whine of a phaser adjusted to a fine cutting edge.

Scott didn't reply, but glanced from the console to the tricorder and back. Finally he nodded his nearly white head. "Aye, that looks about right. I'll take it from here, lad."

"Maybe I can help?" Skalli said.

"You've been useful indeed, lass," Scott said. "Step in here and have a look."

A tiny hole appeared in the heavy metal door, surrounded by a shower of sparks. Kirk and Chekov exchanged glances. They still had some time, but not much. Kirk adjusted his grip on the phaser.

"Uncle Jim?" Julius's voice was surprisingly quiet, devoid of its usual surly undertones.

"I'm a bit busy, Julius," Kirk replied.

"I'd like to help. Scott and Skalli are busy at the console. Let me have a phaser. I'll stand with you."

Kirk glanced at him sharply. The blood had dried on his now-swelling face, but for the first time since Kirk had seen him his expression was almost tranquil. He knew they could all die here. And he knew what he was asking.

"All right, Julius. Take Mr. Scott's phaser. It will be an honor to have you at our backs."

Slowly, despite the pain it must have caused his damaged jaw, Julius smiled, and for the first time, Kirk saw the boy in the face of the man.

The black line had grown to an inch now.

The howling siren stopped. Kirk's ears felt hot from the cessation of the sound. Then came another sound.

"Captain Kirk," came Lissan's voice. "So, I have found you at last."

Chapter Twenty-three

"Kal-Tor Lissan," Kirk said. "I have some information for you."

"Unless it is where you have hidden all your colonists, I have no interest in anything you might say," Lissan said. His voice echoed in the chamber, quiet save for the Kal-Tor's voice and the steady, high hum of the phaser continuing to cut through the door.

"We know about your plot to destroy all dilithium crystals except the stash you are planning to take from the Huanni," Kirk said.

"You figured that out? Very clever. Did the Huanni female help you out? Did she tell you what her people had done to ours?"

"There's no time for this, Lissan," Kirk snapped. "Your scientists have made a fatal mistake. There's a flaw in your research. I believe your only desire was to control the flow of dilithium in the galaxy. But you're going to kill thousands, maybe millions, of people doing so."

Harsh laughter rang through the room. The cut in the door was now a vertical six-centimeter gash, and as Lissan replied, the unseen guard on the other door moved his phaser horizontally. The cut continued in a straight line to Kirk's right.

"We have been planning this for years," Lissan said. "We have run every test imaginable. There is no flaw. You would say anything to try to halt our triumph and keep the Federation's advantage in the quadrant's affairs."

"We studied your data," Kirk said urgently. "We know that you utilized an extremely pure crystal, that indeed all of your tests were performed using splinters of that single crystal. Did you do any tests on any other crystal? One with more impurities?"

"There was no need. A dilithium crystal is a dilithium crystal. This is nonsense, Kirk. I am not cruel. If you surrender now, I give you my word you will not be harmed."

Kirk glanced over at Scott, who was still working frantically. Skalli shook her head; the engineer hadn't been able to get a message out yet.

The cut was now three centimeters across. The angle again went down. Sparks sputtered.

"We ran simulations on our dilithium crystals," Kirk continued. "Crystals of only about seventy-five percent purity. They shattered like common glass, Lissan. If that had been a real crystal in a real matter-antimatter chamber, it would have caused a warp core breach. You know what happens then."

Lissan was silent. The cutting sound continued.

"That's not possible." There was hesitancy in the Falorian's voice.

"Think about it, Lissan. If you activate this virus and a ship goes into warp, you're going to be responsible for the deaths of every single person on that vessel. Is that really what you want?

Is that the legacy you've dreamed of for the Falorian people? To go down in history as the worst mass murderers of all time?"

"We are not killers, Kirk."

"I don't think you are, Lissan," Kirk said truthfully. "I don't think you knew that this would happen, but it will."

"All we want is what was rightfully ours!" Lissan cried. "We died in the mines on Huan. We discovered that dilithium, we *earned* it. This story you have fabricated—you just want to help your precious Huanni. You lie, James Kirk, and promise to the Federation or no, the moment my guards break into the control center I swear, we will activate that virus!"

Kirk glanced at the door. The cutter was making steady progress.

"Let me talk to him," Skalli said unexpectedly. Kirk looked at her sharply. "Please," she said. "Let me talk to him."

"This is a very delicate situation. What are you going to say?" Kirk wanted to know.

"Something that should have been said a long time ago," she replied.

Kirk hesitated, then nodded. Skalli cleared her throat and spoke more loudly. "Kal-Tor Lissan? This is Skalli. The Huanni."

A long, cold silence. "There is nothing you have to say that I could possibly want to hear, Huanni. Save your dignity and don't beg for your planet."

"I'm not going to beg." Her chest hitched with short, shallow breaths. "I want—I w-want—" She gulped and wiped at her eyes, cleared her throat, and squared her narrow shoulders. "I want to apologize."

Again, silence. Then, shockingly, laughter. It was malicious and sent shivers down Kirk's spine. Skalli visibly shrank away from the sound.

"I had no idea Huanni had such a sense of humor," Lissan said. "Of course, that makes everything all right, now, doesn't it? Centuries of laboring under Huanni domination, of taming a world to which we were never born simply because you got tired of us—well, we'll just put that all behind us because one Huanni child practically still slick from her mother's womb says she's *sorry*."

Skalli was crying so hard that tears spilled down her face from all four corners of her eyes. Kirk reached to put a hand on her shoulder.

"Stop," he said softly, for her ears alone. "There's no sense in torturing yourself." She wrenched away from his comforting touch.

"Oh, listen to the little Huanni girl, so sad she's crying. Poor little thing. Too bad you're not on your home planet, you'd really have something to cry about."

Kirk winced at the venom in the words. He knew that he was hearing more than one individual's words. He was listening to centuries of pent-up hatred stream out. Skalli swallowed and somehow summoned the wherewithal to reply. Her voice was so thick that her words were almost unintelligible.

"I . . . don't th-think this will change anything," she cried. "B-but that doesn't make any difference. This is something I need to say, and I need you to hear w-whether you believe it or not. Lissan, I *am* sorry. So terribly, terribly sorry for what my people did to yours." She laughed shakily. "It's not even as if we're different people, we're the same, and yet the people from whom I'm descended did terrible things to the people from whom you're descended. We never speak about it because we're so ashamed. We think that if we don't say anything, then it's almost like it didn't happen. I don't blame you for rejecting our offers of friendship. How can we truly think

235

to be your friends when we can't even admit we did anything wrong?"

She dragged a sleeve across her streaming nose. "So now you're doing something just as bad to us, but at least you've got a reason. I just wanted you to know. That there was someone, at least, who is able to acknowledge what the Huanni did to the Falorians and say it was wrong, and I am very, very sorry."

Again, a long silence. Finally, Kirk broke it. "Lissan, are you still there?"

"It was you, wasn't it, Kirk? You put her up to this."

"Skalli is her own person, Lissan. I'm as surprised as you are by what she just said. It's not too late. Promise me you won't detonate this virus and we will arrange for negotiation between you and Huan. Maybe we can—"

"This conversation is over."

"Lissan? Lissan!" But the Kal-Tor was gone. "Scotty, how far are you—"

"It's no use, Captain. We can't get a message out," Scott said glumly. "Someone's blocking it. This was all for nothing."

Kirk stared at him, feeling the horrified gaze of everyone else upon him. This couldn't be! They couldn't have come this far and not be able to at least warn the Federation. But Kirk had known Scott for decades, and he knew every expression that flitted across that face. There was nothing Scotty could do.

"This isn't *fair!*" wailed Skalli, finally surrendering to her grief and sobbing into her hands.

The Falorian guard was done with his second vertical cut. He moved to complete the rectangle. Once that was done, they'd be in.

"Scotty, give me something. Anything."

Scott remained silent. Kirk's thoughts raced. He looked around the vast room again, seeing it with fresh eyes.

"We're in the control center," Kirk said. "The *control center.* Julius, you said the Falorians were very organized. Do you think they would create this virus and then put the ability to launch it anywhere but here?"

Julius's blue eyes glittered. "Not a chance," he said firmly. "This is where it was made, this is where it will be activated. I'd bet my life on it."

"You may well be doing exactly that," Kirk said. If they had time, maybe even a few more minutes, they could probably determine which console controlled the activation of the virus and destroy it. But they didn't have time. Time was running out. They had a few seconds remaining, a moment or two at the outside.

"You've broken into the communications system, right, Scotty?"

"Aye," Scott said. "But I told you, we can't—"

"We can't get a message out, I know. But within the complex, can this system talk to the others?"

Skalli's tears were drying and now her eyes gleamed. "I think they can," she said, clearly seizing onto the merest shred of hope.

"We don't have time to find out where the activation of this virus is centered," Kirk said. "But if this entire complex is destroyed, the Falorians won't be able to send the activation signals to the nanoprobes. The virus will remain dormant."

The faces that turned to him were grim, but unafraid. Everyone knew what was at stake here. Even Julius didn't offer a protest.

"I can link up all the consoles throughout the facility so that one short will send the whole kit and caboodle sky-high. This whole pit will be one big ball o' flame. We won't be needing to worry about what our relatives will do with our remains."

"I don't give a damn about what happens to me," said Julius. "But the other colonists—Alex—how can we justify making this decision for them?"

"Alexander knows what's at stake here," Kirk said. "What do you think he would want us to do?"

Slowly, Julius grinned. His eyes were shiny. "Stop these bastards," he said.

"Then that's what we'll do. Scotty, get on it now."

Kirk had never seen the engineer move so quickly. Kirk glanced from Scotty's flying fingers to the cut in the doorway. For the moment, it seemed to have stopped. They had reached some kind of bolt or barrier within the door, and the cutting was taking longer.

"Got it, Captain." Scott edged out from under a console. "I crosswired with the security system that blew up Mr. Chekov's console the last time. Press that blue button up there and it'll send a command to all the consoles to self destruct."

Kirk nodded to show he understood. He took a deep breath.

"Commander Sabra Lowe," Skalli said softly. She had stopped crying and had a strange, calm expression on her face.

"What?" asked Chekov, but Kirk understood immediately what Skalli was referring to.

"Yes, Skalli," Kirk said. "We are indeed in the same situation as Commander Lowe was so long ago. It seems the more things change, the more they remain the same."

"You have the same choice as she did, Captain," Skali said. "Continue to fight and eventually be overwhelmed, or destroy this control center now, sacrificing all our lives to save the lives of millions of other innocents."

She smiled softly. "A true command decision, just like hers was. I believe that Commander Lowe did the right thing then, and I believe that what you are about to do is the right thing now. It's funny, but up until this moment I always thought of Commander Lowe as a hero. But I guess she felt just the same way as we do now—scared, worried, hoping this is the right thing, hoping it'll work."

Kirk gazed on her with pride and affection. "Skalli," he said, "you would have made a wonderful ambassador."

Her ears pricked up and her eyes shone.

Kirk heard the whirring noise and knew that the Falorians had gotten past the obstacle. In a matter of seconds, the guards would be in. Kirk looked from face to face, taking them in at this last moment of his life.

Scotty, his face weathered and his eyes bright. How very many times had he saved Kirk's life before? But now, there was nothing even he could do.

Chekov. Kirk had watched this man mature from an enthusiastic boy into an intelligent, experienced man, one Kirk was proud to have served with and to now call friend.

Skalli, who had grown more than he had imagined possible. She was so young, had had so much to offer.

And Julius. As he locked gazes with his nephew, Kirk saw no reproach, no regrets, only a steady determination. Julius had many black marks against him, but in a moment, his selfless sacrifice would wipe that slate cleaner than the youth could have dreamed. Kirk regretted that only now, in these last few hours, had he felt truly close to Julius.

It was time. Push the button, Scott had said, and the threat to the Federation, to innocent lives, would be over.

He moved calmly, his finger steady. But when he was only an inch away from the glowing button, Kirk suddenly paused.

He was thinking about that strange, brief burst on his communicator as they fought to enter the complex. What had that been? Or rather, *who* had it been? Kirk knew that Starfleet was aware that he and the others were being held hostage. What if they'd sent out a rescue ship? Under the circumstances, it wasn't logical, but Kirk knew at least one friend who, despite his professed devotion to logic, would have come if there had been any possible way. He would have done the same for Spock and the others—*had* done the same in the past. Would they do less than he?

Kirk felt keenly that he had not particularly distinguished himself recently. He'd botched experiments, gotten in the way, been responsible for a severe injury to Chekov, alerted Lissan that they knew about the complex and caused Lissan to destroy their only escape vessel, failed to prevent his nephew's capture and beating, failed to convince Lissan to stay his hand, couldn't get a message out, and was now about to be responsible for the deaths of both Kirk brothers.

His time on this planet had been one failure or problem after another. He was fine commanding a starship—he knew what to do there. He'd done it for years, and no amount of false modesty would make him feel that he didn't deserve the accolades he had achieved for his service on the bridge of a starship.

But here, it seemed that all he'd done was make one mistake right after the other. Every time he'd tried to act, all he had done was make the situation worse.

Maybe he shouldn't act.

Maybe his command decision would be to decide *not* to destroy the complex.

Maybe he should trust his friends.

Slowly, Kirk leaned back, and curled his extended finger into a loose fist.

Skalli uttered an incoherent cry and sprang forward, determined to push the button herself. Quick as a snake, Kirk seized her wrist.

"What are you doing?" Skalli shrieked.

"Trusting," Kirk said. The door burst open.

And the room dematerialized around him.

Chapter Twenty-four

When his environment again solidified, Kirk found himself face to face with a Klingon.

Before he could react, a familiar voice said, "Welcome aboard, Captain. Chancellor Azetbur will be pleased to see that her vow of *DIS jaj je* was successfully completed."

Kirk whirled to greet Spock, noticing as he did so that Skalli, Chekov, Julius, and Scott had also made it safely to the bridge of this Klingon ship. The Vulcan stood with his hands clasped loosely behind his back, his head cocked at an angle that Kirk knew very well indeed. Kirk stifled his impulse to hug the Vulcan and instead said, "Mr. Spock. Have I ever told you that you have impeccable timing?"

Spock lifted an eyebrow. "We await your orders, Captain." The Vulcan indicated the command chair. Kirk eyed the Klingon who was probably the real captain of the vessel, received an almost imperceptible nod, and took the proffered seat.

"We've got some hostages down there who—"

"We have already transported everyone in the complex,

including the Falorians, to this vessel and our accompanying bird-of-prey," Spock said.

So Spock had come riding over the figurative hill with not just one, but two Klingon ships? This *DIS jaj je* was obviously of great importance to Azetbur. Kirk supposed he should be grateful.

"Very good. I can assume that the Falorians are all in custody and the injured hostages are being attended to?"

"You may indeed," Spock said.

"The rest of the colonists are hiding in the cave system. Kate Gallagher rigged up a system to block their life signs from the Falorian tricorders, but the Klingons should—"

"We have already scanned for and located them, Captain."

Kirk wondered if there was anything that *hadn't* already been efficiently taken care of.

"That complex is the heart of the Falorian plan," Kirk informed his former first officer. "But I don't think it ever included mass murder." He sought out the Klingon captain, figuring the biggest, meanest-looking of the bunch would hold that rank. "Captain . . . ?"

"I am Karglak," the Klingon said. The opera singer? Here? "That is Captain Q'allock."

Kirk turned to face the real captain. "Captain Q'allock. I need you to send down your finest crewmen to secure that complex. Mr. Scott, you will accompany them. Sanctuary is in Federation hands now."

The Klingon saluted. "It is already done," he said.

"What?" Kirk said, amazed.

"Not actually," Spock said. "It is a figure of speech. A slight exaggeration."

"I'm glad to hear it," Kirk said. "I'd like to think I had something to contribute." He swiveled in his chair, speaking as he did so. "Communications, open a channel to—Uhura!"

The elegant, beautiful African woman gave him a slow, wide smile, positioning her long dark fingers expertly on the console. For a second, Kirk grinned stupidly, then composed himself and said, "Contact the president of the Federation. Use every encryption key in the book. This conversation needs to be completely secure."

Turning to her console, Uhura said teasingly in her warm voice, "It is already done." Karglak moved to stand by her side, looking at her affectionately.

"Any more surprises up your sleeve?" Kirk asked Spock. The Vulcan looked slightly nonplussed at the phrase and was about to reply when the unmistakable voice of Kirk's favorite country doctor came through the intercom on the chair.

"Jim!"

"Bones?"

"Got my hands full here, but I wanted to make sure they'd really managed to get a hold of you."

"We're all fine, Bones. My nephew. . . ."

"We've got Alexander here, he's fine." A pause, then in a more sober tone, McCoy continued, "He keeps asking for his brother. What should I tell him?"

Kirk looked over at Julius. Julius glanced away, fidgeting, trying to hide his emotions beneath his don't-give-a-damn exterior. But Kirk knew him better now. Come to think of it, the boy needed to see the doctor, too. "Tell him that Julius will be right down."

"He'll be glad to hear it."

Kirk hoped so. "Mr. Chekov, you go with him. I'll feel better about those burns if I know Dr. McCoy has looked at them."

"Aye, sir." Chekov, Scott and Julius stepped briskly toward the turbolift.

Kirk's eyes followed Julius. "Commander Uhura, open hailing frequencies throughout both Klingon vessels."

"Hailing frequencies open, Captain."

"This is Captain James T. Kirk to the crew and passengers of the Klingon vessels—" Kirk suddenly realized he didn't know their names.

"The *Kol'Targh* and the *K'Rator,*" Spock said helpfully.

Nodding his thanks, Kirk said, "—the *Kol'Targh* and the *K'Rator.* The colonists of Sanctuary and I are profoundly grateful for your assistance here today. You have quite literally saved all our lives, and we thank you. It is my understanding that many of the colonists successfully eluded capture by the Falorians. I know that many of you took with you valuable information regarding the present danger we all face. I would like for you to upload all information you have to the Klingon computer databanks, and make sure that both ships have complete copies of this information. Captain Spock was put in charge of this mission—" it was a guess, but as Spock didn't make any move to naysay him, Kirk knew it had been a good one "—and upon my arrival, has passed command on to me. You are to take everything I have said as an order. Kirk out."

"Captain, I have the president," Uhura said.

"Onscreen." The image of Sanctuary slowly turning in space was replaced by the reddish skin and white hair of the Federation President.

"Captain Kirk," he said. "It is a great pleasure to see you alive."

"You'll be even happier when I tell you that Sanctuary and its Falorian research facility is under Federation control," Kirk said. "I have a group of Klingons securing it even as we speak."

The president brightened visibly. "That is the best news I have heard in a long, long time."

"This virus is more dangerous than we thought. The Falorians did all their testing with extremely pure crystals. Anything less pure would shatter and—"

"Yes, and cause a warp core breach. We found that out ourselves." Kirk tried not to show his disappointment. He should have known that anything he'd been able to learn, Starfleet would have been able to learn.

"What is the status of the virus?" continued the president.

"As far as I know, it hasn't yet been activated, and I believe that it can't be as long as we're in control of that facility."

"That's part of the problem solved, but not all of it," the president said. "If the nanoprobes remain dormant, someone could learn how to activate them. We must find a way to render them completely useless."

Kirk nodded his agreement. "And if they remain intact, someday someone could learn how to recreate the virus. I don't believe it was intended to be used as a method of mass destruction, but as we've discovered it certainly could be. If the nanoprobes aren't completely destroyed, the danger exists that this could happen again. What's the status on Huan?"

The president sobered. "Not good. They've been bombarded for eleven hours now. So far it's mainly infrastructure that's been destroyed—their fleets, military bases, and so on. Minor casualties, but that could change at any minute."

"Who's at the perimeter of Huanni space?" Kirk asked. "You can safely give them orders to attack now."

"Them? Kirk, the only ship close enough to do any good that we could be certain wasn't infected was the *Excelsior.* We'll of course notify every ship we can now, but it will take them hours to get there, perhaps even days."

"Do you mean to tell me there's only one Starfleet vessel standing ready to defend Huan?"

"I'm afraid so."

Kirk digested the news, then said, "Inform Captain Sulu of the situation."

"Kirk, he's only one man with one ship."

"Respectfully, Mr. President, I served with Hikaru Sulu. He'll think of something. In the meantime, we'll be doing our best to make sure this virus is obliterated."

"Good job, Captain. Best of luck." The image disappeared.

Kirk turned to Spock. "You said that the Falorians were all in custody?"

Spock nodded. Kirk rose. "You have the bridge. Captain Q'allock, I'm less familiar with the layout of your vessel than you might think I would be. Could you escort me to the brig?"

Q'allock snarled. "It would give me great pleasure to behold the quailing scum with my own eyes."

Kirk took that as a yes.

The confines of a Klingon brig made those of Starfleet ships look like luxury suites. Dozens of Falorians, most of them clearly confused and frightened scientists, were crowded together so tightly that Kirk wondered how they could breathe. Dim red lighting provided little illumination. Kirk scanned the crush for Lissan and was about to give up, thinking that the Falorian leader had been transported to the other vessel, when he spied the Kal-Tor in the back.

"Him," Kirk said, pointing. The guards looked at Q'allock for confirmation. *DIS jaj je* or no, Kirk wasn't their captain. The Klingon nodded, and the guards deactivated the force field. One pointed a disruptor at the crowd while the other one shoved into the press of Falorian flesh, seized Lissan, and pulled him out roughly.

For an instant, Kirk could hardly believe that this was the

selfsame being that had strutted about Sanctuary so arrogantly. He was bruised and cut, his once-crisp uniform wrinkled and soiled. Then Lissan straightened, and Kirk realized that even though everything had changed, nothing had changed.

They eyed one another for a moment, then Lissan spoke. "I suppose this is the part where you either beg me to cooperate and save your precious dilithium, or you set your hired thugs on me and bully me into submission?"

"Neither," Kirk said shortly. "Which one of these people is your top scientist? The one who had the greatest part in creating the virus?"

Lissan folded his long, thin arms across his narrow chest and said nothing.

"If you want to play it that way," Kirk said. He turned to the crowd of Falorians. "Which one of you is the top scientist?"

"Say nothing, any of you!" cried Lissan, and before Kirk could stop him, a Klingon had slammed the butt of his disruptor into Lissan's gut. The Falorian doubled over. The Klingon drew back for a second blow.

"Stop it!" Kirk cried.

The Klingon shot him an angry look. "These people are dishonorable! They would see us all dead!" he spat. "They deserve far worse than this!"

"That's not for you or me to decide," Kirk said. "The Falorians will be tried fairly. Until then, you will treat them with care and respect."

The Klingon reluctantly subsided. Kirk turned again to the prisoners. "I ask again—Who among you is the top scientist?"

They simply stared at him with large, frightened eyes. Kirk sighed. He had started to turn away when a small, timid voice said, "I'm the one you want."

Kirk glanced over to see a small, slender fellow push his way to the front. Judging by Lissan's expression of annoyance and disgust, Kirk felt that this was indeed the man he wanted. The force field was again deactivated and the scientist stepped out.

"What is your name?" Kirk asked.

"Don't tell him," Lissan warned.

The scientist swallowed, and then said quietly, "I'm Kalaskar."

"Well, Kalaskar, I have a few things I want you and Lissan to see."

Under heavy guard, Kirk and the two Falorians entered the engineering section of the ship. While the layout was different, the huge pulsing warp core was familiar to Kirk. He asked for and was given a tricorder.

"This vessel is a Klingon *K't'inga* class battle cruiser. It's one of the finest ships in the Klingon fleet. Wouldn't you agree that such a vessel would be equipped with the highest-grade dilithium available?"

Lissan only glowered, but the more timid Kalaskar said, "That would make sense."

Kirk tossed him the tricorder. "Scan it," he ordered. Hesitatingly, Kalaskar did so. He frowned. "What poor grade," he said, with a hint of Lissan's arrogance.

"What's the quality?" Kirk asked.

"A mere ninety-one percent," Kalaskar said.

The chief engineer bridled. "Ninety-one percent is excellent! Our ship is equipped with a superior grade crystal. Better than ninety-five does not exist!"

"But it does," Kirk said. "It exists on Huan. But the rest of us have to make do with a purity rate of sometimes as low as seventy-two percent. You're the scientist, Kalaskar. What do you think this crystal would do if your virus was activated?"

"I—don't know," the Falorian stammered. "We didn't know that a crystal this impure even existed."

"Don't give me that," snapped Kirk. "You're a spacefaring race, you've used dilithium crystals in your ships!"

"We have only been a spacefaring race for two centuries, Captain," Lissan said, his tone equally as sharp. "And even for that, we have had to subsist on the *charity* of the Huanni. What ships we have, they gave us, along with the crystals to power them. We never examined their purity; we assumed that they were all the same. All like the single crystal we have kept since the day we were stranded on Falor."

Kirk searched his eyes. In them he found coldness and dislike, but no lie. He nodded to himself, convinced of Lissan's truthfulness. Kirk waved them over to a console.

"Some information about the virus was recently downloaded to your computers," he told the chief engineer. "We ran several simulations. Call them up."

The engineer complied. Kirk had seen the simulations before; he was more interested in watching the reactions of the two Falorians. Both of them looked upset, but Lissan continued to mingle his distress with defiance. The scientist had no such constraint.

"This is terrible!" He turned to his superior. "Kal-Tor, we never intended this. The virus was only supposed to make the dilithium useless, not destroy it!"

"I told you, I never thought you were a killer, Lissan," Kirk said quietly. "Julius seems to think that the virus can only be activated from that site down on that planet. I'm betting that only you know the command codes. Am I right?"

Lissan didn't answer. Finally, Kalaskar could stand it no longer. "You are right," Kalaskar said. "There's no way to activate the virus except from Sanctuary. And yes, only Kal-Tor Lissan has the command code."

"Is there any way to get the nanoprobes to self-destruct?" Kirk pressed.

"Oh, yes," Kalaskar said. "It was one of the safeguards I insisted we have, just in case the virus got tracked onto one of our own ships. It, too, can only be executed from Sanctuary, and again, Kal-Tor Lissan is the only one that knows the correct code."

"Lissan," Kirk said, "You see what's at stake. If those nanoprobes aren't destroyed, someone with less conscience than the Falorians could figure out how to activate them. What would happen if that level of technology fell into the hands of a race like the—" Kirk stopped himself. He had almost said *Klingons.* "The Orion Syndicate, or the Romulans, or another racist species? Someone who thinks every other species is beneath them?"

"As I see it, Captain," Lissan said coldly, "that is your problem, not mine. We are a dead race now. You have utterly ruined our chance to gain the wealth that should have been ours from the beginning. You will halt our attack against our ancient enemies, the Huanni. The Syndicate knows that we tricked them, and do not think for a moment that we will escape their wrath. The Federation will never consider us as potential members now and will probably not permit us to conduct any kind of outside trading. We've lost everything. I don't care what becomes of you."

He folded his arms and held his head high. "I wish to return to my cell now."

Kirk stared. "You can't mean this," he said. "You know that someone will figure it out. The Falorians may yet be indirectly responsible for wiping out half the galaxy!"

Lissan's eyes glittered. "The corpse cares not who follows him, Kirk. My people and I are as good as corpses. And soon, you will be, too."

Chapter Twenty-five

Wordlessly, Kirk escorted the two Falorians back to their crowded cell. Lissan vanished into the crush of bodies without a backward glance. Kalaskar wasn't as certain, but he too went silently.

"Guards, these two may speak with me at any time," Kirk said. "Lissan, I hope you change your mind."

"You may rot, Kirk, and all your Federation friends with you," was Lissan's retort.

He returned to the bridge and met Spock's gaze. He shook his head. "Any word from Mr. Scott?" he asked.

"Negative," Spock said. "The complex is quite large. It will take even our Mr. Scott some time to determine how the controls work."

The door to the turbolift hissed open. Skalli stood there, her tall, willowy frame looking desperately out of place aboard the sharp angles and shiny metal of a Klingon ship's bridge.

"Captain? May I speak with you?"

He opened his mouth to say no, but then thought better of it.

She'd proved herself many times on Sanctuary. If she wanted to talk to him, she probably had a good reason. It amused him to think of how much his attitude toward her had changed.

"Of course." He indicated what served the Klingons for a ready room, and they entered. The door hissed shut behind them. "What is it, Skalli?"

She hesitated, her ears flapping. Finally, she said, "You did not act."

For a second he was confused, then understood what she was saying. "In the control center? You're right, I didn't."

"I watched you. We talked about Sabra Lowe and agreed that destroying the complex was the right thing to do, and yet you didn't do it. You gambled that there would be someone to rescue us, which made no sense. You didn't know anyone would even be looking for us. It was an illogical decision."

Kirk smiled. "Illogical," he agreed, "but the right one. There are always . . . possibilities. Commander Lowe did the right thing. She had a choice, just as I did. Her decision was the best choice she could have made, the one that would save the most lives. Going out in a blaze of glory is noble, but death is a rather final option."

She cocked her head, trying to make sense of it. "Then . . . you are saying that sometimes it takes more courage to live, to find another option, than to die."

"Exactly. Had I pressed that button, we'd have destroyed the complex, certainly. And we'd have destroyed the Falorians' ability to activate the virus. That would have stopped the immediate threat. But you know and I know that as long as those nanoprobes are out there, someone is going to figure out how they work. Oh, we'd do as much cleanup as possible. We'd find most of the probes, but we wouldn't find them all. And one day, maybe not tomorrow, but in a year, or two, or ten—someone will discover how to activate the virus and we'll be right back where we were. But as it stands, because the facility is still intact, we now have the chance to determine how to completely destroy the nanoprobes once and for all."

She brightened. "We do?"

"There's a signal and a code. If I could just convince Lissan to give it to us." He sighed.

Skalli was silent for a time. At last, she spoke. "I have decided that I need to know more about these things, these command decisions and why they are made. I'm going to return to the Academy and continue my training. A diplomatic career will no doubt be full of such . . . options."

"I'm glad to hear it. Anything else?"

She thought about the question carefully. "No," she said at last.

Kirk opened his mouth to dismiss her, and then he paused. The words died in his throat. *There are always possibilities. . . .*

"You really want to be an ambassador?" he asked.

"Oh, yes!"

"How'd you like to start right now?"

"What do you mean?"

"Lissan is refusing to assist us. You might be able to get through to him."

She recoiled as if he'd struck her. "Oh, no! I tried, down on the planet . . . and he was so mean to me. . . ."

"He was so mean because something you said affected him," Kirk said, pressing his point.

Her ears flapped wildly and her eyes bulged. "I'd mess everything up . . . I'd get him angry with us again. . . ."

"Skalli, he's not willing to help us as it is. You can't possibly make anything worse. And you might very well make it better. You're the same species. He's got more reason to talk to you than to anyone."

He could tell she wanted to believe him. "But I . . . oh, Captain, what would I say? What would I do?"

Kirk smiled and squeezed her shoulder. "Trust," he said. "Trust yourself."

She was silent, then said, "If I do this, you have to promise me something. I don't want the conversation monitored. He needs to know that I am the only one who'll hear what he has to say."

Kirk was confused. It would be safer if they could keep tabs on Lissan. "I'm . . . not sure where you're going with this, Skalli."

"Neither am I, but it feels like the right thing to do." She looked at him, her large eyes pleading. "You said trust."

"So I did. All right. But I will post guards. And if you are in any danger, I want you to call for help."

"Aye, sir." She saluted smartly. "I'll do the best I can, Captain."

As she left and he returned to the bridge to give the peculiar order, Kirk desperately hoped he was doing the right thing. He walked down with her to the room the guards had secured, and for a moment, they stood together outside. She shuffled her feet. She looked very, very young.

"He can't physically hurt you," Kirk reassured her. "The minute you call for help these two gentlemen," and he indicated the towering, muscled Klingons on either side of the door, "will be in immediately."

"I know," she said.

"But he can and very likely will say some very hurtful things. I know your people are very sensitive."

"If I ever want to be an ambassador, I'll have to learn to live with people saying hurtful things." She placed a hand on his arm and squeezed, then took a deep breath. "I'm ready."

The guards tapped the controls that unlocked the door and it hissed open. In the back of the room, Lissan stood staring out the window at the stars. His hands were clasped behind his back, and he faced away from the door.

Skalli stepped forward. Slowly, Lissan turned. Their eyes met, and then the door closed behind her.

"What have you got for me, Scotty?" Kirk asked.

Scott's face filled the screen. "Well, I've figured out how they were going to do this, at least," he said.

"Let's have it."

"It looks as though your little scientist told the truth. The signal was to be sent from this console through the main subspace relay tower. It consisted of a certain code and a keyword that apparently only Lissan knew. Now, that signal's not strong enough to go very far on its own, but there's a series of subspace amplifier buoys scattered throughout Falorian space," Scott said. "And they just happen to be Starfleet issue."

"One of the things that Julius got for them. All the better to penetrate Federation space," Kirk said grimly.

"Aye," Scott said. "The signal would hop along from buoy to buoy, and every single nanoprobe in the area would be told to turn its little self on. The good news is—"

"The self-destruct code works the same way," Kirk finished. "Keep working on it, Mr. Scott. I want to be able to send the signal immediately if we can convince Lissan to aid us."

Scott gave him a dubious look. "The difference between the two orders is probably nothing more than a single word, Captain. Even if you could get Lissan to agree to give you the code, there's no telling if he'd give you the one to activate the nanoprobes or order them to self-destruct."

Kirk nodded. "Understood. Kirk out." He glanced at the chronometer. Skalli had been in with Lissan for over twenty minutes. The guards had reported no sounds of violence. Kirk could only hope that somehow, the Huanni could get through to him.

All their lives depended on it.

Hikaru Sulu, captain of the starship *U.S.S. Excelsior,* sat alone in his ready room, sipping tea and thinking furiously. A few moments ago, he had learned that the immediate threat posed by the Falorian nanoprobe virus had been halted. While at the present time the *Excelsior* was the only vessel in the area, the president had assured him that more were on their way. The first should arrive within forty-eight hours. In the meantime, Sulu was to use his own best judgment as to how to proceed.

He drank his tea without sugar, lemon, or cream, and the slightly acidic flavor mixed with the sweet jasmine scent never failed to both calm and stimulate his thinking.

Sulu's mind raced. He desperately wanted to charge forward, phasers blasting, to defend the Huanni. But that would only result in every Falorian vessel targeting him and, probably, blowing him right out of the sky. No help to the Huanni from a destroyed ship.

He reached forward and tapped a button. Instantly he saw what was on the main screen on the bridge: an image of a green, pleasant-looking planet being bombarded by a hodgepodge of vessels. Apparently the Falorians dealt in trade; there was no uniform look to the ships. Debris from the destroyed Huanni fleet floated in space. As Sulu watched, a ship approached a vessel that appeared to be only slightly damaged and locked a tractor beam on it.

Sulu frowned as he gazed intently at the scene. He hadn't seen that before.

He kept watching, the tea growing cold, as another ship approached and did the same thing to another small vessel.

And then Sulu figured it out. "Sulu to communications," he said.

"Aye, sir?"

"I need to send a message out. Top security clearance. Stand by for coordinates."

A few moments later, a face appeared on Sulu's screen. The green-skinned Orion wore a mask to hide his features, but his species was obvious.

"Well, well. Hikaru Sulu. It's been a long time. The console signature says, *Excelsior.* So, what are you, captain now?"

Sulu nodded. "I am indeed the captain. Otherwise I'd never have the authorization to initiate this pleasant chat." He leaned forward. "And pleasant as it is, I'm afraid we have some serious matters to discuss."

"What is it you want, Sulu?"

"I just saw some of your scavengers hard at work in Federation territory," Sulu said. "Around a nice little planet called Huan which, incidentally, is under severe attack."

"I'm sure you're mistaken," the Orion said.

"I'm sure I'm not." Sulu shook his head in mock sympathy. "I have to say, it looks pretty bad for the Syndicate. I'm well within my rights to open fire, seeing your people brazenly operating in Federation territory like this."

The Orion, Sulu knew, liked playing the game almost as much as he did. But this time, Sulu knew that he was the one with all the cards.

"So why aren't you attacking?" Sulu's contact pressed.

"You know violence isn't what the Federation is about,"

Sulu said. "I'm actually contacting you to do you a favor . . . even though *you* still owe *me* one." He smiled. "But who's keeping count?"

"Who indeed?" Sulu had him on his guard now. Good.

"You see, the people attacking Huan just tried to get a corner on the dilithium market by creating a virus that would kill anyone aboard a ship that launched into warp drive. Now, with those Syndicate ships waiting around to pick up what the Falorians leave, it sure looks as though you're involved. And if it comes out that you've assisted a mass murderer. . . ." He let his voice trail off and sighed deeply in false sympathy. He spread his hands. "Much as I'd like to help, you know I'd have to report what I saw here. Unless. . . ."

The Orion's face didn't move a muscle, but his eyes gleamed behind the black mask.

"You always were a good bluffer, Sulu."

"Hey," Sulu said. "I'm sure you've got someone working on it, but let me send you the information we've got. You'll be able to see that it's genuine. Get back to me if you're interested in talking further."

Sulu had barely gotten himself a fresh cup of tea when his Syndicate contact reappeared. He looked utterly furious, which was exactly what Sulu had hoped for.

"The Falorians are no friends of the Syndicate," the Orion snarled.

"I take it you were able to verify my information?" Sulu said smoothly, taking a calm sip.

The Orion, unsure as to what to say, said nothing.

"Look," Sulu said. "Your organization is not allowed to traffic in Federation space. I've caught your people red-handed. Further, I've got a feeling that you weren't here by accident. I'm betting you allied with the Falorians and they've double-crossed you. And I'm also betting that that makes you pretty mad."

He put down the cup. The delicate china clinked against the saucer.

"If indeed we were ever working with the Falorians," said the Orion, and by his choice of words Sulu knew that the Syndicate had been, "you may rest assured that we knew nothing about the virus." In a quieter voice, he said, "They would have, as you said, double-crossed the Syndicate. On the level, Sulu, we would not have participated in a scheme such as that. Dead men can't pay their debts, and mass murder is bad for business."

Sulu believed him. The Syndicate was all about money, and while murder didn't particularly disturb them, he knew better than to think they'd risk the ruination of their carefully crafted empire.

"Federation heat would be pretty bad for business too, I'd imagine," Sulu said. "I have a proposal for you."

Kirk couldn't take it anymore. He had just arrived at the room in which Skalli and Lissan were closeted when the door hissed open. Skalli staggered out. She was pale and exhausted and almost collapsed into Kirk's arms. Her face was streaked with tears, but she was smiling.

Behind her stood Lissan. His face was a mixture of emotions, and he trembled violently.

"Skalli," Kirk said, helping her stand. "What happened?"

She gazed up at him with pure happiness in her large eyes. "Kal-Tor Lissan will help us," she said in a thick voice.

"Yes," Lissan said. "The Huanni child . . . Skalli . . . has convinced me that I cannot be part of something that will claim so many lives." His voice was hoarse and cracked a little. If Kirk didn't know better he'd think Lissan had been crying. He looked more closely and saw the Falorian's eyes were wet.

"Good God, Skalli," Kirk said, unable to believe the turn of events. "What did you do?"

She steadied herself against him and extended a hand to Lissan, who grasped it swiftly. Squeezing the hand of the being who had hours ago called her a sworn enemy, she smiled.

"You were right. I needed to trust what I felt, and I did. I listened," she said simply.

And then Kirk understood. Skalli was a Huanni, a highly emotional creature. Lissan was descended from the same genes. For centuries the Falorians had lived in isolation, nursing grudges both real and imagined, while the Huanni tried to cover their wrongdoings by simply pretending they hadn't happened. And now, a Huanni sat and listened as a Falorian poured forth the pain of those centuries, listened with her wide-open heart and taking Lissan's anger and pain as her own, healing them both as she did so. It would take more than this to completely mend the rift between the estranged cousins, but it was one hell of a start. It was a tactic that would never have occurred to Kirk, and it was the only tactic that had a prayer of working.

"You'll give us the codes to order the nanoprobes to self-destruct?" Kirk asked.

Lissan met his gaze evenly. "I will," he said.

"Then let's go."

Chapter Twenty-six

They materialized in the control center, and Kirk couldn't help but think that although the room looked exactly the same, things were now very, very different.

He knew he was taking an enormous gamble in trusting Lissan. Spock had been against the idea from the outset. He claimed there would be time later for the Federation to meet with the Falorian government and discuss the nanoprobe technology. Kirk had argued that every moment was one in which someone, somewhere, was analyzing the tiny machines. They had a chance to forever remove the possibility of the virus harming anyone, and he wasn't going to miss it.

Spock had then offered to perform a mind-meld, but Lissan refused, looking frightened. Skalli had intervened, tearfully insisting that to force Lissan to submit would be to cause him extreme torment. Despite their open emotions, Huanni possessed brains with natural barriers that prohibited easy telepathic contact. Falorian brains would likely be constructed in the same way. Spock might eventually be able to tear down the barriers, but at a cost to both him and Lissan.

"We have to show him that he can trust us, and that we trust him," she had pleaded.

Kirk had been saved by his intuition more times than he cared to admit. He was a big believer in building bridges between peoples, and he knew what happened when a Vulcan forced a mind-meld.

It was a time for trust. And the stakes had never been higher. If he gambled incorrectly—if Lissan was playing both him and Skalli for fools—millions could die.

Lissan seated himself at a console while Kalaskar busily went about entering an obviously lengthy list of code. Finally, the scientist sat back. For a long moment, no one moved.

"Lissan," Kirk said. "Now would be good."

"It is not so easy, Kirk," the Falorian Kal-Tor said. "When I enter this code, I will have willfully destroyed all chance of my people ever rising to their rightful place."

"That's not true," Kirk said. "There'll be an investigation. Some of you will be imprisoned. But we'll not hold an entire race responsible. And what you are about to do will go a long way toward mitigating our response."

"Imprisoned," Lissan echoed. "I am sure I will be. How long do you think, Kirk? Forever?"

Kirk wanted to lie, but he couldn't. "I don't know, Lissan," he said honestly. "I'll do what I can for you and your people. As will Skalli. But I can't stand here and tell you that there won't be consequences for what you tried to do."

Slowly, Lissan nodded. "Good," he said. "Had you lied to me I would have known that none of you were to be trusted, and that you would probably have decimated my world. I would have entered the activation code."

He turned and looked at Skalli. She gave him a tremulous

smile. Returning his attention to the console, his fingers flew as he entered a series of code almost as lengthy as that which Kalaskar had.

"Preparing to activate self-destruct sequence," the computer said in a clipped male voice. "Awaiting proper authorization."

"Lissan, series one one four one seven one eight eight four two."

There was a long moment where lights chased each other around the console. Kirk realized that every muscle in his body was tense, expecting betrayal. Had he made the right choice? He was gambling now with lives other than his own.

Then, "Self-destruct sequence activated. All nanoprobes destroyed. Virus rendered harmless."

And Kirk permitted himself to breathe. He clapped Lissan on the back. Skalli wriggled happily in her seat. Kirk flipped open his communicator.

"Report."

"The chief engineer informs me that the nanoprobes have harmlessly imploded," came Spock's calm voice. "Apparently, there is not a sufficient amount left of them for analysis."

"That is . . . exactly what I wanted to hear, Mr. Spock. Beam us up and let's get to Huanni at top speed to give Captain Sulu a hand. I'm sure he'll appreciate the assistance."

Sulu was practically humming when he stepped onto the bridge. Ensign Tuvok, the junior science officer on duty, regarded him with barely concealed contempt. Sulu stifled a grin. For someone who claimed to have no emotions, Tuvok certainly gave the appearance that he had quite a lot of them. More than once, Sulu had received what could be called a "dressing down" by this very Vulcan Vulcan. He'd never put the fellow on report; he enjoyed teasing him too much. In a way, it was a very familiar relationship. Sometimes, Sulu could imagine Kirk's voice coming from his own lips, and hearing Tuvok utter Spocklike retorts. No, he'd not chastise a Vulcan for simply being who he was.

He settled into his chair and gazed at the screen. Huan was still under attack, but as Sulu watched he saw several of the mismatched Syndicate ships stop their scavenging. In a few moments, they were joined by several others. More and more odd, cobbled-together ships appeared.

Sulu's first officer, an elderly woman named Janine Clark, looked over at him. "Captain, care to let us in on what's going on?"

"There's an old saying," Sulu said. "The enemy of my enemy is my friend. The Falorians right now are our enemies. And those ships out there—well, they're the Falorians' enemy too."

"I don't understand," Clark said. "Aren't they all Falorian vessels?"

"Patience," Sulu said. It was obvious to him that the Falorians had obtained the shoddy looking but actually well built ships from the Syndicate. Such ships were typical of the Syndicate, but they were also typical of small, independently owned vessels. It was one of the reasons that the Syndicate was so hard to track down. Sulu thought of the early days of sailing, about which he enjoyed reading. Back then, pirates prowled the seas. They didn't have clearly identifiable "pirate ships." They had ships they stole, like the Syndicate did. It was part of what made them so dangerous. A captain would see a ship in the distance that appeared to be a member of his own country's fleet. The hapless captain wouldn't know he was about to be attacked by pirates until and unless they flew the famous skull and crossbones.

At that moment, a dark spot began appearing on the hulls of some of the vessels around Huan.

"What the hell . . . ?" Clark's voice trailed off as the *Excelsior*'s crew stared. Sulu knew what was happening and in a moment they'd figure it out too. A false panel covered those hulls, which was now being retracted to reveal something painted beneath. Gradually the dark blot formed itself into a clearly recognizable shape of a circle with a lightning bolt shot through it— one of the recognizable symbols of the Orion Syndicate.

"But—but—" Clark began.

"Skull and crossbones," Sulu said.

"Those ships are members of the Orion Syndicate," Tuvok said crisply. He apparently did not suffer from Clark's present inability to find the words.

"I'm glad you can identify them so promptly, Mr. Tuvok," Sulu said.

More clearly marked Orion ships had appeared. Sulu waited . . . waited. . . .

"Shields up," he ordered. "Lock phasers on the weapons and nearest Falorian ship. Those are the ones without the Syndicate symbol."

"Sir," said Clark, "our orders are to—"

"On this ship, my orders are the only ones that count. Lock phasers."

"Phasers locked, sir."

"Fire."

The minute red phaser fire hit the Falorian ship, every single Orion vessel began to attack as well. Once the order had been given to fight, the *Excelsior* crew dived in with gusto. Sitting here waiting had taken its toll, and now they were more than eager to take action.

The Federation ship rocked. "Shields down fourteen percent," Sulu's tactical officer said. "Some damage to decks eight and nine."

"Return fire," Sulu ordered. It was a direct hit, and the Falorian ship that had damaged them spun slowly and then came to a halt, hanging dead in space.

The battle continued, but the tide had definitely turned. The Orions knew all the weaknesses of the vessels they had sold to the Falorians, and exploited them mercilessly. More than once, Sulu felt a stab of pity for the Falorian fleet. He targeted only weapons and engines, but the Orions aimed to kill.

Finally, Sulu turned to his communications officer. "Open hailing frequencies and send this message: This is Captain Hikaru Sulu of the *U.S.S. Excelsior* to the Falorian vessels. Several dozen Federation ships are on their way, and the Orions and I can certainly keep you here until they arrive. Surrender at once, or prepare to continue to fight."

A pale, female face crowned with long ears filled the screen. She was bleeding from a cut on her forehead. "This is Commander Yalka," she said, gasping. "The Falorian fleet surrenders."

"Stand by for terms. Jackson, reenter the coordinates I gave you a few moments ago and put it onscreen." Time to let these children know just how roughly their captain was willing to play.

The masked face of the Orion filled the screen. "So, are there really Federation ships on their way, or was that just a nice bluff?"

"Oh, they're coming, all right," Sulu replied. "Which means that your people should probably clear out."

The Orion cocked his head. "You didn't let me off so easily the last time," he said.

"I didn't let you off at all, as you'll recall," Sulu said. "You—er—left the party early."

"So why are you doing so today?"

"Let's just say that I'm glad the ships of my fleet can go into warp without going into the next world," Sulu said. "I imagine your people are, too. And we'll leave it at that." He grinned. He held up the first two fingers of his right hand. "That's *two* favors you owe me now. Sulu out."

The image of the Orion was replaced by that of a now-safe Huan. The Orion ships covered their telltale symbol again and went into warp.

Stunned silence reigned on the bridge. It was, predictably, Tuvok who found his voice first.

"Sir . . . you collaborated with known criminals, and permitted them to escape."

"Yes, Tuvok, I did. As captain, that decision was mine to make. We've saved countless innocent Huanni and had the entire Falorian fleet delivered right into our hands."

He smiled softly, a fond memory in his mind. "And besides—it's what Jim Kirk would have done."

"Good God," Kirk said, as the *Kol'Targh* dropped out of warp. He hadn't realized the odds had been this bad. There were dozens of dangerous-looking ships, and the *Excelsior* sat exposed. He had just opened his mouth to order the shields up when Uhura said, "Captain, we're being hailed. It's Captain Sulu."

"Onscreen."

For someone who was clearly outnumbered, Sulu certainly looked calm and relaxed. "Hello, Captain Kirk. Glad you could make it."

"Captain Sulu," Kirk said, puzzled, "do you require assistance?"

"Indeed I do. We've got an unconditional surrender

and we'll want to interrogate some of the commanders."

"You've . . . got an unconditional surrender," Kirk repeated. "I see." He groped for words, then simply said, "Very well done, Captain."

"I had a little help," Sulu smiled. "And I see you did too. Why is it I'm always seeing you on a Klingon ship?"

"I've no idea," Kirk said, and meant it. "It looks like you have everything under control, Captain. I'll send some people over to give you a hand, and then I'd very much enjoy it if I can transport over and ask you . . . how you did it. Kirk out."

He leaned back in his chair and looked over at Spock. "Well," he said. "Nothing like racing to the rescue and arriving just in time to help with cleanup. Mr. Spock, you know the crew better than I. Send someone over to Captain Sulu. I'll be in sickbay."

Sickbay was crammed full, with many people all talking at once. Yet over the din, McCoy's distinctive voice could be heard: "Good God, man, do you people still use *needles*? You'll punch a hole right through his arm with that thing! I'd pay real money for a decent hypospray along about now. Yes, I know I was supervising the medical exchange, but we were still working on anatomy when Spock high-tailed it out to this godforsaken part of the galaxy. Now show me how to use that."

It was music to Kirk's ears. He threaded his way through the crush of colonists, most of whose injuries appeared quite minor, and tapped McCoy on the shoulder.

"Alex, I told you to—Jim!" McCoy laughed brightly and embraced his old friend.

"Sorry Spock dragged you out to this godforsaken part of the galaxy," Kirk said.

"Nah, wouldn't have missed it for the world."

269

"How are my nephews?"

McCoy sobered a bit. "Physically, they're fine, but emotionally—well, you probably know better than I do what they've been through."

"They both down here still?"

"Yep. Told them to stay put until whatever was happening happened. Sounds like we dodged a phaser blast today."

"We did indeed." Kirk searched the crowd, then caught a glimpse of two fair heads at the far end of sickbay. He made his way toward them. They were sitting on what passed for a Klingon diagnostic bed. Physically, they were almost touching, but by their expressions and body language, they were trying to put light-years between them. Julius's face was still slightly swollen, but the blood that had turned his handsome face into a ghoulish mask had been washed off and the lacerations were healed. Alex looked fine; as Kirk had thought, the wounds the boy had incurred during the staged beating had been minimal and easily treatable.

"What are a couple of nice boys like you doing in a place like this," Kirk said lightly.

As one, they glanced up at him, and their expressions were so similar Kirk almost laughed. Why hadn't he realized before how much they resembled one another, despite their great differences? He'd been so busy patting Alex on the head and worrying about Julius's sullenness, he'd missed how very much alike they were.

"The doctor says you're both going to be all right. How do you feel?"

Neither one answered. Kirk sighed. "All right, boys, this is your Uncle Jim speaking, and he's a starship captain. You're both very lucky to be alive. You ought to realize that."

"It's all ruined," Alex said. "I was such a fool. It's all ruined now." He ran a hand through his thick fair hair. His father Sam had had that same habit, and for a moment he looked so much like Kirk's dead brother that Kirk's breath caught. "God! How could I have been so stupid! I put everybody in danger because I was too blind to see what was right before my eyes, that the Falorians were just using me and that my own brother . . ."

He closed his jaw with an almost audible snap and looked down at the floor.

Julius swallowed hard. "That your own brother was dealing with criminals in order to get you the colony," he finished. "You're kicking yourself because you believed in me. I've always been good at lying, Alex. You know that."

"But I never thought you'd lie to *me*." Alex's voice cracked on the last word.

"I'd have done anything to help you realize your dream. I'd have killed for you. I'd have *died* for you."

"Don't you get it, Julius?" Now Alex did look at his baby brother, raw pain in every line of his body. "I never wanted anyone to suffer, to, to get hurt, to die for what I wanted. I wanted a peaceful colony, one where technology could be invented and used to benefit everyone. Instead because of this damned colony technology nearly killed millions of people. I'm a failure."

"You didn't fail, Alex," Kirk said, softly so as not to shatter the moment. "Your dream was and still is a worthy one. So what if this one venture didn't work out? Do you know how many times colonies had to be founded before they hit on the right combination of ideas, resources, and people? I'm certain there would be many species willing to fund another attempt. Technology for peaceful, humanitarian means is a noble and brave ideal, one from which you and your people never deviated. You could have fought, and you didn't. You always sought a peaceful solution. That's going to resonate with a lot of people when the story gets told."

Julius snorted. "Yeah, and when the story gets told, Julius Kirk is going to be a big black mark against his uncle's legacy. Piracy, information trafficking, theft—"

"Courage," Kirk said. "A willingness to own up to his mistakes—mistakes that he only made in the first place because of a deep love for his brother. True remorse and every effort to help correct the wrongs he'd done. And an uncle who's very proud of him, and who would be honored to stand by his side during his trial."

"Nice pep talk, Uncle Jim," Alex said. "But a pep talk isn't going to make everything all better."

"I know," Kirk said. "Just like I know that showing up once or twice a year for a few hours wasn't really being any kind of an uncle to you. I've made my mistakes, too. But mistakes don't have to scar you forever. Life's too short, too precious. What happened on Sanctuary can be a beginning, not an ending, if you let it."

He looked at them for a moment longer, then sighed and turned away.

But out of the corner of his eye, he saw Alex slowly lift an arm and put it around his brother's shoulder. And he saw Julius wipe clumsily at suddenly full eyes.

Chapter Twenty-seven

"You're a sight for sore eyes," Admiral Laura Standing Crane said as she smiled at Kirk from the viewscreen.

"The feeling's mutual," Kirk said. "You still owe me that drink."

"After what you've done, I think I owe you dinner *and* a drink," Standing Crane said. "Although that will have to wait until I get back from the Huanni/Falorian conference."

Kirk uttered a mock groan. "That could take years. I'm getting old, Laura, I don't have that much time left!"

Now she laughed aloud. "Jim Kirk, you're the youngest man I know."

"I'm not sure how to take that."

"Take it as a compliment."

"All right, I will. I don't envy you, Laura. The Federation's got a big job ahead of it in trying to sort out the Huanni/Falorian mess."

"Truer words were never spoken," she admitted, "but it's not as bad as it could be. A lot of lives were lost in the Falorian campaign against Huan, but far fewer than it could have been. I'm a little fuzzy on the details—how did Captain Sulu manage to defeat the fleet?"

Now that was a sticky issue. Kirk kept his face carefully neutral as his mind raced, trying to come up with an answer for that one.

"You'll have to talk to Captain Sulu about that. I'm not sure about all the details myself and I'd hate to tell you something that might not be correct." The response was so smooth that even a Romulan would have been proud of it, he thought.

"Fair enough. Regardless, the Huanni infrastructure took a lot of damage and it's going to take time and resources to get them on their feet again. And there's going to be an inquiry, of course."

"About the fact that they enslaved the Falorians and pretended it didn't happen," Kirk said.

"You have to admit, that's a big omission."

"If Skalli's a fair representative of the Huanni, then they're a good people."

Standing Crane nodded her dark head. "I'm inclined to agree with you, but we can't let this pass without notice."

"What about the Falorians?"

"They're being extremely cooperative. Good job on coaxing Lissan into destroying the nanoprobes, Jim. That's a big point in their favor right now. They might be great actors, but I'll tell you, the Kal-Toreshi seemed stunned by how close they came to mass murder. On their own, before we could even request it, they destroyed all information relating to the development of the virus, so that such a threat might never again occur."

"I assume you're trusting but verifying," Kirk said.

"Of course. We'll have our own teams there to make sure of it. For the present, the planet's under martial law."

Kirk nodded. He had expected as much. All the members of the Kal-Toreshi, including and especially Lissan, had been detained and would be brought to Starfleet headquarters for questioning and, most likely, some term of imprisonment.

"Sounds like it's all over but the shouting," Kirk said.

"Just about. I've got to get going, Jim, but I wanted to see with my own eyes that you were all right."

"I'm fine. But I'm hungry. Don't be too long on that dinner."

She smiled. "I'll do my best. Standing Crane out."

Kirk leaned back in the torture device the Klingons called a "chair" and touched a button on his personal recording device.

Captain's personal log, addendum:

Despite the messiness and the scope of this situation, I have high hopes that the two separated people will be reunited. If not, then at least they will be able to live in peace. Skalli's courage in repeatedly extending the hand of friendship to Lissan, despite his initial harsh rebuffs, is largely responsible for this development. I'm glad she's coming back to finish her education, though it might take a while since both Huan and Falor have requested her involvement in future proceedings.

My nephew Julius is also returning for trial. While I cannot condone his actions, his subsequent behavior will count in his favor. He's a good man. Sam would have been so proud of all his boys. And I understand that despite what they went through, all the colonists, down to the last man, have assured Alexander that if he can get them another opportunity, they will be willing to sign up again.

Kirk didn't want to talk about the rest. It all still irked him. He turned off the recording device and sat back in the hellishly uncomfortable chair in his private quarters.

There was a harsh, grating buzz, and Kirk realized that

someone was requesting admittance. "Come in," he called, and the door hissed open. Spock and McCoy stood there. McCoy grinned and lifted an amber bottle.

"I invited the rest of the old gang, but they're all busy. Good thing, too. Scotty would have wanted us to drink his Scotch instead of this sweet stuff."

"Well, let's not let that fine Kentucky bourbon go to waste," Kirk said, waving them in. As he located three of the hefty mugs the Klingon used to drink a beverage called "blood wine" he noted with amusement that he was becoming used to Klingon ships.

"Boy, the Klingons don't do things by half measures, do they?" McCoy said, eyeing the massive steins. He poured a little into each one. What would have been a generous shot in any other glass barely covered the bottom.

"So I assume Scotty's busy reading up on what is left of the Falorian technical information," Kirk said. Spock nodded. "Where are the rest?"

"Commander Chekov's over talking with Sulu," McCoy said. "I wouldn't expect him to return with us if I were you, Jim. Seems Sulu's first officer is due to retire in six weeks and he needs a first officer."

"Chekov was holding out for a captaincy," Kirk said.

"Chekov has always valued service and friendship above the advancement of his career," Spock said. "I believe he would serve Captain Sulu well and loyally."

"I know he would. And I understand the multitalented Uhura is going to be performing in less than a week."

McCoy chuckled. "You should see how she handles that Klingon opera star," he said. "She's got him under her thumb, that's for sure."

"I saw a little of that on the bridge. I've never seen a smitten Klingon before. I don't suppose the feeling's mutual?"

"I doubt it," McCoy said. "Uhura's a tough cookie, and she's admitted that Karglak's voice makes her weak in the knees, but I just can't see her walking around wearing all that armor and eating *blech*."

"The term for that particular food item is *gagh*," Spock said.

McCoy fixed him with a gaze. "You call it what you want, I'll call it what I want."

"Looks like Uhura has developed some unique negotiating skills," Kirk said. "Perhaps we should permit her to conduct all negotiating sessions with the Klingons."

Spock looked a tad offended. "I do not think that would be appropriate."

Kirk and McCoy looked at each other and grinned a little. "I propose a toast," McCoy said. "To old cowhands on the last roundup. May they always bring their charges safely home."

"Cowhand?" Spock asked, raising an eyebrow.

"Shut up and drink, Spock," McCoy growled. Spock did.

Kirk swirled the liquid in the mug and sipped, trying to ignore the strange, musky scent that still clung to the mugs. "The last roundup," he mused. "Is that it? And are we the cows or the cowhands? Going back to the bunkhouse or going out to pasture?"

McCoy set his glass down and stared at Kirk. Spock, too, looked sharply at his former commander.

"Captain," Spock said slowly, "I perceive that you feel unhappy with the level of your involvement in recent events."

"Damn right I do." Kirk knew he was bone-tired, or he wouldn't have let the words spill out so freely. And again, it could be the strength of Bones's bourbon mixed with whatever might still be in the bottom of the mug. "I've done nothing right since the *Enterprise* was decommissioned. I'm . . . lost without her, Spock. I don't know how to be anything other than a starship captain. I feel useless and worse, I feel like I'm a hindrance.

"I didn't do anything. I didn't save the colonists—they saved themselves. Veta and Gallagher came up with the technology that allowed them to disappear into the cave system. You and Spock saved us when I was just about to blow up the control center. I didn't save the Huanni from Falorian attack—Sulu did. I didn't convince Lissan to cooperate—Skalli talked him into it. Hell, even the *Klingons* played a more active part than I did. I've just had my life saved by the Klingon High Chancellor and her people. Klingons, Bones! Who deserves the credit? My old shipmates and my old enemies. I can't contribute anymore. I can't make a difference. Maybe I *should* be farmed out to pasture."

McCoy glowered. "Now that's poppycock and you know it, Jim."

"Although he may be surprised to hear me say it, I completely agree with the good doctor. You are a valuable resource and a magnificent teacher. Your students are extremely fortunate to have you as a presence in their lives."

"Spock's right," McCoy said. "I am surprised he agrees with me." He grinned. "And damn it, he's right about the other stuff, too. Do you have any idea, Jim, of the amazing vastness of your sphere of influence?"

"Well, maybe I can share what I've learned, but—"

"No buts. Let's take a brief look at just a couple of your students. Skalli managed to take her hyperactive emotions and put them to good use instead of falling apart in the midst of a crisis that would have challenged anybody, let alone a Huanni. She may be responsible one day for single-handedly uniting the two separate races. She learned that discipline from you. She wouldn't have even gone in to talk to Lissan if you hadn't put her up to it."

Kirk opened his mouth to object—Skalli had had that in her all along—but McCoy said "Ah, ah, I'm not done yet. Sulu goes in there and manages to wrangle the slipperiest characters in the galaxy into fighting alongside the Federation. Think that would have occurred to him if he hadn't spent years watching you pull stunts like that?"

"I wouldn't call them stunts," Kirk began, but again McCoy waved him to silence.

"And then there's the Vulcan and me and Uhura. You think we'd be hauling our tired old bones halfway across the galaxy if some idiot named Jim Kirk hadn't put that fire in our bellies years ago? Hell no. I wouldn't get out of *bed* for most people, Jim." He lifted his glass. "To Jim Kirk, who's a walking, talking inspiration." He narrowed his blue eyes and added, "And don't you *dare* say a word to contradict me."

Kirk glanced at Spock, but the Vulcan merely said, "As it is illogical to falsify and exaggerate one's virtues and importance, it is also illogical to deny them when all evidence supports their existence."

A slow smile spread across Kirk's face as, for the first time, he allowed himself to think that maybe, just maybe, Spock and Bones were right. Maybe he didn't have to save the day all the time. He couldn't deny the truth of what Spock had said. He *had* done a great deal in his life. He'd helped a lot of people, trained so many to "get out there and do some good."

Eventually, he knew, the day had to come when the baton would be passed. Kirk realized now how deeply he had dreaded it, how he feared in the deepest recesses of his soul that if he wasn't on the bridge of a starship, he might as well be dead for all the good he could contribute.

Maybe that line of thinking was, as Spock put it, "illogical." And damned selfish, too.

Perhaps simply by being himself, Kirk could continue to have a positive influence on those around him.

And whether or not it's true, he thought, *it sure as hell beats playing solitaire.*

He lifted his mug. "Gentlemen," he said, "far be it from me to contradict the sage words of two old friends. To the last roundup, and a warm bed at the end of a cold hard day."

As their mugs clinked, Kirk added, "Either of you ever try skydiving?"

EPILOGUE

Kirk was shrugging into the coat of his dress uniform when a message came. It was Standing Crane.

"Laura! Good to see you. What's going on? I'm just about ready to leave for—"

"I know, and I won't keep you." Her expression was somber. "I've got some bad news. Kal-Tor Lissan was found dead in his cell this morning."

"Oh, no." Kirk was genuinely sorry to hear that. He had hoped that Lissan would be one of the architects of the peace accord that might someday be hammered out between the Falorians and Huanni. He had respected the man. "What happened? An illness?"

"A murder," Standing Crane replied, chilling him.

"How did that possibly happen? He was in a Starfleet security cell!"

"We're investigating that right now, but it looks like a hit." She took a deep breath and said, "It was pretty messy. His throat was slashed and someone had carved the number 858 into his chest."

"Damn it. He didn't deserve that. He was only trying to do what he thought was right for his people. Any idea what the number means?"

She shook her head. "No. We'll do everything we can to find the killer, but it looks like a professional job. I don't know that we will."

"Can you inform Skalli?" The young Huanni was on Falor right now. Huan was busily rebuilding its fallen buildings and mining the incredibly pure dilithium that the Falorians had revealed was there. It was Skalli who had suggested that part of the wealth be shared with the Falorians whose difficult physical labor had discovered it centuries ago, and who had been appointed head of a team to negotiate the exchange.

"She already knows. She cried buckets."

"Of course she did. I'm glad. Lissan deserved someone to weep for him."

"On a brighter note, your testimony really helped Julius Kirk," Standing Crane said. "A decision hasn't been reached, but it looks like his sentence is going to be reduced. He might even get out on time served with community service."

"That *is* good news," said Kirk. "He made some mistakes, some bad ones, but he's done what he could to atone."

"And that's going to be taken into account. Well, I won't keep you, Jim. I know you're looking forward to this afternoon."

Kirk rolled his eyes. She grinned, and then her image disappeared.

As he finished dressing, Kirk thought about the other colonists. Last he heard, Alex was in negotiations with the

Vulcans about backing for a possible new venture. Now that would be a good match. He hadn't heard much from the others, but for some reason the words that Kate Gallagher had spoken before she left with Alex to hide in the cave system came to mind. He was suddenly curious: Why would she want to look at her thesis?

"Computer," he called. "Find information on Katherine J. Gallagher. Specifically, the title of her master's thesis."

"Gallagher, Katherine J. Known as Kate," the computer said in its crisp female voice. "Title of master's thesis is 'The Devil in the Dark: Starfleet's Blackest Moment Becomes Its Finest Hour.'"

"Display." Kirk began reading and then smiled to himself, touched. The rough, angry Kate had written her master's thesis on James Kirk's intervention on Janus VI to save the Horta. Apparently, it was this single incident that had captured the young Gallagher's imagination and set her feet on the path to protecting endangered species. No wonder she was so prickly around him when she thought him just another Starfleet bully. He made a mental note to drop her a line when he got back this evening.

Kirk put his medals on and examined himself in the mirror. Not bad for a retired legend. He was looking forward to seeing Scotty and Chekov again . . . and to walking the deck of a certain ship that he would always passionately love.

"Come on," he said to his reflection. "I hear Captain Harriman isn't a patient man. And besides, I hate to keep a lady waiting."

About the Author

Award-winning author Christie Golden has written twenty novels and fifteen short stories in the fields of science fiction, fantasy, and horror. Among her credits are three stand-alone *Voyager* novels, *The Murdered Sun, Marooned,* and *Seven of Nine,* the Dark Matters trilogy (*Cloak and Dagger, Ghost Dance,* and *Shadow of Heaven*), the *Voyager* segment of the Gateways series, *No Man's Land,* the novella *Hard Crash* for *Have Tech, Will Travel,* and the Tom Paris short story, "A Night at Sandrine's," which appeared in *Amazing Stories.*

In addition to *Star Trek* novels, Golden has also written three original fantasy novels, *King's Man and Thief, Instrument of Fate,* and, under the pen name Jadrien Bell, *A.D. 999,* which won the Colorado Author's League Top Hand Award for Best Genre Novel of 1999.

With *The Last Roundup* and its cast of original *Star Trek* characters, Golden feels she has come full circle from her days in junior high math class when she furtively wrote *Star Trek* scripts instead of taking notes. She hopes readers will enjoy the ride.

Golden lives in Colorado with her husband, two cats, and a white German shepherd. Readers are encouraged to visit her Web site at www.christiegolden.com.